WREAKING HAVOC

DEMON BOUND
BOOK 1

GRAE BRYAN

Copyright © 2024 by Grae Bryan

All rights reserved.

No part of this book may be reproduced in any form or by any electronic or mechanical means, including information storage and retrieval systems, without written permission from the author, except for the use of brief quotations in a book review.

Cover designed by MiblArt.

This is a work of fiction. Names, characters, and incidents are the products of the author's imagination. Any resemblance to actual persons, living or dead, or actual events is purely coincidental.

Content warnings: Moderate violence, aftermath of off-page torture (non-MC), implied homophobia, references to human trafficking, parental death (past, off-page), panic attacks

PROLOGUE

Kai

Kai gasped for breath, dagger in hand, body convulsing as he bent over at the knee. Of all the damned things in either realm, was there anything worse than the dizzying panic of being returned to the Void?

"You're back."

Kai looked up to find the incubus staring at him, his tail flicking rhythmically against the stone walls of the cavern. "The others?" Kai asked.

"Sleeping."

Of course. What else was there to do between contracts but sleep? Even their little chaos demon grew tired of peering into the human realm eventually.

Kai straightened, wiping his bloody dagger off on his trousers before placing it carefully in its sheath. There was the soft sound of a throat clearing, and he glanced up again to see the incubus still staring intently, purple eyes aglow. "How was it?"

Kai cast a pointed glance to his sheathed dagger, then to his blood-soaked chest. "A success."

The incubus leaned closer. "What did they want?"

"What do they always want?" Kai shrugged. "Power. Glory. Carnage."

"How deliciously greedy," the incubus murmured, licking at his lips.

That was one way of looking at it. Not Kai's way. Why had he ever thought the human realm could be fascinating? That it might relieve the bone-deep apathy he'd been plagued with in his home realm? Almost a thousand contracts later and he could no longer remember. When it came down to it, the human lust for power was predictable. Boring.

Meaningless.

"How many left?"

The rasping question came not from the incubus—who'd leaned back and shut his eyes, lost in some fantasy of his own—but from the shadows, where eerie white eyes were open and glowing.

So Nightmare wasn't asleep after all.

Kai bared his teeth in a sharp smile. "Just the one."

"How fortunate for you."

Kai supposed so, especially as he'd just been summoned. How long had it been since the others had been called?

Nightmare retreated back into the shadows, his brief flicker of curiosity apparently appeased. That suited Kai well enough—he wasn't one Kai would have picked as a companion, given the choice.

But there was no choice. Only four remained, out of the hundred who had first started. Stuck with one another until they could complete their final contracts.

Kai left the daydreaming incubus behind to wash the rest of the blood off in the lake. As the rivulets of red swirled away, he considered taking a taste. But he didn't need it—not here. He didn't need anything here.

One more contract, as he'd told Nightmare. Just the one. And then...freedom. The freedom to return to his home, to never think of humans and their predictable, tedious desires ever again.

When the last of the human carnage was rinsed off his skin, Kai left the lake behind, settling in the cave he'd claimed for himself.

He allowed his eyes to shut for the first time in days.

All that was left to do was wait.

1

Sascha

There should be a special place in hell for people who called before ten a.m.

Sascha rolled over and groped for his offending phone, horrified to see that not only was it before ten, but it was only *seven thirty in the goddamn morning.*

Definitely straight to hell.

"Sergei, you son of a bitch," he grumbled, putting the thing on speaker so he didn't have to hold it to his face.

"Ivan wants you," Sergei's gruff voice told him evenly, unfazed as ever by Sascha's less-than-enthusiastic greeting.

Of course. What other reason for his brother's right-hand man to be calling than to do his brother's bidding? Like it was so hard for Ivan to pick up a phone himself.

Sascha stretched, luxuriating in the delicious ache of his well-used body. All thanks to the dumb hunk of man meat beside him, the one that wasn't even faintly stirring from the noise of the phone call next to him.

Poor man. Sascha must have tired him out.

He grinned at the thought, even as his tone stayed petulant. "Ivan never *needs* me, Sergei."

"He requests your presence, then."

Ugh. Sascha threw the covers back in one decisive motion, stumbling out of what's-his-name's bed. He knew better than to assume a request from Ivan was only that—a request.

"Why?" he asked—well, more whined, really, but Sergei would have to forgive him a little peevishness at this ungodly hour.

"Damned if I know, zaychik."

"Don't call me that," Sascha griped, more out of habit than anything else. "Keeping things close to his chest these days, is he?"

"Maybe he wants you to take a more vested interest in the family business."

That earned a real laugh from Sascha, one that finally had his companion rolling over with a grunt. *Sascha* an active member of the family business? No way in hell. Whether or not he had a head for numbers, he was about as intimidating as a wet kitten, and the thought of a gun in his hand had bile rising in his throat.

Not exactly the makings of a Mafia man, was it?

"Ivan knows better than to depend on another brother," Sascha pointed out, pulling on the skintight jeans he'd been wearing the night before.

Sergei scoffed. "Not much family left in the family business, then."

"Sure there is." Keys. Where were his keys? "What about Cooper? He's a—what—distant cousin?"

Sergei let out a very Russian-sounding grunt. "I suppose he does his part. Behind those screens of his."

Poor Sergei. So old-fashioned. The thought of a hacker as part of the team had gotten him all in a tizzy, once upon a time.

Really, Ivan was lucky to have *anyone* on his side, with what an unbelievably major dick he'd been the last few years. Well, since birth, really, but he'd amped it up lately, even for him.

Sascha supposed betrayal did that to a man. Not that dear middle child Alexei had seen his actions as a betrayal—survival, more like.

Never mind that he'd left his little brother here all alone to deal with their oldest brother's hissy fits.

"When should I tell Ivan to expect you?" Sergei asked, the faintest hint of impatience finally creeping into his voice.

"Give me an hour," Sascha told him, slipping out the door. "I'm not decent."

He'd need to find a cab too. He'd dismissed his driver the night before, not wanting to get an earful from Ivan about his extracurricular activities. It wasn't exactly a secret that the guy reported all Sascha's movements to his brother. And while Ivan wasn't against those activities, exactly—not in the way their father had been—he didn't appreciate Sascha "flaunting" them.

Sometimes Sascha thought Ivan wouldn't have minded so much if Sascha had been some uber-masculine top. It seemed to be the lack of machismo of it all that fucked with these old gangsters' heads more than anything.

Poor Ivan. Papa had messed him up good, hadn't he?

Sascha ended the call over Sergei's exasperated spluttering. Really, Sergei should be grateful. Nighttime activities aside, Ivan would blow a gasket if Sascha came in wearing what he was. While he may technically have been following the unspoken approved list—jeans and a black shirt, no color, no frills—neither item left much to the imagination. And Sascha was in no mood for a lecture.

His brother would simply have to wait.

And if Sergei got punished for it...

Well, that was the price of working for a mobster, wasn't it? He'd chosen his path, after all.

Sascha had never had that luxury.

ONE WOULD THINK, after paying five figures for a suit, said suit would be, at the very least, not only exquisite to look at, but *comfortable*.

But no. The damn thing itched and tugged and constricted like any other of its cheaper brethren. Suits were a fucking scam was what they were. Designed to keep men on edge so they didn't miss any important nuances of their busy business dealings or whatever.

Which was why it was so utterly fucking pointless for Sascha to be wearing one, wasn't it? He had no business dealings to speak of, and being on edge only made his stomach hurt.

But Ivan insisted, like their almighty father had before him, and so here Sascha was, in yet another overpriced, uncomfortable suit, miserable and pissy.

Not that anyone would know, he thought, breezing through the glass doors of Ivan's office building with a smile plastered on his face, nodding amiably to the guard who scanned his key card. Sascha was pampered, rich, and carefree, without having to work a day in his life for it, as Ivan loved to remind him. It was only in the privacy of his own home that he was allowed to be sulky or demanding.

Or the privacy of Ivan's office, as was often the case.

Ivan's office that had been relocated from the shabby warehouse to this sleek monstrosity the second their father had croaked. Ivan had said he was dragging their family business into the modern era, but Sascha knew what he was *really* doing: putting his power on display. Poor brute couldn't resist.

Still, there were perks. It was close to more than a few designer shops, for one. And it didn't smell like black mold, for another.

But there were other places Sascha would rather be this fine sunny morning. Like the bed of his current dalliance, for example—the one he'd been so unceremoniously dragged out of. Sascha didn't do morning cuddles, not with any of his disposable men, but he wouldn't have minded another round. The man was hung like a horse, for all that his head seemed to contain more skull than brain matter.

Sascha pressed the button for the elevator just as his phone buzzed. He fished it out of his pocket.

Where the fuck are you?

God, Ivan really had been on a tear since Alexei had run off, never mind that it had been almost two years since their brother had fled.

Ivan hadn't even summoned Sascha himself, and yet here he was pestering him like he was late when it had barely been forty-five minutes. If he expected Sascha to arrive dressed appropriately, then he had to wait for the results, didn't he?

Keep your boxer briefs on, brother dearest, Sascha texted back, just as the elevator arrived.

Oh, that would piss him off. But it wasn't like he'd actually *hurt* Sascha. And Sascha was maybe the only man in all of New York who could say that.

His allowance, however, was another matter.

Shit. Was it too late to take that text back?

Sascha nodded distractedly to the other elevator occupant—some middle-aged man in a workman's uniform—as he considered whether to apologize over text or wait until he was facing him in person.

"Floor?"

"Oh!" Sascha startled at the gruff voice, then cleared his throat, trying to cover up his less-than-suave reaction. Ivan was probably monitoring the security camera like a creep, and he was sure to call Sascha out on his lack of composure later. "Um, fifteen, please."

The man pressed the button for the fifteenth floor. No other buttons were lit up. Huh. Maybe Ivan was installing new security cameras in his office as well, assuaging some of that rampant paranoia of his.

Sascha's stomach dipped as the elevator rose. He was regretting his text, and it was giving him a tummy ache. He hated that. And his goddam *shoe* felt loose, to top it all off.

He glanced down to see his shoelace had come undone. See? Even the expensive shoes that came with the expensive suit were bullshit.

He bent down to tie it, a whoosh of air brushing past his torso as he did so. And then—

Fuck.

A fiery burn erupted out of nowhere in Sascha's upper arm, leaving him choking on air. He glanced down, already afraid of what he'd find.

There was a handle sticking out of him.

He looked up at the workman, as if another person could help make sense of the situation—the workman who was now gazing at him with an intensity that no ordinary person should be looking at him with.

Something clicked in Sascha's brain. "Did you just *stab* me?"

He might have been embarrassed at his pouty tone at any other time, but his arm *hurt*, goddamn it.

"Not where I intended," the man muttered. Then he pressed a palm into the handle sticking out of Sascha's limb, raising his voice to be heard over Sascha's scream. "We have a message for your brother."

Sascha's scream trailed off into a whimper, his gaze drawn to his arm again. The stupid suit was darkening around the knife in a telltale pattern.

Oh God, that was blood, wasn't it?

His vision started growing mercifully fuzzy at the edges. "Well, you picked the wrong way to go about it," he sniped, his words already slurring. His head was beginning to feel too heavy to hold up. "You should know I faint at the sight of—"

And then everything went dark.

2

Sascha

Two months later

The thing about adorable Maine tourist towns was that apparently half the town shut down for the off-season.

Sascha stared at the "Closed for Winter" sign on his favorite coffee shop—the only one he'd found that knew how to make a decent espresso—his lower lip pushed out into a pout.

Well, what the hell was he supposed to do now?

Five minutes later, his answer was apparently the Bakeshop, a bakery Sascha had passed almost daily the past six weeks here but had never entered because he could already tell from the sidewalk that it was most decidedly *not* his scene.

There were *doilies* on the counter, for God's sake.

But as he peered in the window now, he could see a coffee pot percolating behind the pastry case, so he was going to have to brave the doilies, wasn't he?

The aproned teen behind the counter, all round cheeks and bouncing curls, smiled brightly at him as he entered. "Morning!"

"Morning," Sascha replied, maybe a little sulkily, but what did it matter? No one here knew him for who he was. He could be as sulky as he wanted, damn it.

His phone buzzed in his pocket. Sascha ignored it for the tenth time that morning. "You don't happen to have an espresso machine hiding back there, do you?" he asked without much hope.

"Nope. Sorry. Marjorie doesn't like them," the teen answered, as if Sascha was supposed to know who Marjorie was. Sascha didn't even know who *this* person was, except his name tag said Seth, with a little "He/Him" underneath. "But what we've got is freshly brewed."

"I'll take a large cup, then. Very large. And—" Sascha perused the pastry case, which didn't look nearly as despairing as he'd first assumed "—one of those chocolate croissants."

"Coming right up!"

God, he was perky. Weren't teens supposed to be sullen assholes?

"We don't usually get many tourists off-season," Seth pointed out chattily as he grabbed the croissant from the case, further proving Sascha wrong.

"I'm not a tourist. I live here." *For now*, was the part Sascha left unspoken. *Until Ivan deems it safe to return.*

Which would perhaps be sometime in the next million years.

Seth's eyes widened in apparent delight. "Oh! You're going to love Seacliff in the winter. Gets real cozy. And don't worry, there's still a ton to do. Cross-country skiing…"

Sascha would *not* be doing that.

"Skating on the lake…"

Nope.

"Ice fishing."

Fuck no.

Seth seemed to see something in Sascha's expression as he handed over the croissant, because he suddenly grinned. "Or, you know, indoor stuff. Weekly karaoke. Drag night at the Lighthouse. But not the literal lighthouse," he told Sascha, like that was a common mistake people made. "The bar."

Sascha perked up a little at that. He'd known the town hosted a gay bar, but he'd avoided it like the plague, assuming it would be too tragic to bear.

But a drag night was promising.

He noticed for the first time, as his coffee was placed in front of him, that Seth's nails were painted lime green. Seth saw him looking and wiggled his fingers. "You like?"

God, Sascha did. He'd never been allowed to paint his nails. His father would have chopped his fingers off, probably.

But Papa wasn't here, was he? Neither was Ivan, the controlling fuck. "You get that color at the drugstore?" he asked.

Maybe he'd need to make another stop.

"Yep! But I've got the bottle in my bag. One sec." Seth disappeared into what Sascha presumed to be a back room of some sort and reappeared, setting two bottles of nail polish—one lime green and one electric blue—onto the counter next to Sascha's pastry and coffee.

Sascha eyed the bottles skeptically. "You're awfully friendly, aren't you?"

Seth shrugged. "It's a small town, especially in the winter. Everyone's friendly."

That was true enough. But so far everyone had been treating Sascha with the vague, distant friendliness given to tourists. This was the first time he'd been treated like he actually lived here.

It made him vaguely uneasy. Like any second friendly Seth was going to pull a handgun out from behind the counter.

God, he was damaged.

His phone buzzed again. Almost like it *knew*.

Fuck it. Sascha grabbed the nail polish bottles, pocketing them both in his oversize coat. "Thanks. I'll bring them back tomorrow."

Seth smiled brightly. "No rush."

Sascha paid for his goods. As he was walking out the door, Seth called out, "The restaurant down the street—Darcy's—they make a killer cappuccino. And they're open all winter."

Sascha nodded his thanks and walked out the door to the sound of his phone buzzing again.

He yanked it out of his pocket. "*What?*"

A familiar cold voice was on the other end. "I've been trying to reach you all morning."

"My apologies, brother dearest. I just have so *many* social engagements here, in the middle of bumfuck nowhere. It's hard to keep track."

"You chose your own hiding spot," Ivan reminded him.

He had, it was true. Ivan had given Sascha a choice: a bodyguard contingent or temporary exile. And when Sascha had picked exile—fuck no was he going to agree to being trailed twenty-four seven by any of Ivan's goons—Ivan had told him to pick somewhere no one would expect. Sascha had pointed a finger on a random town on the map. Seacliff Harbor, Maine. Population: 11,000.

But it was Ivan's stupid fault he'd needed to point to any town at all.

Sascha made a quick about-turn and headed down the path that left the small downtown to run along the cliffs.

He needed some dramatic ocean views in order to deal with his brother this morning.

"How's the arm?" Ivan asked, sounding like he couldn't care less about the answer.

Sascha winced, his pinky finger all pins and needles around the warmth of the coffee cup. He didn't like thinking about his arm, or the lingering nerve damage. Thinking made him remember, and remembering made his stomach hurt. It was easier to pretend his pinky finger just...fell asleep sometimes. "It's fine," he grumbled.

"You're doing your exercises?"

"Maybe." Sascha did a little roll of his shoulders. There, did that count?

There was a long, dangerous silence. "You will answer when I call from now on."

"Of course I will," Sascha drawled, adding a cheeky, "Sir," just to be a dick.

Ivan tsked at him. "Did you ever think I might worry?"

"The thought never even crossed my mind," Sascha answered truthfully.

Ivan's sigh was heavy, like he had the whole weight of the world on his shoulders. "Everything I do for you is in your best interest."

Sascha rolled his eyes as dramatically as possible, almost wishing Ivan was there just so he could see him do it. "You wouldn't even let me tell Alexei I'd been stabbed."

"Because he would have come to coddle you, and then I would have had to kill him. And then you would have sulked endlessly. So, as I said—in your best interest."

"When can I come home, then?"

"Not yet."

"Don't you already know who ordered it? Can't you just...deal with it already?"

"I *believe* I know who ordered it," Ivan corrected him, in the same tone beleaguered adults used with overly curious children. "And the man who stabbed you *has* been dealt with. But he was a disposable pawn—he didn't have the intel about the cameras in the elevator. I doubt they expected him to escape. It's the person giving the orders we need to worry about, and I can't just start a mob war because you're getting antsy in your rustic paradise, zaychik."

Sascha suppressed a shiver. He knew he'd been the one to lead the conversation in this direction, but he didn't like thinking about people being "dealt with," even if they *were* assholes who'd stuck a knife in him. He didn't like thinking about the family business at all, if he could help it. And why should he? Their father had made it clear from the beginning Sascha wasn't expected to participate. Too delicate.

Too weak was what he meant.

But Ivan, in his rampage after Alexei had tanked a business deal and fled into the night, costing them millions, had apparently pissed some *other* family businesses off, and now Sascha was caught in the crossfire.

Someone was trying to make a message out of him.

He, who had never even held a gun. Some mistaken asshole seemed to think his death would actually put a damper on Ivan's day. And now he was stuck in this town until Ivan deemed it safe to return. He was concerned he had a mole in his operation, someone who'd spilled the beans on the timing of Sascha's arrival to his office.

Of course, Ivan could always decide he was better off with Sascha out of the picture entirely and keep him there indefinitely.

And would that be so bad? Alexei escaped it all, and he's happy enough.

But Alexei had found love and purpose and all that jazz. All Sascha had found so far was a too-large house desperately in need of renovation and an overly friendly teenager who thought cross-country skiing was a legitimate pastime.

He sighed loudly into the phone. "I'm hanging up now."

"Pick up next time."

"Ta-ta." He slid his phone back into his pocket and sipped his coffee. It was surprisingly good—dark and rich. What was a fetus doing making such good coffee?

Sascha stared out at the restless ocean, shivering as a breeze hit him. The joggers he'd thrown on were too thin for the changing weather.

But they were comfortable.

Sascha grinned as he took another sip. That was one thing a life in hiding had going for it, he supposed.

No fucking suits.

———

Sascha took his time returning to his house, a shabby number in the Queen Anne Victorian style—two whole stories, not including the attic, all of it shaded by the enormous trees surrounding it.

He wasn't sure why Ivan had insisted on paying cash for a whole-ass house, rather than just renting him a place, especially since Sascha was without his usual maid service to keep the damn thing clean. It no doubt fit into his nefarious schemes somehow, in some way Sascha wasn't privy to. It had come fully furnished, and Sascha was fairly certain the former owner had died in there, but he tried not to think about that part too hard.

Either way, it was…a lot. Sascha's apartment in New York had been nothing to sneeze at, but this was a whole goddamn *house*. One that made a lot of noises. Which he'd been assured—by both Ivan and the plumber who'd come to fix the pipes—was just the sound of the house's bones settling with the changing weather.

Although, frankly, Sascha didn't like to think of his humble abode as having bones at all. It made him think too much of the house as a monster, ready to devour him.

Not that he was scared, or anything. He was almost thirty, for fuck's sake. He just didn't like old, weird houses that seemed to talk.

Like now.

Sascha paused, bottles of nail polish in hand. He'd been setting up a station for himself—sheets of newspaper on the coffee table in case he made a mess—but he'd just heard a strange rustling sound, maybe coming from the attic room in the front turret (because, yes, his house had a *turret*).

There it was again.

Sascha frowned up at the ceiling. "If you're a ghost up there," he called out, shaking the bottles vaguely in the direction of the attic, "I'm asking you kindly to get the fuck out of my house."

There was no answer, only the same strange noise again. It was probably the old owner, wasn't it, come to tell him to fuck off back to New York?

Or, even worse...

Sascha stood in a hurry, setting the bottles on the table. "Oh, fuck no. There better not be rats up there."

If there were rats in that goddamn attic, he was moving out, no matter what Ivan said.

He headed upstairs, turning on each light as he went, no matter that it wasn't dark yet outside. He wasn't facing a ghost *or* rats in anything less than complete brightness.

He climbed up the ladder into the attic room, pulling the cord to turn the one pathetic light bulb on once he got up there.

He was met with a few pieces of dusty furniture and a whole stack of boxes. And...more boxes, more than he had the energy to get into anytime soon. Couldn't the house's seller have cleared it of *any* of the previous owner's junk?

He paused. There was that rustling sound again.

Sascha peered around the boxes, barely daring to breathe. There were scattered books on the ground, dusty and a little water damaged. Had they been knocked over?

But he didn't see any droppings or—actually, Sascha had no

clue what other signs to look for when it came to rats. A ratlike smell, maybe?

But the attic smelled just fine. A bit musty, but not rank or anything. Sascha bent down and picked up one of the books. It was a real fancy number, leather-bound, with intricate designs etched into the cover. Skinny though. Barely a hundred pages.

He flipped it open. What words there were, were written in a language he didn't recognize. It almost looked like it could be Latin. But Sascha knew Latin—one of the takeaways of boarding school, along with how to give and receive furtive blow jobs after hours—and this wasn't it.

The book was mostly illustration, with pretty designs on almost every page. They looked like runes of some kind. Huh.

Sascha held on to the book while he did one more cursory look around the room. He didn't find anything worth freaking out over. The noise must've been the house's old, creepy bones after all.

He took the book down with him—it would give him something to stare at while he painted his nails. Six weeks in this tiny town and he was sick to death of trash TV.

And he'd never thought he'd see the day when he could claim *that*.

Sascha set the book on the coffee table and perched on the edge of the couch, ready to get to work. He'd decided to go with the electric blue—Seth seemed nice and all, but Sascha didn't know him well enough to get all matchy-matchy with him when it came to nail colors.

He painted his left hand as best he could and studied the results, which weren't half-bad. Although it did make his clothes —his beige sweatshirt and black joggers—look a bit boring in comparison.

Maybe he should get something a little more fun to wear, just for at home. Some looser pants, maybe. Something flowy and...pretty.

Bright.

After all, what Ivan didn't know couldn't hurt him.

Sascha flipped through the book he'd found while he waited for his left hand to dry enough to start the other. There was one pattern in particular that kept catching his eye, a swirly blue number that almost seemed to move when he stared too hard.

He set one of the newspaper pages he'd been using to catch any stray drops next to the book, using the nail polish brush to copy the design. It looked pretty nice, actually. The thing had seemed complicated when looked at as a whole, but each individual part was easy enough.

When he'd finished his doodle, Sascha leaned back to compare the two. The only difference was the stanza of poetry or whatever under the design in the book.

Sascha tried sounding it out phonetically. "Too-ah-thun fay-mon..."

He continued mumbling while he traced the pattern over again with a second coat of polish. When he got to the end of the little poem, he flipped the page to see if there was any more.

Fuck.

Sascha hissed and flinched back, a familiar burning on his index finger. "Ouch."

He'd gotten a paper cut.

Sascha's stomach turned over, and he looked to the side as quick as he could, holding his finger out of sight. A paper cut alone probably wouldn't be enough to make him faint, but he didn't want to risk it. He could feel the drops welling up, dripping onto the newspaper.

Gross.

He'd wait for the bleeding to stop, then put a paper towel over it. He could wash it in the sink without looking and then—

BOOM.

Sascha startled, a yelp escaping his lips. *What the fuck?*

BOOM.

He straightened in his seat. The noise—and this was no subtle *rustling* anymore—seemed to be coming from everywhere and nowhere all at once.

BOOM.

Sascha stood, bleeding finger forgotten. That definitely wasn't rats. And if it was a ghost, it was a goddamn poltergeist.

He made to exit the living room, to see if maybe there was some construction going on outside, but the noise sounded again, this time accompanied by a thick blue smoke filling the room, obscuring Sascha's vision completely.

Oh God, was he under attack? Had Ivan's stupid enemies found him and now instead of stabbing him they were going to give him a heart attack via haunted house special effects? Should he run? Hide? Throw a bottle of nail polish into their eyes?

But before he could decide, the smoke cleared in an instant, like it had never been there at all. It might have been reassuring—the unnatural speed of it all aside—if not for what the cleared smoke revealed.

Oh. Oh fuck.

There was a goddamn monster standing in Sascha's living room.

3

Sascha

Sascha had been in front of some terrifying men before. Dead-eyed, callous, trigger-happy.

But now he was standing less than two feet away from an actual monster.

Like, in the flesh—all sevensome feet of it, plus whatever extra inches the black horns twisting out of its head added.

Good thing this place has such high ceilings. Sascha let out a hysterical giggle.

As he stood there, his giggle trailing off into a weird, choked gasp and his feet seemingly frozen to the living room floor, the monster blinking at him calmly, Sascha had to eventually admit that it was at least a *hot* monster.

Its face was human-looking, if you ignored the strange color, and almost eerily beautiful, in a harshly masculine way. Like a statue, all sharp lines cut from stone, with its dark slashes of eyebrows pulled together in a slight frown. The black hair trailing down to the middle of its chest looked unbearably soft and smooth, like a waterfall of silk.

And holy fuck...he—Sascha couldn't think of him as "it" anymore, not with that face—had clearly never missed a day at the gym. A fact that was made abundantly clear by his weird getup, wherein his broad shoulders were covered with some strange leather armor but his chest and arms were bare.

How the hell is that practical? Sascha had to wonder.

The armor was paired with loose, almost flowy black pants held up with an array of mismatched belts, more than one of which had a wicked-looking dagger sticking out of it.

Sascha frowned at that, his heart catching in his chest. He wasn't exactly a huge fan of daggers lately.

The monster's revealing outfit showcased not just his physique but a dark-blue mass of tattoos that ran up his chest and shoulder all the way up the right side of his neck. They weren't like any tattoos Sascha had seen, mostly because they didn't stay still, instead swirling like smoke over his skin.

Skin that had a decidedly blue tint to it, although a much paler shade than the dark ink of his markings. And lighter than the blue of his eyes, which were glowing like little monster light bulbs.

Overall, the effect was a tad unsettling, to say the fucking least.

Sascha tried to clear his throat, but all he managed was a strangled cough. How long had they been standing there? The monster was just staring back at Sascha, one dark brow—the same black as his hair—arched as if to say, "Well?"

Rude. It wasn't like Sascha had *invited* him, was it?

Eventually the monster seemed to tire of Sascha's frozen indecision. He opened plush lips. "Human," he said, his voice so dark and deep it sent a shiver running down Sascha's spine.

Well, at least he could communicate.

Sascha swallowed hard, grateful when he didn't cough again.

"Yes. Human," he agreed, pointing to himself in demonstration. He pointed back at the monster. "And you are?"

The monster gave him a deeply unimpressed look. "Explain your purpose, *human*."

Explain his...purpose? *Sascha's* purpose? "E-Excuse me?" Sascha sputtered. "You just—just *appeared* in my living room."

The monster's glowing blue eyes narrowed. "You summoned me."

"I did *not*!" Sascha argued. "I wouldn't! I don't make a habit of summoning monsters into my living room."

The monster gave him a concerned frown, like Sascha was daft. "No monsters here."

Sascha gaped at him. "What?"

"I'm not a monster, pup. I'm Kai." He bent his absurdly large torso into a weird half bow. "Kaisyir, at your service." He said the last part grudgingly, like at Sascha's service was the last place he wanted to be.

Sascha didn't know what to say to that except, "Well, I don't summon Kaisyirs either."

Oh God, what was happening? Maybe Sascha had never woken up from his stabbing. Maybe he was in the hospital, still comatose, and this whole small-town reverie was just that: a figment of his imagination. That would explain Ivan sending him to Maine, wouldn't it?

He hadn't let Sascha leave New York in years.

Except everything felt so...real. The smoky scent in the air, lingering long after the clouds of it were gone. The heat of the room, which had gone up at least ten degrees on Kai's arrival. The almost palpable weight of Kai's stare. The way Sascha's stomach was twisted into knots.

Surely Sascha's imaginary, comatose self wouldn't still be having tummy aches, right?

Kai cocked his head toward Sascha's coffee table, where the bottles of polish and newspaper still lay. "You painted my mark."

Now that he mentioned it, the design Sascha had traced did bear a remarkable resemblance to Kai's weird smoke tattoos.

Still. "I was just doodling with nail polish!" Sascha protested.

Kai huffed, like Sascha was the one being unreasonable. "You said the words, did you not?"

"I didn't know what I was saying!"

"And you spilled your blood upon the symbol."

Sascha's stomach roiled. He held up a hand. "Please don't say that word right now."

"What?" Kai crossed his arms, biceps bulging, a smirk on his face. "Blood? If you mean to master me, you can't be squeamish, pup."

"I don't mean to master anything!" Sascha shook his head, irritated that all his statements were coming out as screeches. "And I'm not a pup," he said, his voice a little more even. "I'm a grown man."

Kai looked him up and down, the act of which made Sascha terribly aware that while he may have been a respectably average five foot ten, he was a little speck compared to this massive brute, especially considering Sascha had missed quite a few days at the gym. Like, all of them. Which had never bothered him before—he was naturally thin, and he had no interest in being all muscly—but he was suddenly feeling very...inadequate.

What if this thing wanted to *fight* him?

His assessment finished, Kai's smirk only deepened. "You're barely grown, *pup*. Have you even held a sword?"

Something about Kai's piss-poor attitude had at least a bit of Sascha's fear dissipating. Monsters were one thing, but he was no stranger to toxic masculinity. He sniffed haughtily. "I wasn't aware that was a criterion for manhood. Where would I even find one in this day and age?"

Kai's smirk turned into a frown. He glanced around Sascha's living room. "What century is this?"

"Um. The twenty-first?"

"Mm." Kai hummed thoughtfully. "I lost track, I suppose." He caught Sascha back in that alarming gaze. "Now, about our contract."

Sascha resisted the urge to step back. "Contract?"

Kai nodded. "You can't summon without a contract."

Sascha threw his hands up, giving in to the urge to screech again. "I didn't mean to summon you in the first place!"

"You really didn't?" Kai shook his horned head skeptically. "Well, I'm here now, aren't I? Any enemies in need of vanquishing? Havoc in need of wreaking?"

"No, I—" Sascha paused. Truthfully, he did have enemies. Although, he wasn't sure if throwing a gigantic, horned, supposed non-monster at them was the way to vanquish them.

He peered up at said gigantic, horned non-monster. "If you're not a monster, what are you?"

Kai flashed a smile at him, revealing two rows of bright white, pearly, *pointed* teeth. "I'm a demon."

Oh. A demon. Of course.

Sascha leaned into the wall, suddenly feeling like standing solely on the strength of his own two feet wasn't such a good idea. "From—from hell?" he asked faintly.

"From—" Kai said a word that sounded an awful lot like "Muck-lake." At Sascha's confused look, he clarified, "The demon realm."

Right, right. The demon realm. Not hell, then. That was a plus, right?

Sascha noted for the first time that Kai was standing in a circular ring, one that looked almost painted onto the floor, the same swirling blue of his tattoos. And that he hadn't stepped out of it—not to walk toward Sascha or around the room or anything else.

Sascha peered up at him. "Am I right in thinking you can't leave that circle?"

Kai eyed him warily. "Not until our contract is finalized."

"Oh! I see." Sasha nodded frantically. "Okay, cool. Perfect."

And then Sascha did the only sensible thing he could do.

He straightened from the wall. He took a deep breath.

And he ran right the fuck out of the house.

Sascha shivered as he speed-walked, putting as much distance between himself and his cursed residence as possible. He missed having a driver at his service. And why hadn't he thought to bring a jacket during his dramatic exit? Compared to the extra warmth Kai had brought with his arrival, it was practically the arctic outside.

He did an abrupt about-face, turning in the direction of downtown. Sascha would go to the bar, warm up, and call Ivan to get him the fuck out of here. He'd beg if he needed to.

Because surely a little Mafia squabble was nothing in comparison to a literal demon summoned from some hell dimension, right?

But there was someone else Sascha wanted to speak to first.

He pulled his phone out of his pocket—giving a quick little prayer of thanks to the technology gods that he'd had it on him when he'd run out—and dialed the only number other than Ivan's he actually had memorized.

"Sascha?"

A wave of relief ran through Sascha at the sound of his brother's voice. "Alexei," he sighed. "Alyosha," he amended, switching to the rarely-used Russian diminutive of his brother's name, weirdly comforted just saying it.

He should have known that would be a dead giveaway.

"What's wrong?" Alexei asked, alarm in his voice. "What's happened? Where's this area code you're calling from?"

There was so much Sascha wanted to say that he didn't even know where to begin.

Everything's wrong. I was stabbed. I'm in a strange place. Someone's after me, and I didn't even do *anything. There's an honest-to-God demon waiting for me in my living room.*

Alexei had always been the one Sascha had turned to, growing up. Seven years older, Alexei was the only one in their family who'd looked after him without asking for complete subservience in return. He'd been a safe space. A haven.

But then he'd left.

He'd *left*.

Sascha hesitated. "Nothing's wrong. I—" He paused. He remembered, just then, something that had happened shortly after Alexei had left. Sergei had gone after him and had come back with his tail between his legs, claiming that Alexei was a monster and that his boyfriend was too. He'd clearly meant it literally but wouldn't say anything beyond that.

"The eyes," he'd kept saying.

Glowing, freaky blue demon eyes, perhaps?

Sascha nibbled on his lower lip. "Hey, Alexei. Is your boyfriend by any chance a demon?"

"Excuse me?" All the warmth and concern left Alexei's voice in an instant, leaving it cold and eerily similar to Ivan's.

Sascha pressed on. If he'd let himself be intimidated by cold, eerie voices, he'd never have done anything remotely fun in his entire life. "You know, a demon. Giant dude with horns and smoke and weird, moving tattoos? Possibly summoned from an old book you found? Ring any bells?"

"I've sent you photos of Jay. Does that description really fit?"

Oh, right. Sascha let out a sigh. "I seem to have summoned one accidentally. A demon, that is. He's waiting for me at my house. Says he needs a contract. Do you think he means, like, my soul?"

There was a long pause. When Alexei spoke again, he no longer sounded cold. Just...tired. "Listen, I'm sorry I haven't been checking in more. I did try calling your old number last week, but it didn't go through."

Of course. Alexei thought this was just a cry for attention. What else was he supposed to think? Sascha tried to keep his voice light, even as his heart sank. "Oh, that's okay. You know me. Always landing on my feet, with the help of Papa's money. Or Ivan's, now, since Papa's dead and all. Which you know!" He let out a laugh. "You were at the funeral and everything."

"Sascha..."

"Anyway, got to go! Demon in my living room and all. Ta-ta."

He dropped the call, mortified to find he was holding back tears. What had he really expected? For Alexei to drop everything and run back to him because Sascha was spouting deranged nonsense about demons?

He was a grown man, for fuck's sake. He shouldn't be asking for Alexei to clean up his messes in the first place. And more than that, he knew better. People left—left Sascha—and they never, ever came back. Not his mother. Not any of his dozens of nannies. Not Alexei.

Ivan would probably do the same someday, most likely by way of a bullet through his head.

"Hey, you all right?"

Sascha took his eyes off the ground and looked up to find he'd made his way downtown after all, his feet apparently on autopilot. There was a handsome buff dude standing in front of the door to the town's one and only gay bar.

Sascha cleared his throat, blinking back his traitorous tears. "I'm fine."

"You don't have a coat on," Buff Dude pointed out.

"I...dropped it."

"Oh. Bummer." The guy nodded, apparently convinced. Maybe not the brightest crayon in the tool shed. Sascha knew the type—it was one of his favorite types, actually—good-looking and built and dumb as rocks.

No matter that Buff Dude didn't hold a candle to Kai's unearthly beauty.

Sascha would have to be twelve kinds of crazy to lust after a literal demon.

Buff Dude tilted his head toward the inside of the bar. "You going in? It's cold out. Especially if you dropped your coat."

Sascha glanced at the door. The place didn't have any windows, at least not on the front side. But he could imagine it would be, at the very minimum, warm inside. He could pick this himbo up, get him to take Sascha home, leave the worrying about the demon for another day.

That would be the familiar, cowardly way out. Push it aside. Pretend not to see it. Leave it for someone else to deal with. He'd continue hiding out, Ivan would clean up his mess eventually, and Sascha would get to go home.

Until the next time Ivan pissed off someone powerful, that was.

Sascha held up a finger to the nice, muscled man. "One sec, champ."

He fished out his phone and sent a text.

I've summoned a demon.

Ivan's reply was prompt and predictable.

I don't have time for your games right now.

Sascha didn't have to bite back any tears this time. Of course

Ivan wouldn't take him seriously. No one did. No one ever had. But with Kai at his disposal...

Sascha sent one last, longing look at the hottie in front of the bar.

And then he turned around.

This demon wanted to be at Sascha's beck and call, form a contract, wreak havoc on Sascha's enemies?

Then maybe it was finally time for Sascha to start doing things a little differently.

4

Kai

The human had just...left. With Kai still in the damned summoning circle.

Kai growled, smacking at the invisible barrier that surrounded him. He would have liked to be able to at least pace his frustration out, but the boundary wouldn't allow him even that much.

Was this a negotiation tactic of some kind? Leave Kai to stew and hope for better terms? If so, the pup had another thing coming to him—contracts only went one way.

But the little human had seemed more frightened than wily.

Had he truly summoned Kai by accident?

Kai grinned wolfishly. *Poor pup.*

He certainly wasn't anything like the humans who had summoned Kai before. Kai had always been called by warriors, chieftains, leaders of men. Battle-weary and bloodstained and almost always arrogant to a fault. But this human? He was slender and soft, with delicate features and clear blue eyes, his hair a pale white-blond that was rare to see on a man grown. He looked more likely to warm a man's bed than lead him into battle.

He was different. Almost...interesting.

Although, anything would be interesting after being stuck in the Void for centuries. Kai had looked through the portal into the human realm enough to know that time had progressed, but he hadn't paid much attention to the details. He wasn't like the incubus or Chaos, enraptured by every little thing the humans did. Kai had wanted to be done with this world.

And if he could get the pup to bite—to take the contract—he would be.

As if the human was summoned by his thoughts, the front door opened. Kai's muscles tensed in anticipation. He could smell him on the air, strangely sweet and almost floral.

And then there he was, the towheaded beauty, his fists clenched in determination, even as his knees visibly trembled.

Kai did his best to look as unintimidating as possible, but it was most likely pointless—he couldn't revert to human form without a contract in place. He supposed he could have crouched down to the little one's level, but he'd only feel foolish doing so.

The pup approached the circle, every step small and cautious, like Kai would grab him if he came too close.

He just might, at that. The human smelled good—soft and sweet, just like his pretty face. A far cry from the smoke and ash of the Void.

When he didn't speak right away, Kai couldn't resist asking, "What's your name, pup?"

The human's eyes narrowed. "It's Sascha. So you can stop calling me *pup*."

"Sascha," Kai repeated, tasting the sound of it on his tongue. It was a soft sound. Everything soft. Everything sweet.

If Kai had been allowed this kind of variety all along, he might not have tired of his summonings so soon.

"Yes. Sascha," the human repeated, his tone haughty, like he hadn't run away less than an hour before. "And I have questions."

Kai tipped his chin in acknowledgment. "Of course."

Sascha peered up at him. His lashes were pale, like the hair on his head. "What does the contract entail?"

Kai shrugged a shoulder. "Just as it sounds. A mere bargain."

"Yeah, likely story." Sweet Sascha placed his hands on slender hips. "What *kind* of bargain?"

"That's up to you, isn't it?" Kai waved a hand. "Most want me for exactly what I told you—destruction of their enemies. Aid in battle."

"Aid in battle?" Sascha repeated, disbelief coating his every word. "Who's asking you for that? The knights of the fucking roundtable?"

Kai frowned at him, recognizing again that he was in a very different time from the last era he'd been summoned into. "Clansmen. Kings. It's been...perhaps some time since I've been in the human realm."

Sascha took a moment, seeming to digest that fact. "And what do you get in return, in this bargain?"

"Only a small piece of your essence." Kai put his thumb and forefinger a smidgen apart in demonstration. "A tiny little piece, you see?"

"My essence?" Sascha's brow furrowed in confusion, and then his pale eyes widened. He stepped back. "You mean my soul? You want my *soul*?"

Kai attempted a reassuring smile. He'd never had to coax someone into a bargain before. "Just a piece, as I said. You won't miss it."

"Says you!" Sascha cried, his voice taking on a shrill tone again.

He was a loud little thing, wasn't he?

"Yes, says I," Kai confirmed. "It's only to tether me here, in the human realm."

"And I get it back when the contract's done?"

Kai cleared his throat. "Well, not exactly. But as I said, you won't miss it. Think of it like a strand of your hair." Kai reached out, itching to see if that hair was as soft as it looked. But of course the summoning circle stopped him, his hand hitting that invisible barrier. He lowered his arm. "Would you notice one missing strand?"

Sascha gave him a suspicious glance. "You don't take the whole thing when you leave?"

Kai shook his head. "I have other pieces already, from other summonings. This is my last contract." Kai didn't know what compelled him to give that truth, but it didn't seem to mean anything to the human anyway. His eyes were still narrowed warily.

"Don't I need every piece of my soul?" Sascha asked, teeth worrying at his lower lip.

"Do you?" Kai asked softly, his gaze narrowed in on that pink mouth. "When was the last time you used it?"

"You don't use it. It just *is*." Sascha let up his nibbling and threw his hands in the air. He seemed to waver strangely between hesitation and boldness. It was rather entrancing, in a dizzying way. "I haven't had enough coffee for a theological debate."

Kai straightened abruptly. "Coffee? You have coffee here?" He craned his neck, trying to find evidence of the brew. He'd had it just the once, an offering from one of his last bargains, and he'd longed for the taste ever since.

"Not here in the house. I'm a civilized man." Sascha crossed his arms with a sniff. "I have other people make it for me."

"Your servants have it, then?" Kai continued to search the room with his gaze, as if maybe one would appear, steaming mug in hand.

"What servants?" Sascha shook his head like he was clearing it of cobwebs. "Stop changing the subject. Okay, so a piece of my soul—which I will *not* miss, according to you—and you take care of my enemies?"

Kai nodded, anticipation zipping down his spine. They were getting somewhere now. "If that's what you wish."

"That's what I wish."

"Perfect. I, Kaisyir of the Demon Realm, will vanquish Sascha —" He paused, looking to the human. "What's your clan name, pup?"

"My clan name? Oh. Um, Kozlov."

"I will vanquish Sascha Kozlov's enemies to his satisfaction, in exchange for one piece of his immortal soul."

"Oh God," Sascha moaned. "Okay." Then he straightened, seeming to steel himself, and met Kai's eyes. Perhaps he wasn't completely soft, this human.

Kai grinned at him, his smile only widening when Sascha's gaze caught on his sharp teeth. "And now we seal the bargain."

"How?"

"The same way you called me. Blood."

Sascha began shaking his head furiously, stepping back. "Oh no. Nuh-uh. No way. I don't do blood."

"It's only a few drops," Kai argued, trying to keep the frustration from his voice. He was so close, damn it.

But Sascha kept up his furious shaking. "I can't. Not on purpose. I can't—can't look at it."

"Then I'll help you," Kai soothed, unwilling to lose this chance. "You may look away."

Sascha halted his retreat. "How?"

Kai beckoned him closer. "Place your hand into the circle."

"It won't stop me?" Sascha asked, cocking his head.

"No part of me may leave it, but any part of you may enter. Give me your hand, pup."

Sascha's limb trembled, but he did as Kai asked. He had a remarkably slender wrist and delicate fingers. Kai took hold.

The human gasped. "You're warm."

"Always." Kai kept his voice soft and low, as much as he was able. "Look away now."

Sascha turned his head, and Kai brought Sascha's index finger to his lips. "Deep breath," he instructed. Sascha obeyed, inhaling and holding it.

Kai bit down, ever so gentle, slicing the tip of Sascha's finger with one of his teeth. Copper dripped into his mouth and—unable to resist—he sucked gently, just for a moment.

Delicious.

Sascha made a strangled sound, head still turned away, and Kai released his finger from his mouth, allowing a few drops to fall onto the summoning circle.

There was a flash of bright light, a puff of smoke, and then Kai felt the boundary ease.

He was free.

He let out a joyful cry, stepping out in one long stride and sweeping the human up, tossing him in the air. "It's done!" he crowed, catching him as he fell.

There was no reply.

He looked down to find Sascha limp in his arms.

The human had fainted.

———

IT TOOK ONLY A BRIEF SEARCH—THE human a negligible weight in his arms in the meantime—for Kai to find the only bedroom in the house with a made bed, presumably where the human slept.

He set Sascha down gently on top of the covers. He found himself strangely reluctant to let go—it had been so long since he'd had any sort of touch at all, and it was oddly soothing to have that warm bundle in his hold.

But Sascha would no doubt sleep for a while yet—the act of sealing a contract tended to take it out of a human, even those who weren't squeamish at the sight of blood.

It was almost beyond comprehension: Kaisyir summoned by one who fainted at bloodshed.

What possible enemies could such a slip of a thing have?

Opportunists, perhaps? Aggressors looking to take advantage of his slight build and frail disposition? A hot surge of anger rose in Kai's chest at the thought of it. He ran his tongue thoughtfully over sharp incisors.

Whoever they were, they had another thing coming, didn't they?

The pup had protection now.

The contract had seen to that, as it always did. Kai could feel it, deep in his chest—that kernel of Sascha's essence he had taken. A warm weight just as soft and sweet as the feel of Sascha in his arms had been.

Strange. Kai had never enjoyed the feel of a soul piece before. Nor the taste of one. But Sascha's...

Delicious.

Kai watched that sleeping form a moment longer, his gaze focused on the gentle, steady rise and fall of Sascha's chest. There was a sliver of pale skin where his shirt had ridden up—Kai could tell, just from looking, that it would be like silk to the touch.

He wasn't boring, this human. Even in his sleep, he wasn't boring, his face contorting into little frowns, his hands clenching and unclenching. Bad dreams? Nightmare could have had quite a feast with him, if so.

But it wasn't Nightmare who'd been summoned, was it?

Just the thought of it sent a strange wave of possessiveness through Kai. He shrugged it off—the beginning of a contract always left one a bit unsettled—studying the rest of the human, from top to toe. The fingernails of his left hand were painted blue. But only the one hand. A strange custom, that. It brought to mind what he might look like with other embellishments. And his clothing was oddly drab—it didn't fit the essence of him at all. He'd be better suited to bright colors and soft silks, surely. Perhaps fine jewelry as well.

Kai had once seen a man with a gold chain around his middle, one end of it dangling down, dipping low, all the way to...

He shook his head, purging such thoughts. He was becoming just as bad as the incubus. This was not about physical desire. It was a bargain—one boon for another.

Kai did not fuck his bargains.

Although, he'd never had a bargain like Sascha before...

No. It was past time to leave this room. Too long in the Void had left him susceptible to weakness of the flesh; that was all. Best to occupy his mind with other things. Perhaps a search of the house would give him a clue to Sascha's predicament. The faster Kai could deal with it, the faster he would be free to return to his own world.

And then what?

Kai shook the thought away. If nothing else, a cursory look through the house might help orient him to this time. He'd seen the centuries pass, more or less, from looking through the portal. He knew in his mind the human world had changed. But being immersed in the reality of it was another matter, wasn't it?

All the plastic doodads, for one. Technology, as they called it. Like the little handheld devices that allowed humans to speak to someone a world away. Or the Internet, however that damned thing worked.

Why hadn't Kai asked the others to teach him better?

But he already knew why. It was because he'd begun to lose hope he'd ever be summoned again. He'd thought the Book must have been lost or somehow destroyed, no matter that it was supposed to be indestructible.

But clearly not. Sascha had found it.

Sascha had saved him.

He made his way back to the living room. There was his symbol, painted in... Kai picked up the bottle with one clawed hand and sniffed at it, immediately recoiling at the chemical scent. He'd seen this same color on Sascha's fingernails.

This was what Sascha had painted himself with? How strange.

Kai set the bottle aside, far out of reach. There, next to his symbol—the Book. Kai stared hard at its leather covering, as if to glean its secrets. He couldn't touch it himself—no demon held within its pages could, lest they attempt to tamper with their own mark.

After a time, he sighed, diverting his gaze. There were no secrets to be learned there, other than the mess Sascha had made of crumpled newspaper and spilled nail paint.

Kai went from room to room after that. He fiddled with the television, turning it on before immediately shutting it off when he was met with painted women screeching at each other from couches. They sounded a bit like Sascha when he was worked up.

After that he played for a while with the burners on the stove. He supposed it was impressive that humans had figured out a way to summon fire in an instant.

But then again, Chaos could do the same, and he didn't need a stove to do it.

Kai spent a good amount of time searching the cabinets for coffee, but Sascha had been truthful: there was none to be found. He'd have to ask Sascha who made it for him—he certainly hadn't been lying either about the house holding no servants.

Overall, Kai recognized more than he'd thought he would. He must have absorbed quite a bit vicariously from the others' viewings. Maybe it wouldn't be hopeless. He could ask Sascha to fill him in on the rest.

Sascha.

Kai's hand kept returning to his chest, over the place where the soul piece resided. He found himself strangely impatient for the human to wake. He'd never been that way before—it was usually a relief when his bargains slept, their demands on hold for a number of hours.

But he found himself returning to the bedroom and pulling up a chair. Watching. Waiting.

He told himself it was for Sascha's protection—Kai didn't yet know who the pup's enemies were. It was best to stick close, so as not to muck up the contract.

Yes, that was the reason for his vigilance.

Nothing more.

5

Sascha

Sascha woke with a start, eyes blinking open to soft morning light.

Huh. He must have forgotten to close the curtains last night.

He was tempted to roll over and go back to sleep—it wasn't like he had anything he had to do today anyway. Or any day, for that matter. And he'd had such a weird fucking dream: a big, hot, horned demon promising him protection or vengeance or whatever.

And if he was going to dream about built, beautiful monsters, couldn't those dreams be about them fucking him into the mattress? Otherwise, what was the point? Maybe if he closed his eyes again and thought real hard about thick, muscled arms and huge pecs and bare—

"You're awake."

Sascha shrieked, eyes flying back open. *What the fuck.*

He looked to the side. There was that same massive blue beast sitting in his bedroom chair, staring at him with glowing blue eyes.

Once, as a child, Sascha had woken to his dad at his bedside, loaded gun in hand.

He wasn't sure which experience was more disconcerting, really.

"Oh God," he moaned when some furious blinking didn't make the apparition go away. "You're real."

Kai let out an amused rumble. "Did you think me a figment of your imagination?" A massive hand landed on top of Sascha's, where it was clutching the bedspread. Kai's nails were black and pointed at the tip, like talons. "I'm as real as you."

Sascha snatched his hand back—were all demons so hot-blooded their touch practically burned?—and tossed the covers over his head. "I really can't be doing this before coffee."

"You said you could procure some. Where? When?"

The naked longing in Kai's voice had Sascha peeking out from under his blankets. God, he looked *hungry*. Or thirsty, as it were. "You really like coffee, huh?" He sat up, the strange normalcy of the demon's craving somehow giving Sascha the strength to face this supremely weird day. "I need to get it from the bakery, then."

"I'll accompany you."

"What? No. You're not exactly someone I can bring around town. You're all..." Sascha gave up on finding a word for it, waving a hand in demonstration instead. Like, seriously, how did Kai look even more massive sitting down?

He wasn't just sitting on top of Sascha's furniture. He *was* furniture. Furniture Sascha wouldn't mind climbing on top of and—

No. No horny morning thoughts. He is a literal *demon.*

He focused back on the present to find Kai frowning down at him. "I can't allow you to go alone."

"Why not?" Sascha asked, sliding out of bed, careful not to brush one of Kai's overly long legs on his way out.

"How am I to protect you if I'm not by your side?"

"My enemies aren't *here*." Sascha laughed at the thought, walking over to his dresser and grabbing a fresh stack of clothing, a pair of leggings and an oversize sweater he wouldn't be caught dead in outside the house.

"Where are they?" Kai asked.

"I don't know."

"*Who* are they?"

"I'm not sure."

"Why are they after you?"

"Oh!" Sascha snapped his fingers. "I know this one. My brother pissed them off."

Kai did not look suitably impressed by his knowledge. "Your brother," he repeated.

"Yeah, he's the leader of the, um, family business."

"Business."

"Yeah. You know..." Sascha lowered his voice to a whisper. "The mob? Russian Mafia?"

"His business is leading a mob of men?"

"Oh Lord. Coffee. We need coffee."

Sascha grabbed his phone. Seacliff was small, sure, but not small enough not to have at least one meal delivery app that was usable. He put in the order before heading into the bathroom with his clothes, shutting the door on Kai when he tried to follow him.

"No enemies in the bathroom," he called out through the door.

See? This was why he hadn't wanted his brother's stupid bodyguards, either. No privacy. Not a moment alone.

Although, his brother's bodyguards weren't anywhere close to the piece of terrifying eye candy Kai was, so there was that little perk, he supposed.

Sascha got dressed in a flash before brushing his teeth and

splashing some water on his face. His usual skincare routine would have to wait for a day he didn't have a seven-foot behemoth lurking at the bathroom door.

Sascha exited the bathroom, narrowly avoiding smacking his face into an absurdly broad chest on his way out.

"So!" he said brightly, leading Kai down the stairs and doing his best to avoid thinking about motorboating giant demon pecs. "The mob. Or Mafia. You know, take your pick on the terminology. Basically my brother is in charge of...a business, of sorts, like I said. But, um, illegal stuff. Like, we have legitimate fronts—nightclubs and the docks. But there's also gambling, and a decent amount of drugs, and maybe weapons, but I can't remember if that's still going on. No people though. We don't do human trafficking."

Jesus. Was he really trying to justify his family's shady dealing to a demon? "We're not the biggest game in town, but we're not tiny either. And there are a few families we deal with on a regular basis. Or compete with, depending how you look at it. And my brother pissed one of them off."

"And what do you do?"

Sascha missed a step in the hallway. "What?"

Kai's massive hand landed on his shoulder, righting him like a wayward tenpin. "You keep saying it's a family business. What do you do?"

"Oh. Um, nothing," Sascha told him, shrugging off the touch, a little disconcerted by the part of him that wanted to push up into it instead. "I'm not really involved. Our dad didn't want me to be."

"Because you faint at the sight of blood."

"No. That's—" Sascha turned in his tracks, scowling up at the demon. "I didn't *always* faint at the sight of blood. There was an incident." He cleared his throat. "Anyway, he just...didn't. Said one of his sons should be paving the way for legitimacy. Sent me to school instead. Schools plural. Boarding school, then college to get a business degree. But when I graduated, he never gave me anything legitimate to do, so I guess that was all bullshit. I think what he really wanted was to be a real father to at least *one* of sons, and I needed to not be his goon for that to happen."

Kai was staring back at him intently, his face unreadable. Why was Sascha even talking about this? There was no possible way the demon cared about any of his—or his brothers'—daddy issues.

Not to mention the mommy abandonment issues.

The doorbell rang, and in an instant, Sascha was flung against the wall, Kai looming over him, lethal-looking dagger in hand.

"What are you doing? Put that away. It's not a hit man, it's our coffee order." Sascha pushed his way out of Kai's grasp, ignoring the warm tingling at each of the places Kai's body had touched. "Stay here, you lunatic."

He opened the door to find the same buff dude from the bar the other night, coffee order in hand. "It's you," Sascha said with surprise.

Buff Dude nodded amiably. "You bought the old Eisner place. Right on." He held up his closed fist, presumably for a bump of some kind.

Sascha narrowed his eyes, his own hand remaining at his side. "I thought you were a bouncer."

"Oh, I do a lot of stuff," Buff Dude told him with an easy grin, lowering his arm. "But my passion's fitness. I post my routines online and everything." He gave Sascha a once-over. "If you ever want to bulk up some, I'm your guy."

Sascha hummed noncommittally. He would *not* be doing that. Twink death might be inevitable down the line, but that didn't mean he had to go and help it along.

He was about to politely shut the door in the guy's face when Buff Dude's eyes widened comically, his gaze fixed past Sascha's shoulder.

Oh fuck.

Sascha turned, expecting the worst. Would they have to erase the guy's memory like the suited dudes from *Men in Black*? Where did one go about acquiring a memory-erasing pen?

But it was not a giant horned monster in his entryway, after all.

It was a giant human man instead.

A giant human *Kai*, presumably, unless he had a human twin he'd been stashing away somewhere. He had the same unnaturally gorgeous face, but he was about half a foot shorter than his demon form—topping off at an almost reasonable six foot five—his armor gone. He was just as shirtless, with miles of tanned skin on display and that gorgeous hair falling to his chest. His weird swirling tattoos had turned into ordinary dark-blue ones that didn't move at all.

He still looked fierce as hell, reminding Sascha of some legendary Highlander from a trashy romance novel.

What he was, when it came down to it, was sex incarnate.

Sascha swallowed with a dry throat. Oh God. This was just a disaster, wasn't it? There was no use denying it anymore.

Sascha really wanted to fuck this demon.

Sascha wasn't sure what he said to get rid of the delivery guy, only that he was suddenly back in the kitchen with a still-human-looking Kai, who was making absolutely obscene noises over his coffee.

At least Sascha knew he'd gotten the order right: large black coffee, no sugar, no cream.

He held his own oat milk latte—still too hot to drink—between his hands, praying to whoever would listen he didn't spring a hard-on over a demon and his caffeinated beverage.

"Why didn't you tell me you could do that?" he asked. "Change into human form?"

Kai took a break from his pornographic coffee moment to shoot him an amused glance. "How else did you think I appeared on the battlefield without causing a panic?"

"I don't know! Turn invisible or something?"

"Invisibility is a challenge," Kai mused, casually blowing Sascha's mind. "Although, I can merge with the shadows well enough. Not like Nightmare, but..." He shrugged a shoulder. A massive, muscled shoulder, all tattooed and lickable and no longer covered by any armor.

Sascha took a huge swallow of his latte, burning his tongue and throat and possibly his entire digestive tract. "Can you turn back?"

Kai arched a dark brow. "Why?"

"Just turn back, please," Sascha pleaded. "It's...disconcerting." Mostly because it looked like a model from the cover of a cheesy romance novel had appeared in Sascha's kitchen like a wet dream come to life.

Kai let out a heavy sigh, like Sascha was being unreasonable, and set down his coffee. "All right then."

It turned out it was equally disconcerting to watch him transform from human to demon—it was almost too fast for Sascha's eyes to follow, the way he grew half a foot in a split second, horns sprouting from his head, Sascha's kitchen chair suddenly looking like dollhouse furniture beneath him.

Oh God. He was still hot. Why was he still so fucking hot?

Unfairly oblivious to Sascha's inner turmoil, Kai threw his head back and downed the rest of his coffee, throat working in ways that weren't helping Sascha's sexual panic a bit.

Maybe he should have gotten him a gallon of the stuff.

But no. Sascha needed a distraction. He found himself asking a question that had been niggling at the back of his mind. "If you haven't had a bargain in centuries, why do you speak modern English so well?"

"It's part of the magic of the Book," Kai explained. "I speak whatever language needed for my bargain." He gave Sascha a strange look, then added, "Zaychik."

The familiar nickname—one given to him as the baby of the family—coming out of the demon's mouth had Sascha's brain going haywire. Had he even heard that right? "What was that?" he asked faintly.

"Zaychik," Kai repeated perfectly, setting his presumably empty cup down with a mournful look.

"There's no reason for you to speak Russian," Sascha told him snippily, ignoring the way his traitorous heart was racing. "That's one of the only words I know. And it's just a stupid nickname."

Kai ran his tongue over sharp teeth, looking amused. "I know. *Bunny*."

"It can also just mean, like, darling. Or honey or whatever." Sascha gave him a stern look. All the more reason for the demon to stay away from using it. Sascha was an *adult*, goddamn it. "You better not start calling me bunny. Pup is bad enough."

Jesus. This wasn't the distraction Sascha had been looking for. "There's pastries too," he offered, holding up the white paper bag the delivery man / bouncer / online exercise sensation had brought. "I didn't know what you liked, so I ordered a few different kinds."

Kai shot the bag a disinterested glance. "I don't eat human food."

"What do you live off of, then?"

"In the human realm?" Kai placed a taloned hand on his pec. "The piece of your soul sustains me."

Sascha brushed that aside immediately. He couldn't think too hard about a chunk of his soul existing in someone else's chest. "That's all you need?"

"All I *need*, yes." Kai gave him a heated glance, his eyes beginning to glow slightly. "Sometimes our bargains will give us a bit extra for a job well done."

"More of their soul?" Did people really part with their spiritual bits so willy-nilly? Sascha was no stranger to impulsive decisions—he often made bad calls when scared, or angry, or sometimes just when he was particularly hungry—but damn.

"I can feed off other things," Kai mused. "Strong emotions, particularly anger or rage. Blood."

Sascha choked on a sip of his latte. "Demons drink…blood?" He'd been very much hoping that finger biting was a one-off.

Kai leaned back in his chair, seeming to get into the topic. "Different demons specialize in different things. My kind are warriors. So rage, violence, bloodshed." His eyes took on a faraway look. "Once, after a particularly fruitful battle, a chieftain cut open his wrist for me over a goblet. That was a good day."

What. The. Fuck.

Sascha clutched his hands to his chest, scooting his chair back as far away from Kai as he could manage. "Oh, I think the fuck *not*."

Kai only gave him a sly grin. "That was a special occasion. An incubus, however—just as an example—would feed off your lust."

Oh shit. Sascha cleared his throat. "But you don't—you don't do that?"

"It's not my specialty." Kai's grin turned positively wolfish. "But that doesn't mean I can't smell it on you."

"Um…"

Kai leaned forward, his eyes beginning to glow again. "You desire me, pup," he crooned, sounding entirely too pleased with that fact. "There's no use hiding it."

"I—What—I—" Sascha searched for the appropriate denial, only able to come up with a blurted, "You're not my type!"

"Oh?" Kai asked coolly, not seeming at all convinced. "And what is?"

"I like my men like I like my coffee: big and dumb and always nice to me." Sascha gathered the shreds of his dignity around him and gave Kai an exaggerated, appraising look. "You're big, but I don't think you're dumb. And you haven't been very nice to me either."

Kai's stupidly pretty lips formed into a mock pout. "But I put you to bed ever so gently."

"After you cut me!"

"A mere scratch. A nibble."

Sascha straightened in his chair. This demon was teasing him, the wretch. He sniffed haughtily. "I'm used to a certain level of treatment. I'm very spoiled, I'll have you know."

"Spoiled how?"

That caught Sascha short. He'd never had to explain how before. It was just a given. Sascha was the baby. Sascha was the weakling. Sascha was spoiled. He thought it over. "Well, mainly they give me money and don't ask me to do things I don't like to do."

Kai cocked his head. "They spoil you by ignoring you?"

Sascha let out a groan. "Ivan hardly *ignores* me, the controlling bastard."

"Then I don't understand."

"Well, just—I've never had a finger broken for flinching, or been forced to shoot a man, or—" Sascha broke off there, suddenly finding it hard to get air. His stomach had twisted into knots, and his throat wasn't working properly for some reason.

He didn't like talking about this stuff. Why was Kai making him talk about this stuff?

"Hey. Human. *Human.*"

Sascha opened his eyes—when had he closed his eyes?—to

find a glowing blue gaze locked onto his. Kai's hands were hot on his cheeks. "Breathe, pup. With me. In. Out. Just breathe."

Sascha did as Kai said, focusing on the unnatural glow of those eyes, the strange shifting tattoos on his neck.

Eventually, when breathing came naturally again, he attempted a smile. "See?" he said, unable to help how petulant he sounded. "You got me all worked up. Not very nice of you."

Kai's voice was low, his tone soothing. "No, I see you're correct. I don't meet your criteria at all, do I?"

Sascha sniffed, shaking his head out of Kai's hold. "No, you don't."

Although, that didn't explain why Sascha wanted nothing more than to bury his head in that massive chest, to let himself be held and comforted by a literal demon.

Stupid. It was so stupid of him, to want that.

Maybe *he* was the dumb one after all.

6

Kai

Kai sat in front of the small machine—the "laptop," Sascha had told him—staring at the image on the background. There were green, rocky hills with sheep scattered all around. The land looked familiar: modern-day Ireland, or Scotland, possibly.

Had Sascha been there? Kai had been summoned in those parts, a time or two. Perhaps they'd walked over the same land, centuries apart from each other.

Kai smiled at the thought. He'd have to ask in the morning. Sascha had retreated into his room for the night, after setting up another bedroom for Kai and insisting haughtily that Kai was under no circumstances allowed to watch him sleep this time.

He was a strange creature, this Sascha. Fearful one moment, brave the next. Bold beyond reason, then unaccountably shy. Full of contradictions at every turn.

As when Kai had called out his attraction—Sascha had been

red-faced and strangely flustered, even as he'd shamelessly insisted Kai was mistaken. That Kai was "not his type."

A lie if Kai had ever heard one.

He saw the way the human couldn't keep his eyes off him, sensed the simmering lust in his soul piece, smelled it on his person. So why the foolish denial? Was Sascha perhaps nervous their bodies wouldn't fit?

They would fit. Kai would make sure of it.

Perhaps he needed to convince Sascha of that fact...

And perhaps Kai should have been alarmed with how quickly he was changing his own mind—telling himself one moment that he didn't fuck his bargains, then spending the next considering how best to seduce sweet Sascha. But it was only natural, wasn't it? Kai had been alone a very long time, and Sascha was so very...tempting.

Kai brought a hand to his chest, where Sascha's soul was lodged. Was it perhaps the little soul piece's fault? It had settled so well within him it was hard not to think how else they might merge.

Kai had heard rumors, of course. Of demons meeting a compatible human and choosing to stay in the realm, to bond with that human only. He'd figured the compatibility part had been an excuse—those demons had wanted to remain, and they'd found their way. All souls had always tasted the same to him.

But no longer. Sascha's soul piece was like no other he had tasted: sweet and juicy, with little salty or bitter pockets hidden every which way.

Or maybe the problem was all the tempting thoughts Sascha had brought up with his talk of being pampered. His definition was so lacking it made Kai want to rectify the situation. Sascha thought money and a lack of responsibility made him so? What of being brought the freshest kills? Having his naked form draped in the brightest furs of the demon realm? Being bathed in warm rivers and massaged with fine oils?

Of course, that was mating behavior...

But Sascha had brought the subject up, whether he'd intended to or not. His talk of *niceness*. Niceness was a human construct. *Sweetness* was what he really craved, to match the sweetness in his soul. And demons of Kai's ilk were sweet only with their mates. Mostly because the females of his species were twice as large and three times as ferocious. If one didn't want their head bitten off—quite literally—sweetness was the only option.

But Sascha? Kai wouldn't *need* to be sweet with him—Sascha could hardly lay a scratch on him, even if he wanted to—but there would be a certain...pleasure to it, wouldn't there? Watching those pale cheeks redden in delight? Seeing if he lashed out in haughty embarrassment?

It would be delicious to try.

As delicious as the rage simmering alongside Sascha's lust— rage that Sascha didn't quite allow himself to feel but that bubbled up each time he spoke of his family. Rage as dark and tempting as the bitter brew he'd procured for Kai that morning.

Kai sighed, licking his lips. All in its time. For now, he needed to focus. They'd whiled the rest of the day away with Sascha educating Kai on the modern world, explaining how the various modern doodads worked, giving Kai the password to his laptop so he could "goggle" what else he might want to learn.

As to what Kai *really* wanted to know—who was after Sascha and why—Sascha had been as unforthcoming as ever. He claimed he needed to consult his brother but made no attempt to do so. As if he feared involving him.

Which was odd in itself. If this Ivan was his kin, and they were in no contest for power (as Sascha insisted they were not), why wouldn't he want to aid him? Maybe it had something to do with

Sascha's reaction that morning, when discussing how his family "spoiled" him.

Kai had seen it before, in those who had experienced battle too young. There were different words for it in different eras: battle-dazed, shell-shocked. He supposed now they would simply say the pup was traumatized.

And maybe Ivan had something to do with that.

Kai growled, turning his attention back to the laptop. He opened the browser, as Sascha had shown him, and typed in the name: Ivan Kozlov.

It was frustratingly slow work. Sascha had typed with both hands, but Kai's fingers were too large for the little plastic button letters; he had to press only one at a time.

But when it was done...

There wasn't much information, only a few businesses listed. Nothing about mobs or Mafias. But there was a photo. Kai clicked on it carefully, and it grew on the screen. He studied it.

Ivan looked remarkably similar to Sascha—the same pale-blond hair, the same blue eyes, the same pink lips and almost delicate features. There were signs of his older years—light markings of crow's-feet around his eyes, a certain solidity to his form. He was taller as well, from what Kai could see. And meaner.

With the eyes of a killer.

Sascha's eyes may have been the same icy color, but they didn't exude coldness, not like that. Kai found himself oddly grateful for that fact. He wouldn't have wanted Sascha to have a killer's eyes. Sascha didn't need them anyway. He could continue to be strange and varied and sweet.

He had Kai to do his killing for him.

At that thought, Kai found himself eager to be closer, no longer content to poke around with the laptop. Why play with machines when there was better entertainment so close at hand? He wished Sascha hadn't demanded he sleep in his own bedroom. They wouldn't even have had to mate—Kai could have simply crawled into bed with him, shared some of his warmth.

He crept up the stairs on silent feet, stopping at the door to Sascha's bedroom. He wasn't technically disobeying Sascha's order—he wasn't watching him sleep, was he? He was only standing at a door.

It was the best location for standing guard anyway. He was there for Sascha's protection.

And, as he was there, he couldn't help listening. He already knew Sascha was still awake—he could feel a pulsing awareness from Sascha's soul piece. What was he doing in there all by himself? Playing on his little magic phone?

Kai pressed an ear to the door. There was the rustling of sheets, the quiet sound of heavy breaths, and then...

Was that a moan?

Kai held his own breath. Yes, there it was again—a soft, little sigh of a moan. Was the human pleasuring himself? Kai's cock grew heavy at the thought.

He breathed in deeply now, as quietly as he could. The door was in the way, but he could still make out the buttery tang of a human's lust, deeper and richer than what he'd scented in the kitchen earlier. And as Sascha continued with his task, his noises grew less careful, and Kai grew even more sure.

If only Kai could see. Was Sascha stroking himself? Or perhaps playing with his entrance? Were his eyes closed, thinking of Kai? Sascha desired Kai's body; that much was clear. But did he imagine Kai filling him? Did he prefer Kai in his demon or his human form?

No matter. Kai could give him either. Or both.

He grasped his hard cock through his trousers. His ridges were pulsing now, almost in time with Sascha's desperate gasps. He could stroke himself right here, if he wished, mark Sascha's door with his release.

He let out a long, low growl at the thought.

All at once, the noises inside the bedroom stopped.

Kai held back a curse. Would Sascha yell now? Order him to his own room?

But after a moment, the familiar sounds of pleasure started up again. They were even louder now, as if Sascha were perhaps nearing the end. Losing control.

Kai bared his teeth in a grin. He kept his grasp on his cock, his thumb playing with the slit through the soft fabric of his trousers as he drank in the muffled sounds. Sascha hadn't stopped, but he hadn't acknowledged Kai's presence either. Did he think to play? To pleasure himself to the thought of Kai listening, then deny it in the morning?

That was fine. Sascha could pretend all he liked.

It had been a long, long time since Kai had held desire for anything tangible, but he desired this human. In what way, or for how long—those were questions he could answer later.

But of one thing he was certain—he wanted Sascha.

And what Kai wanted, Kai would have.

7

Sascha

Sascha crept down the stairs. It was possible Kai was still sleeping—God, let him still be sleeping—and Sascha needed every minute alone he could get.

What had he been *thinking*?

He hadn't been thinking, obviously, because why else would he have been jerking himself off to Kai growling outside his door?

Idiot. Dumb, dumb, dumb.

But he'd been hard and horny and weak; may the gods of sexual frustration forgive him. He'd retreated to bed early, hoping to get away from all the stupid temping muscles in his house and distract himself with online shopping (and there were quite a few packages he was most definitely going to regret coming his way in two business days or less). But it hadn't been enough. So then he'd turned to porn, specifically videos of blond twinks getting absolutely railed by massive dark-haired men.

But *that* hadn't been enough either. He'd kept thinking of Kai, Mr. I-Can-Smell-the-Desire-on-You Demon. And look, was it really Sascha's fault he'd been born a size queen? Why would fate tempt him like this?

No, he scolded himself, turning at the foot of the stairs. *Your propensity for big dicks does* not *excuse you lusting after a creature from another dimension.*

Although, it was hard to remember why when he tiptoed into the kitchen to find Kai already there waiting for him, a surprisingly charming grin on his face. "Sascha," he purred. "Good morning."

God, he made Sascha's little kitchen table look like doll furniture.

Kai's expression gave nothing away. It didn't *look* like he'd been listening to Sascha jerk off in his bedroom just the night before. Maybe the growl hadn't been about that? Maybe he'd been… securing the premises or something, scaring off any potential baddies.

And maybe Ivan will show up to your door tomorrow in a rainbow fucking tutu.

Kai was in his demon form, but the shoulder armor was missing. Not sure what else to say that wasn't, "Hey, hear anyone masturbate lately?" Sascha asked the only other thing he could think of. "Why do you only cover your shoulders? Why not your chest or, like, your belly?"

Kai's brow furrowed. "That would cover my most vulnerable areas."

"Um, yeah. Exactly."

"It would be a sign of weakness."

"Oh, of course." It took everything in Sascha to contain his eye roll. Maybe Kai was more his type than he'd thought. That was maybe the dumbest thing he'd ever heard.

Kai waved a dismissive hand in the air. "Besides, no human weapon can kill me. And no demon in this realm would attempt it." Then he winked at Sascha. Which, frankly, should be illegal for someone that hot to do. "So you don't need to worry, pup."

Sascha bristled. "I'm not *worried*."

But Kai was already changing the subject, sidling closer until his body heat was warming Sascha's skin, staring hopefully at the phone in Sascha's hand. "Have you summoned our coffee yet?"

No, because I was hoping you'd still be asleep, you goddamn walking wet dream.

Sascha cleared his throat, the scent of smoke and spice making him a little light-headed. There was too much sexual tension here for one house to hold. They needed to expand their perimeters. "Put your human suit on," he ordered. "We'll get the coffee ourselves."

"We're going out?" Kai's eyes lit up at the suggestion.

It was stupidly endearing.

"Just let me get dressed." Sascha started to head back upstairs, then turned back. "Um. None of my shirts are going to fit you."

Kai stared at him for a moment, then waved a hand, a black shirt appearing on his broad chest out of thin air. He grinned smugly. "I can procure my own shirt."

Sascha gaped. Closed his mouth. Gaped again. He shook his head. "Why the fuck can't you *procure* coffee for yourself, then?"

Kai frowned at him like he was being unreasonable. "How could I? Clothing is simple. Foodstuffs are…complicated."

Sascha had no idea what to say to that. Was it his life now to have his mind blown every day before it was even a reasonable hour? He shook his head again for good measure and went to get dressed.

The walk to the coffee shop was…distracting. Specifically, Kai was distracting. His magnetic pull did not seem limited to Sascha —everyone whose path they crossed stared, with varying levels of subtlety. It had Sascha's hackles raising.

He knew logically that it was only natural. There was something about Kai that stood out, even as a human, even wearing a regular black long-sleeved shirt instead of his demonic armor. There was an air about him that just didn't quite seem to fit in this modern, mortal day and age.

Or maybe it was just the tattoos crawling up his neck.

Either way, people were going to stare.

That didn't mean Sascha had to like it.

And yes, Kai was a giant, tattooed, gorgeous hunk of a man with a waterfall of silky hair down to his pecs, and he looked like sex incarnate, but he was *Sascha's* giant, tattooed, gorgeous hunk of a man, damn it. He'd summoned him, fair and square. He'd even had his finger nibbled to seal the deal. So all these other jerks should just keep their damned eyes to themselves.

He opened the door to the bakery a little more forcefully than he maybe should have, striding in with Kai hot on his tail. The demon did not seem to know much about personal space, barely allowing a few measly inches between them at any given time.

"Oh, hey!" Seth raised a hand in greeting, his eyes on the pastries he was rearranging. Then he looked past Sascha, his eyes growing wide. "Um, hey, did you know there's a real-life Viking behind you?"

Sascha let out a deep sigh. "I was thinking more like a Highlander."

"Oh, cool. So I'm not hallucinating him."

"If only." But judging from the very real body heat at Sascha's back, neither of them were hallucinating anything.

"I see the coffee," Kai whispered directly into Sascha's ear, sending a shiver down his spine.

He stepped forward deliberately, putting space between them. "Yes, of course you do. That's why we're here."

He knew he sounded peevish, but he hadn't slept well, had he? He'd been plagued mercilessly by horny dreams, and it was this giant brute's fault.

"Two coffees?" Seth asked, looking between them with a slight smile on his lips.

"Yes, please." Sascha's eye caught on Seth's green fingernails. "I forgot your nail polish."

"You can keep it longer." Seth's smile grew, showcasing a dimple in one of his round cheeks. "You only got the one hand."

Sascha glanced down at his right hand and the bare nails there. His pinky finger was tingling again. He curled it under the rest of his hand. "Oh, right. I look like a lunatic, don't I?"

Seth shrugged, pouring out two coffees. "Maybe you'll start a microtrend."

Sascha shook his head with a smile. "You're sweet."

He tensed. There was that heat at his back again. Were all demons this clingy? Kai's breath caressed his ear again. "Make him give us all the coffee he has."

"I will not," Sascha hissed. He glanced back, his irritation deflating when he caught sight of Kai's unbearably hopeful expression. He sighed again—he was doing a lot of that these days—and turned back to the counter. "Seth? Better make that four. Four very large coffees."

———

COFFEES SECURED, Sascha led Kai down the path he'd walked the other day, this time taking it all the way to its natural end: a small, sandy beach surrounded by rocky outcrops at both ends, the lighthouse around the bend just barely visible.

In a minor miracle, there was no one else there. Sascha wasn't quite sure why *they* were there, other than the fact that his home still felt too small to contain both the two of them and his own inconvenient lust.

Kai had already finished two coffees just outside the bakery—

and were demons immune to burning their tongues or something?—so Sascha handed the third over now.

Despite the eager greed in Kai's eyes, he hesitated, hand outstretched. "You don't want it for yourself?"

"One giant coffee is enough for me, thank you," Sascha told him. "I prefer lattes anyway." He couldn't help watching as Kai sipped at the offering with open glee, slowing down to savor it this time around. "So what do we do now?"

Kai peered at him knowingly over the cup's rim. "I can't help you until I know who your enemies are, pup."

Sascha turned his gaze out to the ocean. "I need to call Ivan, then."

A shiver ran through him, courtesy of the harsh coastal breeze. Or maybe that was just from thoughts of his brother. What would Ivan do if he knew Sascha had a demon on his side?

He'd see it as a threat, of course. He'd see *Kai* as a threat. And by virtue of that, Sascha as well.

A new weight settled on Sascha's shoulders. He glanced down to find a coat covering his shoulders, over his own jacket. A very large coat. He looked to Kai, in his shirt and soft pants. "You don't get cold?"

Kai grinned at him. "I run hot."

"I bet you do," Sascha murmured to himself. Raising his voice, he pointed out, "Ivan might not be very forthcoming."

"Then we'll keep trying until he is."

It was a little pathetic, how comforting that was. A reminder that Sascha wasn't doing this alone anymore. He had an ally now, didn't he? And sure, he'd had to give up a piece of his literal soul to gain one, but it was the first time in a *very* long time where he felt certain there was at least one person who had his back. One person who couldn't send him away, or brush him off, or run away themselves.

At least not yet. Not until the contract was over.

Sascha took out his phone and hit Ivan's name.

His brother picked up on the second ring. "A phone call? Unprompted? Are you done pouting, then?"

"Jeez. Good morning to you too."

"I'm afraid I'm rather busy today."

Sascha glared out at the ocean. God, typical Ivan. Acting like a loon when Sascha didn't pick up every single one of his calls, then immediately pushing him away the second he actually reached out. "I'll get to the point, then. Which family is it that's after me?"

There was a pause on the other end. "Why so curious?"

"Don't I have a right to know?"

"You've never cared before."

Sascha couldn't help the shrill edge to his voice. "Well, I've never been *stabbed* before."

There was another pause, and Sascha was almost certain Ivan was going to keep his silence. But then he spoke. "The Carusos."

Sascha actually knew that one. "The Italians?" he asked with surprise.

"I cut off one of their shipments. A large one. They lost quite a bit of money." Sascha could almost hear his smile. "They're calling me a tyrant."

"Okay, the Carusos. And?"

"And what?"

"What are you doing about it?"

"At the moment?" There was the sound of rustling paper in the background. Was Ivan even paying attention to Sascha at all? "Nothing."

"Well, why the hell not?" Sascha asked through gritted teeth, vaguely aware of Kai removing the coffee he'd been sloshing about from his hand.

"I already told you." The first hints of true impatience entered Ivan's voice. "One underhanded assassination attempt is hardly a declaration of war. I'm not willing to start one."

"I thought I heard you telling Sergei they were small potatoes." See? Sascha listened. Sometimes. Mostly because the name had sounded a little like the name of one of his favorite restaurants, and he'd been hoping someone was ordering lunch.

"They have connections."

"And those connections are more important than me being knifed?"

"You healed up nicely, didn't you?"

Sascha hung up.

If he hadn't, he would have said something truly regrettable, and then he wouldn't have to worry about the Carusos, because Ivan would kill him instead. Alexei had always claimed Sascha had immunity to Ivan's wrath, that Ivan coddled him, but half of that was just Sascha knowing when to keep his mouth shut.

His phone rang. He turned it off.

"I miss Alexei," he found himself muttering. Alexei would at least have been properly upset that Sascha had been knifed.

The cold ocean breeze was cut off as Kai's body warmth enveloped him once more, his chest pressing against Sascha's shoulder. "Who's Alexei?"

Sascha found himself leaning into that warmth. "My other brother," he said with a sigh. "My *better* brother."

Fuck, that was a mean thing to say. *Good.* He hoped Ivan felt the sting of it, somehow, over in his ivory business tower.

He tilted his head to look up at Kai, the start of a wry grin on his lips. One that fell as soon as he caught sight of the demon's face. He looked furious.

Sascha frowned at him. "What's *your* deal?"

"You were stabbed?" Kai asked, his eyes roaming over Sascha like the wound would reveal itself if he looked hard enough.

"Oh. Yeah. My arm." Sascha held a hand to his right bicep.

Kai's hand covered his, turning Sascha gently to face him fully. "And you kept this from me?"

Was he supposed to give Kai a running tally of all his old boo-boos? "I guess I forgot to mention it?" he said.

"You forgot," Kai repeated, his nostrils flaring.

God, this was like his conversation with Ivan all over again. Pissy alpha males acting all weird and cagey. Sascha huffed. "I didn't mention it because I don't like to think about it, okay?"

"Show me," Kai ordered, his voice rough.

"Ugh." Sascha wrinkled his nose. "Why though?"

"Show. Me."

"You're bossy when you're cranky, you know that?" When Kai only stared back at him, Sascha pushed his lower lip out into a pout. "It's too cold with the wind. Maybe when we get home."

"We'll shelter in the rocks." Kai released his shoulders and grabbed his hand instead, tugging gently. "Come."

Sascha let himself be led to a spot on the beach that was adequately sheltered by the rocks. Kai set their empty coffees to the side and removed the coat from Sascha's shoulders, setting it on the sand before tugging Sascha down on top of it.

Sascha rolled his eyes but settled cross-legged where he was placed, Kai kneeling at his side. He shrugged out of his own jacket, pushing the sleeve of his shirt up to show the scar. "See?" he asked, as pissy as could be.

Warm fingers caressed the pink scar tissue. "It still pains you," Kai said softly. "I had thought you merely uncoordinated."

That wasn't exactly incorrect—Sascha's disastrous two-week stint on his boarding school's baseball team was evidence enough —so Sascha let it slide. "The asshole grazed a nerve," he explained. "They were able to mostly repair it, but sometimes my fingers get a bit tingly. I'm just...aware of it, I guess."

Kai tugged at his sleeve. "Take this off."

"Why?" Sascha asked, eyes widening when Kai shrugged out of his own shirt, revealing miles of bare skin. "What are you *doing*?"

"I can heal it." Kai frowned again at the scar, like it had personally offended him. "Heal it completely."

When Sascha made no move to undress, he cocked a brow. "Don't you trust me, zaychik?"

God, wasn't that the fucking question? They'd made a bargain, sure, but trust was a tricky thing and not one Sascha had much practice with. He loved his brothers—both of them, however flawed—but one had abandoned him without a thought, and the other had the temper of a rabid hyena. His own mother had left him as a baby.

Where was the trust in that?

But there was something about Kai. Something beyond him being a hottie of epic proportions. There was a gentleness to the way he treated Sascha, bossy arrogance aside. Like the way he'd stopped Sascha's imminent panic attack in its tracks. Or the stupid coat Sascha was now sitting on, protecting him from the cold sand.

Sascha had wanted to turn to him for comfort yesterday. It had taken everything in him to stop himself from curling up into Kai's chest like a goddamn kitten. That something about him seemed to scream *safety*.

Was that just a side effect of him holding a piece of Sascha's soul hostage?

Did it even matter?

Sascha reached for his hem and tugged off his shirt.

8

Kai

Kai barely dared to breathe as Sascha settled back down in front of him, this time with a torso that was deliciously bare.

His skin was pale and unbelievably soft-looking, unmarked other than the wound on his arm. Kai shifted closer on his knees, brushing that spot with his fingers again—it was recent enough to still be pink and slightly puckered. Recent enough to be healed.

A visible shiver ran through Sascha's body, as it seemed to do every time Kai put a hand on him. It pleased Kai immensely, the way this human responded to his touch.

Sascha cleared his throat. "So healing is one of your magic powers?"

"You're my bargain," Kai explained. "I can heal any wounds of yours related to battle. I can't cure illness or the like." And for the first time in his long existence, Kai found himself regretting that fact. Humans were vulnerable to too many things beyond the weapons of their enemies. He needed to be able to protect Sascha from it all; otherwise, what use was he?

"Still, pretty nifty," Sascha said. "I could have used you two months ago. Would've saved me some time and money."

Sascha sounded glib enough on the surface, his voice light and airy, but there was tension in his frame. Kai placed both palms firmly on his little human's shoulders. "Relax, pup. Breathe. I'm not going to hurt you."

He kept his hands in place as Sascha began to breathe in and out more slowly, his muscles gradually loosening.

"Good boy," Kai told him. Sascha's head whipped around to showcase a vicious glare. Kai laughed, gesturing with his chin. "Turn back around now."

After another moment of scowling, Sascha did, giving Kai a direct look at the back of his neck. The exact spot a mating mark might lie. Kai ran his thumb over it—another shiver ran through Sascha's frame.

"Does healing really require so much touching?" Sascha asked, his voice snippy.

"No," Kai answered honestly, rubbing his thumb over Sascha's neck once more. He was met with silence. Did his mouthy bargain really have nothing to say to that? Were a few soft touches all it took to hush him up?

How enticing.

But there was business to attend to first. It wouldn't do to continue to let Sascha walk around injured, however minor the effects might be. Just the thought of it filled Kai with rage.

He nudged even closer so the whole of Sascha's back was brushing against his own bare chest. Sascha was slight, fitting so perfectly against Kai's broader frame, just as his soul piece fit so perfectly inside. His skin was cool in comparison to Kai's own body heat. It was oddly soothing.

Kai removed his hand from Sascha's shoulder and set it over

the wound, reaching inward to the piece of Sascha's essence inside him. He could feel the internal injury, the edges of it that weren't healed quite right, the bits that still pained Sascha. Kai sent some of his own essence into that wrongness, bathing it in his own strength.

Sascha let out a small gasp, the sound almost lost in the soft roar of the crashing waves.

"You feel me, pup?" Kai asked in a murmur.

"It feels...hot."

Kai held steady. "Too much to bear?"

Sascha shook his head.

"Good."

Just as Kai had thought. In the past, he'd had seasoned warriors screaming in pain at a healing, but those warriors hadn't had an essence like Sascha's, one that fit so well within Kai's own. Sascha's body didn't fight Kai's intrusion any more than Kai's fought Sascha's.

They were matched well.

He let the healing complete, the small wound requiring mere moments, then brushed his fingers once more over the site. No more scar. Not even a hint of past damage.

"Better?" he asked, his voice rough.

Sascha rolled his shoulder, then flexed and released the fingers on his right hand. "Yes." He sounded awed.

He made as if to stand, to move himself away from Kai, but Kai held him in place with the hand on his shoulder. He asked the question that had been plaguing him since the day before.

"Why do you shy away from your desire for me? Why do you fear it?"

Maybe it was Kai's demon nature—or the restless, yearning part that was just him—but he truly didn't understand wanting something and not reaching for it. He didn't understand how the lust emanating from Sascha paired with his avoidance.

For a moment, it seemed as if Sascha would deny it all again, claim Kai was "not his type." But it wasn't a denial that ultimately left his lips.

"I don't know," he answered quietly, still facing out at the ocean. After a long moment, he spoke again. "I'm not very brave."

Kai wasn't so sure about that. But if that belief was what was holding Sascha back...

Kai stroked the back of Sascha's neck with his thumb again. "You don't need to be. I have bravery enough for the both of us."

He might not have much else to offer, but he did have that.

Sascha let out a sigh, and then he uncrossed his legs, bringing his knees up with his feet flat on the sand, before leaning back fully, resting his weight against Kai.

Kai ducked his head to hide his grin in Sascha's soft blond hair, then slid his hands down and around to clasp Sascha's clothed thighs.

His trousers were of a rough, dark material.

"Your clothes are different today," Kai pointed out.

The tips of Sascha's ears turned a fetching pink. "You mean from what I was wearing at home? That's...not my usual style."

That was a shame. He'd looked delightfully soft and tempting the day before, wearing thin leggings and a stretched-out sweater that slipped off his shoulder again and again.

"Why not?" Kai asked.

Sascha hesitated, fingers toying with the sand. "Well...those clothes aren't very...masculine?"

Kai didn't understand. "Why does your clothing need to be masculine?"

Another deep sigh from Sascha. Kai's bargain was full of them. "That's a good question."

One it didn't seem he was going to answer. "You look nice in pretty things," Kai pressed.

The pink color of Sascha's ears deepened to red, but he didn't turn back to face Kai. "Do I?"

"Mm," Kai hummed, his thumbs stroking against the rough material on Sascha's thighs. "Pretty things for a pretty man."

"You think I'm pretty?" The words were quiet, directed to the sand.

"I think you're lovely."

He was. Lovely and strange and wounded, much deeper and more varied than that simple scar on his arm. Kai could feel it, in that little piece of Sascha's soul he held. Fear and disappointment and sorrow. He'd been pulsing with it all, speaking with his brother. Not to mention the anger. What would it be like, if Sascha let that anger loose?

What Kai wouldn't give to see it.

He lifted one hand and traced the shell of Sascha's ear. Sascha's breath quickened at the touch. Was he sensitive there? Kai leaned in, giving a quick nip with blunt teeth. Sascha gasped.

Kai grinned. Yes, quite sensitive.

He nuzzled at the back of Sascha's neck, breathing in deeply, inhaling the scent of his skin. He smelled clean and vaguely floral. Fresh.

Sweet.

Kai lost himself in it for a moment, only brought back by Sascha's huff. "I thought you said you were brave enough for the both of us?"

"I am," Kai confirmed, giving another nibble of Sascha's ear.

"Seems to me like you're doing a whole lotta nothing," Sascha griped, clearly aiming for snippy but missing the mark when his breath hitched again at another press of Kai's teeth.

"Is that so?"

It sounded like an invitation. Kai ran his hands up from Sascha's thighs to his bare waist. He was slender there, as if Kai could encase it fully with both hands. Perhaps, in his demon form, he could. He ran his nose once again along the short hairs on the back of Sascha's neck, before brushing his lips over his shoulder. "I thought you wanted me to be nice to you, hm? You crave sweetness, don't you, Sascha? Sweetness to match your own?"

"I'm not sweet," Sascha mumbled.

"Oh, but you are." Kai brushed his hand along Sascha's stomach, feeling him tremble. "The sweetest morsel I've come across in a long, long while."

"You make it sound like you want to eat me," Sascha accused shakily.

What could Kai say to that? He did want that, in a way. The small taste of Sascha's soul he'd had so far was not enough. He wanted all of it. All of him.

For as long as Kai could remember, he'd been a restless soul. He'd been restless in the demon realm, volunteering for the Book as soon as he'd been able. And he'd been restless through all his many summonings, eager to be finished. And then he'd been restless in the Void, waiting to be done with it all.

But he could easily stay on this beach, with Sascha trembling in his arms, for another three centuries without tiring of it.

"Would you like me to touch you, zaychik?" He tugged at the waist of Sascha's trousers, but they wouldn't give. He peered over Sascha's shoulder—there was a button there, as well as a small metal tag.

"Oh, for fuck's sake." Sascha straightened, brushing Kai's hand aside to undo the fastenings himself before grabbing Kai's hand and shoving it inside, groaning when Kai's palm settled around the soft skin of his cock.

Kai squeezed with an approving hum. "You're already hardening, pup? From a wee bit of touching?"

"Shut up." Sascha leaned back against him. "I've had a bit of a dry spell."

Kai kissed the side of his neck, bared so conveniently for him, before exploring his prize with his fingers as best he could within the tight constraints of Sascha's trousers. He was a surprising length, for his smaller frame.

Although, his size was nothing compared to Kai's, of course.

Sascha sighed, his head rolling back onto Kai's shoulder. "We shouldn't be doing this."

Kai froze, biting back a growl of displeasure at the words. "Why not?"

"What if someone comes by?"

That was his hesitation? Kai resumed his exploration, bringing Sascha to full hardness, tucking his head against Sascha's outstretched neck. "I'd hear them long before they approached us."

"Oh." Sascha's breath caught as Kai thumbed at the fluid building at the tip of his cock. "Then you should definitely make me come."

Kai grinned against the soft skin of Sascha's neck. And here Sascha had claimed he wasn't brave.

Kai brought Sascha's cock out of his trousers. There wasn't a lot of give with the damned things, so he pressed the hard length back against Sascha's stomach, stroking as best he could, the metal teeth at the opening digging into his hand. "As I said before, I prefer your other attire." Those soft leggings would have been easier to work with.

"I'll—I'll keep that in—in mind," Sascha told him, gasping between the words.

He was so very sensitive. So responsive. It was delectable to witness. Kai's own cock was hard and aching between his thighs, desire thrumming in his veins.

Sascha moaned when Kai twisted his palm over the head of his cock. "Your hand is so hot. Fuck, that feels good."

He liked that, did he? Good. This was nothing. When Kai had

him truly alone? Undressed and bared for his lips and hands and cock?

Kai was going to ruin him for human men.

He pressed his mouth to Sascha's ear. "If you think this is nice," he whispered, "think of how I'll feel inside you. If we weren't at this beach, with all this blasted sand, I'd have you writhing on my cock already."

Sascha let out a high-pitched whine.

Kai hummed his pleasure, squeezing the base of Sascha's cock. "You like that idea? Of course you do. Look how sensitive you are to the slightest touch. You were made to be fucked, weren't you, little human?"

"*God.*" Sascha's head lifted and thumped back against Kai's chest.

It was addictive, the way he was melting into Kai, the way Kai's touch had those outer defenses crumbling so easily.

He wanted Kai to be nice to him? Kai would *worship* him, if this was the result.

It wasn't long before Sascha's hips were jerking into Kai's hold, frustrated whines escaping his lips with each movement.

"Hush," Kai soothed, kissing along his neck. "I have you."

With his free hand, he brushed up along Sascha's chest, pinching one of his nipples lightly. Sascha yelped, his cock jerking in Kai's hold.

"You like that, hm?" Kai brushed his thumb over the stiffened peak. "Would you like my mouth here, perhaps? Would that be *nice* of me, Sascha? To suck your pretty pink nipples?"

Sascha only whined again, his hand clamping Kai's wrist. "Faster," he demanded. "Faster. And your thumb on—on the tip again."

Kai obeyed his bargain's orders, picking up the pace, letting the fluid leaking from Sascha's cockhead ease the glide of his hand.

His own fluids would have been better, but he didn't want to take either hand off his prize, so he made do.

Three strokes more and Sascha arched back against him, crying out, and Kai cupped his hand to catch his release, stroking the skin of Sascha's chest gently to soothe him through his tremors.

When Sascha had relaxed back once more, Kai held up his hand, admiring what he'd wrought. He brought it to his mouth.

Sascha turned back to look at him for the first time since the healing had begun, tracking Kai's movement with glassy eyes. He looked absolutely beautiful, all flushed cheeks and heaving breaths. "Oh God," he whimpered, watching Kai lick him off his fingers.

He shook himself out of Kai's hold and scrambled onto his knees, facing him. Before Kai could mourn the loss of his touch, he begged, "Can I suck you? I think—I think I need to suck you off now."

Kai groaned. He would have been satisfied with just this—planting the seeds for future pleasure between them. But if Sascha wanted to put his eager mouth on him?

He made a move to lower his trousers, but Sascha shook his head. "You said you would hear if anyone came by?" he asked, a bright gleam to his pale-blue eyes.

"No one will surprise us."

"Then change," Sascha ordered.

"Pardon?" Kai was momentarily too aroused to grasp Sascha's meaning, the ache in his cock redirecting all his attention.

Sascha arched an imperious blond brow. "If I'm going to fuck a demon, I want to fuck a demon. Change back."

9

Sascha

Sascha knelt on Kai's jacket, tucking his spent cock back inside his jeans, the sand that had made its way onto the fabric during his writhing prickling at his knees even through the denim.

He was barely holding himself up—he'd always been shaky after orgasms—but still, he needed this, more than he'd needed anything in a very long time.

It had been a stilted, toying hand job, hindered as Kai had been by Sascha's restrictive clothing and their semipublic location. But his hand had been hot, his voice a silky croon, and even that much had worked Sascha up into an embarrassing frenzy.

He'd been trying so hard to resist, and now it was like Kai had opened the temptation floodgates, and Sascha was being swept away by his own desire.

Sascha kept his gaze intently on Kai as the demon changed back into his true form, not even allowing himself to blink. Even with his eyes wide open, the process was still so rapid it was hard for Sascha's brain to process. The growth, the horns, the tattoos transitioning from stationary to their mesmerizing swirl. Kai's eyes didn't always glow, but they were glowing now.

He was beautiful. Otherworldly. And he wanted Sascha.

And fuck, did Sascha want him back.

Why do you shy away from your desire for me?

Sascha had answered the question as best he could. Bravery wasn't his strong suit, and something about this...situation seemed to require it. Something about Sascha's attraction that felt too big. Momentous in some way.

All Sascha's previous relationships had been wholly superficial, attraction without connection. His family life was too complicated for anything else, for one. But Kai already held a little piece of Sascha's soul hostage. How could they get more connected than that?

It was frightening. And while Sascha was no stranger to fear, this was a whole new kind to process. His heart was racing so fast it threatened to gallop right out of his chest.

But if Kai wanted to be brave for them both...

Sascha had already decided to trust him with his body when it came to healing. He supposed he'd have to trust him with the rest when it came to sex. Trust him not to let this thing between them grow too big for Sascha to handle.

He opened his mouth to speak, various pleas running through his head. *Please don't hurt me. Please don't draw me in just to push me away. Please don't crush me like a bug when you leave.*

But Sascha couldn't say any of that. So he said the next best thing.

"Take out your cock," he ordered, making his tone as imperious as he could. "I want to see it."

Kai flashed sharp teeth. "As you command."

He lowered his trousers—the soft material much easier to manage than Sascha's denim—and pulled out his cock.

And holy. Fucking. Shit.

Sascha swallowed, his mouth watering. "You really commit to a color scheme, don't you?"

Kai's cock was... Well, first of all, it was fucking huge. Had Kai really said if they weren't on blasted sand, Sascha would be riding him right about now? Yeah, fucking right. That thing was *not* going to fit. No way, no how. Size queen card revoked. License expired.

And the size wasn't the only difference from a normal human dick. It was blue, for one. A deeper blue than the rest of Kai's skin, darkening to an angry violet at the bulbous tip. And it was...ribbed?

Sascha shuffled closer. Yep, those were ridges running along the length of it, like it had rings around it. *Ribbed for my pleasure*, he thought, with just a touch of hysteria.

And those ridges were pulsing in time with the beads of fluid leaking out of the head. The very large head.

Yeah, that thing is never fitting inside me.

"It will fit," Kai told him silkily, alerting Sascha to the fact that he'd spoken out loud. Kai's hand was circling the base, like he was offering his cock up to Sascha as a treat. There was no hair there— no body hair anywhere, Sascha realized.

"*How* would it fit?" he asked, more than a little mesmerized.

"Come closer," Kai crooned.

Sascha dropped onto his hands, hovering over the monstrosity.

"Touch me."

Sascha raised a hand and brushed it over the fluid beading from that dark, leaking cockhead. He gasped. "It's...thick," he murmured, rubbing his thumb and forefinger together.

Kai's precum was a different texture than a human's, thick and viscous, almost like...

"You have *lube* leaking from your dick," Sascha accused.

An amused rumble emanated from Kai's broad chest. He arched a dark brow. "How else would one mate?"

Of course. How else?

Sascha brought his finger to his mouth. In for a penny, in for a pound. He licked gingerly. Smoke and... He licked again. Spice? Whatever it was, it made his lips tingle.

A low growl had his eyes darting back to Kai's. They were glowing even brighter than before. "Why don't you taste it from the source, Sascha?"

"I was getting to that," Sascha told him, a little peevish. He was usually better at seduction than this, but it wasn't every day he was confronted with demon dick, okay? He deserved a little grace.

He lowered his head and licked at the tip, keeping eye contact with Kai all the while. Oh yes, definitely spicy. He closed his eyes and licked again, smacking his lips a little. They were tingling so much now they were verging on numb.

"You toy with me."

Sascha opened his eyes, narrowing them at Kai. "Just getting my bearings, hot stuff."

He hid his grin as Kai mumbled the words *hot stuff* to himself.

Well, hell. Fortune favored the bold and all that. Sascha sucked the head of Kai's cock into his mouth. Just that much had his lips stretched tight. Good God, he was going to need to make good use of his hands with this one.

He popped off and spread the leaking precum all around the shaft, getting it slippery. The ridges felt nice against his hands, his palms starting to tingle too.

Once it was all appropriately slick, and Kai's growl had become a constant, low rumble, Sascha took the tip back into his mouth. He tongued around the head, sucking gently, gratified when that growl turned into a groan.

He smiled around his mouthful. Okay, he could do this. He hadn't trained himself to deep throat for nothing.

He hollowed his cheeks as best he could, sucking harder, and gradually started taking in more, until he could feel Kai at the back of his throat. It was easier than ever to let his throat open, that tingling, almost numbing sensation from Kai's precum easing his efforts.

Sascha breathed through his nose and met Kai's eyes again. They were heavy lidded and still glowing. Had he looked away from Sascha even once?

Sascha's own dick pulsed, and he realized he was getting hard again, his poor cock trapped back in its denim cage.

And there it would stay, because this was definitely a two-handed job.

And Sascha was no slacker.

"You're good at this, aren't you?" Kai said softly, one hand reaching out to trace the stretched line of Sascha's lips. "Taking me."

What was he talking about? Sascha hadn't even done anything yet. He started bobbing carefully, moving his head along Kai's monstrous cock at the same time as he slid his hands along the shaft.

Kai hissed, his eyes practically boring holes into Sascha's head.

Did the guy not need to blink?

Sascha's lips and cheeks were already aching, but it was that good kind of ache. He closed his eyes, humming as he let himself do what felt right. Spit and precum dripped down his chin, and the texture might have been different from what he was used to, but the effect was familiar. Sascha had always liked this part—the messiness, the filth.

As he licked and sucked and swallowed around all that girth, the ridges started swelling under his hands. Sascha squeezed them as he stroked, rewarded with a grasp or growl or groan every time he did.

Fuck, how was he going to go back to sucking human dick

after this? This was the blow job Olympics, and he was fucking crushing it. He couldn't be sent back to regionals.

Was he doing sports metaphors right?

Distracted, he went too far, choking himself, and Kai's hips bucked.

Sascha pulled off, glaring up at him. "Easy," he chastised.

"I'm close, Sascha." Kai must have been trying to look apologetic, but he just looked wrecked. On his knees in the sand with Sascha between them, his glowing eyes heavy lidded, his massive chest heaving.

"Then stay still and let me work, huh?" Sascha squeezed those ridges harder in warning, but that only made Kai groan.

"As you command."

How did he manage to make that sound so cocky? But no matter, Sascha had a job to finish.

He bent back over, swallowing Kai down. And down. And down.

"*Fuck.*"

It was the first time Sascha had heard Kai swear. He would have smiled, if his cheeks weren't stuffed so full. He placed a hand on Kai's thigh for leverage and with his other started stroking faster, squeezing Kai's ridges harder, swallowing down on that head over and over.

He could feel the tension in Kai's massive leg muscles as he held himself back from thrusting. But he did hold back. Following Sascha's command, as he'd said.

Sascha moaned at the thought, and that seemed to do it—the ridges under his hand hardened and pulsed rapidly, and fluid erupted down his throat. He choked and spluttered, swallowing as best he could. There was more of it than he was used to, and more ran down his chin than made it into his throat in the end.

He came off Kai's cock coughing and looked up with watery

eyes. The expression on Kai's face was something else, dazed and almost worshipful.

Before Sascha could ask him what his deal was—had he never gotten a blow job before?—voices came from their left, their words indistinct but definitely close.

There were people coming onto the beach.

"Holy shit!" Sascha scrambled to get his shirt on, rubbing the demon jizz off his face as he brought the fabric over his head.

He turned to glare at Kai—back in his human form already—just as an older couple came out onto the other end of the beach. "You said you would hear someone coming," Sascha hissed.

"I did hear. But I wanted to let you finish." Kai reached out, rubbing his thumb over Sascha's chin. He smiled, and even without the pointed teeth, his grin looked wolfish. "You have a bit of something there, zaychik."

Arrogant fucking demon.

SASCHA HAD SPENT the rest of the afternoon in a strange haze as they wandered around the town. There wasn't much to see or do, but he'd needed the extra time in the open air. If he'd been worried before, now he was absolutely certain the house wasn't going to be big enough to hold them.

But eventually he hadn't been able to delay any longer.

They'd stopped first at the grocery store and grabbed a restock of microwave dinners and a gargantuan bag of coffee grounds.

Sascha had never made his own drip coffee before (his New York apartment had an espresso maker, like any civilized dwelling should), but he'd seen a coffee maker hiding somewhere in the house's kitchen, so...why not buy what would make the demon happy?

Or happier than Sascha sucking on his giant dick like a lollipop already had.

Because the dude was *glowing*.

Not literally, seeing as he was still in human form, but he was all broad grins and hearty laughs, constantly touching Sascha in a thousand little ways. A hand on his back. An arm around his shoulder. Brushing against his side.

It was bizarre. And not at all endearing.

Not. At. All.

Sascha sighed, placing a filter into the coffee maker. (Had he searched on his phone "how to make coffee in a regular-ass coffee pot"? Possibly.) He poured what looked to be a decent amount of grounds into it.

He'd known this was going to be a problem. It was part of why he'd been shying away from his attraction, trying to use his head for once. He just didn't have the proper defenses for hot demons with huge cocks who said they were going to protect him, let alone hot demons with huge cocks who said they were going to be *sweet* to him.

Because Sascha had lied to Kai before. The men Sascha was into weren't good to him, not in any special way. They treated him like a good fuck and a temporary meal ticket, and that had been working for Sascha just fine. Anything more would have put whoever he was fucking too close to his volatile family anyway. Sascha banged them good, dropped them eventually, and never thought of them again.

Hell, he never even thought of them the next morning.

It was just…easier that way.

But here it had been a whole afternoon since he'd gotten off, and Kai was standing so close in this kitchen that seemed too small for the both of them, giving Sascha all these tiny touches, and it was *doing* things to him.

Sascha pressed the button on the coffee maker, prayed for the best, and stuck his dinner in the microwave, taking a few steps away from Kai as he did so.

Only to have Kai immediately claim those few steps back.

Sascha shot him a wary look, but Kai only grinned, his teeth sharp once again. Whatever. Sascha rolled his shoulder experimentally, flexing his fingers. He'd been so focused on the hookup he'd almost forgotten: his arm was healed. By *magic*. Just the thought of it had him wanting to go to bed already. His brain just wasn't made for processing such things.

The microwave dinged, and he grabbed his mac and cheese, sitting at the kitchen table.

Kai lowered himself gracefully into the chair next to him, wrinkling his nose. "What is that?"

Sascha glared at him. "My dinner."

"If we were in the demon realm, and you were a demon, I would bring you a fresh kill every night," Kai told him. He said the words while staring pointedly, like they were supposed to mean something.

"And if we were in New York, I'd be out having a ridiculously overpriced but perfectly cooked steak." Sascha swallowed a bite of the gluey mac and cheese. "But those are two big ifs, aren't they?"

"Yes." Kai hummed thoughtfully, taking his intense gaze off Sascha to look around the kitchen. "I suppose I'll have to learn how to make human food."

Sascha had no idea why, when he'd already told Sascha he didn't eat it. But he no longer had the energy to parse through Kai's strange musings. "Whatever floats your boat, big guy."

"I have no boat," Kai told him haughtily.

Sascha hid his grin with another bite of his mediocre dinner. It was time to change the subject—clueless Kai was too adorable for Sascha's vulnerable heart to handle. "So how did you get put into that Book in the first place? Were you, like, captured?"

Kai stopped his perusal of the kitchen to frown at him. "To be in the Book is a great honor."

"You chose to be summoned?" Sascha couldn't imagine. "You wanted to be put in the—what did you call it?—the Void?"

"I didn't intend to be in the Void for centuries like that, but yes, I chose it."

"Why? The great honor?"

Kai hummed in thought. "Restlessness." His brow furrowed. "And power, perhaps. When the last contract is finished, when you have a thousand pieces of human soul, you return to the demon realm with quite a bit of it. Your strength grows, as does your reputation. I was young and hungry for more. And...curious, I suppose. It's the only way to spend time in the human realm, via contract."

"The only way?" Sascha remembered something. "And you said this is your last contract." His stomach twisted. There it was. The other shoe dropping. After Kai finished his contract with Sascha, he would leave, and he wouldn't come back.

Kai scooted his chair closer. "Well, there *is*—"

Sascha's phone dinged.

He held up a finger to Kai—any more of this particular conversation and he wouldn't be able to stomach the rest of his dinner. It was already sticking in his throat. Kai's weird cum must've done something to his insides, because they were feeling all scratchy.

It was, predictably, a text from Ivan.

I do not appreciate being hung up on.

Sascha was a little surprised it had taken him this long to message. He must have been cooling down enough to communicate without threatening bodily harm.

Sorry. Bad connection, Sascha typed back. Out of the corner of his eye, he saw Kai rise and pour himself a cup of the finished coffee. The mug looked ridiculously tiny in his massive hand.

Ivan's reply was swift. *You want my help, you'll correct your behavior.*

Anger ran through Sascha again, so hot and swift it almost burned. Ivan with his goddamn strings. Whose fault was it Sascha was in this mess in the first place?

His fingers were moving before he could stop them. *Don't fucking bother. I've found someone else to help me.*

Sascha's phone started ringing immediately. He turned it off, waving a middle finger at it for good measure.

Kai was watching him closely over his mug. "I can taste your rage, pup."

"I don't have rage," Sascha told him wearily. He was suddenly so fucking tired, his head fuzzy and dull. "I'm not allowed to. So taste your coffee instead."

Kai took a sip. His nose wrinkled. "This is not like what the baker made for us."

"Is it better?"

"No," Kai answered mournfully, staring into the cup. "It is not better."

Sascha almost laughed, but what came out instead was a sigh. He pushed his half-finished dinner away. "I'll try again in the morning. I'm tired."

"What of the Carusos? The family of your enemies? Should we not begin searching for them?"

So you can leave me sooner? Sascha almost said. "In the morning," he promised instead, rising from the table.

"All right." Kai set his cup down and made to follow Sascha.

Sascha paused his steps. "What are you doing?"

"Following you to bed."

"You have your own room."

Kai frowned at him. "But I don't want my own room."

Sascha rubbed at his eyes. "What *do* you want, then?" If Kai was going to ask for a repeat performance of their time at the beach, Sascha was going to tell him to fuck right the hell off. He was no longer in the mood for sexy shenanigans with unattainable demonic entities.

But of course Kai refused to be predictable. "I wish to hold you as you slumber," he said firmly. "I'll sip on the rage you claim you don't have. You'll sleep better for it."

Sascha stared at him from between his fingers. Sure. Let a demon hold him as he slept so said demon could literally drink his emotions. Why the hell not?

But of course he was going to say yes. Sascha couldn't remember the last time someone had really held him. He was tired and weak, and he wanted a goddamn cuddle, even if that cuddle included weird demon bullshit.

"Fine," he huffed, trying to sound put out about it. "Come along."

"As you command."

Kai kept saying those words, but Sascha was more than aware he wasn't the one running this show. He could only hope Kai knew what he was doing.

Sascha sure as hell didn't.

10

Kai

Kai waited patiently while Sascha readied himself for bed in the bathroom. He'd told Kai it would be a minute, mumbling something to himself about not letting hot demons interfere with his skincare routine any longer.

Kai was too pleased Sascha still thought him attractive to concern himself with the rest of that statement.

When Sascha came out of the bathroom, smelling fresh and faintly botanical, with soft leggings replacing his stiff trousers, Kai was already in human form under the covers. He patted the bed invitingly, grinning at Sascha's pouty scowl.

He was a little surprised when, after crawling in, Sascha immediately latched himself to Kai's side, throwing his arm over Kai's chest and his leg over Kai's hip.

"No talking," Sascha mumbled, his breath cool on Kai's skin. "And pet my hair."

Kai obliged immediately, running the silken strands through

his fingers as Sascha determinedly closed his eyes and somehow seemed to pretend Kai was not there, even as Kai held him tightly.

So Kai held the human in his arms, breathing in and out deeply, coaxing Sascha into the same steady rhythm as he sipped gently at the anger simmering under the surface.

Perhaps Sascha didn't want to admit to his own rage, but Kai could feel it, turning the soul piece in his chest hot and prickly. It was delicious—rage always was, rich and spicy—but the emotion clearly unsettled Sascha, so Kai drank steadily until that heat dampened and Sascha slumbered in truth, his breaths deepening as he let go of consciousness.

Kai remained awake. He had much to consider, not the least of which was the conundrum of the bargain between them. They now had a name for Sascha's enemies and a general location—it surely wouldn't be too difficult to find them. And once found, Kai would rip them apart as easily as breathing.

But doing so would complete the contract, and Kai would be sent back to the demon realm. Back to what was supposed to be his home. And what had once meant freedom—in those long centuries waiting in the Void—now seemed some sort of divine punishment.

Kai would be sent back, unable to return. The piece of Sascha's soul in his chest would join the rest of his bargain fragments, stagnant and buried. He would no longer be able to taste it, to explore its dark pockets and hidden corners.

It was intolerable to even think about.

Kai had grown attached to the piece inside his chest, as he had to the man in his arms. Something about Sascha grounded him, soothed an itch he'd known his entire existence. If Sascha had been in the demon realm, perhaps Kai never would have entered himself in the Book in the first place.

Kai wanted to keep him. Him and his delicious soul.

But the only way to keep them both would be a permanent

bond. A *mating* bond. And that would be madness to consider with a human.

And yet...

Now that Kai had tasted Sascha—not just his soul, but the pleasure they could have between the two of them—now that he'd felt that eager mouth on him...

What would Kai really be returning to in the demon realm? Power and glory? Perhaps. But no family, no mate match. There was the chance he'd find one eventually, but whoever he found, they wouldn't be like Sascha—soft and sweet and small enough to tuck into his chest. Or full of the same complex human emotions: his hot and bitter anger, the sour tinge of sadness that encased the inherent sweetness of his soul.

Sascha stirred in his sleep, and Kai tightened his hold, pulling him closer to his chest. Kai had to maintain his human form to fit properly in the bed. It was slightly uncomfortable—akin to wearing ill-fitted clothing for too long—but it was worth it to hold Sascha like this. To feel this press of him against Kai, so trusting that he'd sleep in his presence.

No, whoever Kai found wouldn't make him horrible, weak coffee and demand he take out his cock for them to admire. They wouldn't demand anything, not with the prestige Kai would hold, returning after a completed contract.

Kai's cock twitched at the memory of their time on the beach. For one so small, Sascha had taken more of him than Kai would have expected. He was a sensual creature, clearly, enthusiastic and unrestrained when he gave in to desire.

Kai had never had a mouth on him before like that. It wasn't wise, with a mouthful of sharp teeth, and demons didn't fuck each other in human form. What else would Sascha teach him, if he stayed?

Kai fell asleep pondering the possibilities.

He woke to a new weight on him—during the night, Sascha

had draped himself further over Kai until his torso was almost fully on top of him. He had his arms folded under his chin on top of Kai's chest and was studying his tattoos.

"You're awake, pup?"

"Oh." Sascha blinked up at him, a sheepish smile gracing his lips. "Did I wake you? Sorry, you're just...really warm. It's nice." His voice had a husky tinge to it after a night of rest.

Kai peered back down at him. Sascha's cheeks were flushed with sleep, and there were creases on his face from his pillow, his white-blond hair sticking out in all different directions. The sass he seemed to wear like armor was missing in the early morning, as was his surly mood from the night before.

He looked unbelievably delicious.

Kai grabbed him by the hips and settled him more completely on top of him, Sascha's morning erection pressing against Kai's own hard length. "You can take as much of my heat as you want, zaychik."

"Oh." Sascha shifted against him, then paused, like he hadn't meant to do it. "That's very...accommodating of you."

Kai grinned at him. "Would you say it's sweet of me?"

"Stop." Sascha's sleepy flush darkened, and he tucked his head into Kai's neck. "I can't handle your flirting right now," he mumbled against Kai's skin. "Are you like this with all your bargains?"

"No," Kai answered honestly.

There was a long moment of silence, and then Sascha turned his head, so his next words were clear. "You said there were four of you left in the Void. Are they all like you?"

"No, we are different types of demons. Different clans. I come from warriors. The other three have different specialties."

"Hm." Sascha raised his head. "What kind of demon would I be?"

Kai stroked his hand along Sascha's back. "There are no demons like you, Sascha."

A flash of hurt crossed Sascha's face, like Kai had wounded him with his words. But he hadn't meant it as an insult. Sascha would be eaten alive in the demon realm, but that was part of his appeal. Soft, sweet, sulky.

Only the human world could have produced such a creature.

Sascha frowned down at the hands he had folded on Kai's chest. "Because I'm weak, you mean."

"You're not weak," Kai told him firmly. "You may not be as physically strong as some, but you're fierce. Not everyone can harness a demon. It takes inner strength to form a contract."

Sascha's frown deepened. "It didn't feel like much."

Kai kept up his steady strokes along Sascha's back. "That's because we're very compatible."

"We are?"

"Mm." Kai couldn't resist sliding Sascha against his length once again.

Sascha squirmed against him, then narrowed his eyes. "Are you just saying that because you're horny?"

"No." Now it was Kai's turn to frown. "Your soul piece fits very nicely within me, as I've said. As your body fits so nicely against mine."

"Uh-huh," Sascha said skeptically. "That sounds like horny thinking to me."

Kai's frown turned into a grin. "I've been holding you all night. It's been a very tempting arrangement."

Sascha rocked once against him, almost absent-mindedly. "You insisted."

"I did." Kai lowered his voice. "Take out your cock, Sascha. Press it against mine."

Sascha arched a brow. "Bossy."

But he did as Kai asked. Kai hadn't gotten a good look the day before, but Sascha's cock was a lovely sight, with its pink skin and ruddy tip. Its smaller size looked obscene next to Kai's girth, which was substantial, even in human form. "Stroke us," Kai ordered.

Sascha tried, one elbow digging into Kai's chest as he wrapped a hand around both of them. But he had trouble keeping them together. "My hand's too small," he complained.

"Mm." Kai hummed his agreement. Why was that so enticing? He knocked Sascha's hand away, grabbing them both, using his natural lubricant to ease the glide. This position was much better than the one the day before because he could see Sascha's face, see the way his eyes began to grow glassy, his lips parting, the flush on his cheeks spreading down to his neck.

Until Sascha dropped his head down with a gasp, mouthing at Kai's skin.

Kai wanted that mouth elsewhere.

"Kiss me," he demanded.

Sascha raised his head expectantly, and Kai craned his neck to reach, pressing against soft lips. Sascha whined, his hips jerking as he tried to deepen it. "You're too tall."

"You like how tall I am," Kai told him, darting out his tongue to lick along Sascha's lips. "Even more so in my demon form."

"Who says?"

"The way you look at me says."

Sascha dropped his head down, pressing cool kisses to Kai's chest again. Kai sped up his strokes, desperate now for both of them to reach their release.

It didn't take long, and when they'd both emptied themselves onto Kai's stomach, Sascha rolled off to the side, flushed and panting. Kai wanted to tuck him back against himself, but he was filthy, so he rose from the bed.

Even after Kai had cleaned himself with a towel from the bathroom, cleaning Sascha gently as well and tucking him away in his leggings, Sascha remained flushed and panting, sprawled out in the bed.

Kai frowned down at him. "Are you all right?" Was the human's stamina really so poor?

Sascha threw an arm over his eyes. "'M okay. Just getting sick maybe."

Panic tightened Kai's chest. "*What?*"

Sascha waved his free hand in the air weakly. "I didn't play around in the dirt enough as a kid, I guess. I get sick easily. I'd say it's from being out in the cold yesterday, but that's not actually a thing."

Sascha was sick. It was perhaps the most terrifying thing Kai had ever heard. He could protect against soldiers, mobsters, swords, guns—he could do nothing for illness.

Not without a bond.

"What do I do?" he asked.

Sascha sighed. "Nothing. I just need to rest, I think. Drink plenty of water, all that jazz."

But as the day progressed, rest and fluids were useless. Sascha grew weaker and more lethargic, switching between sweat and chills and coughing halfheartedly. When Kai stroked his forehead, his skin no longer felt cool. It matched Kai's own temperature, and Kai knew enough to know a human shouldn't be that hot.

It was unacceptable, all of it. Kai had seen illness take too many men in the human realm. Often after a battle it was the fever that killed, not the wounds themselves. Kai had once joked to the incubus that pestilence did half his work for him.

What was he supposed to do now?

He didn't know how to reach a modern-day healer, and even if he did, he wouldn't trust one.

And Sascha wouldn't tell him what steps to take. When roused, he batted at Kai irritably, telling him to leave off.

By the end of the day, when Kai woken him yet again to sip at some water, he glowered feebly at him. "Just turn the TV on and leave me to die," he moaned, closing his eyes resolutely.

Leave him to *die*? Kai would not. He *could* not.

He needed someone with knowledge of humans, knowledge of Sascha. He had said he'd gotten ill as a child. Clearly the illness had never taken him, if he was still here.

Kai searched and found Sascha's little pocket phone. He held it up to Sascha's sleeping face as he'd seen Sascha do to unlock it for use. He searched through it, cursing his overlarge fingers, but eventually found what he was looking for.

He pressed the contact and held his breath through the phone's little song, relieved when a deep voice answered.

Kai wasted no time. "Your brother is dying," he told them. "Come for him."

11

Sascha

Sascha's tummy hurt.

Throwing up was awful, but he was probably going to anyway. And it would be extra awful because his throat didn't feel too good either. He probably needed medicine, something to make it not hurt so much.

But it was the middle of the night. The nanny had already gone home. And Sascha wasn't supposed to interrupt Papa, even after dark.

Especially after dark.

That was the agreement. That was why he'd been allowed home from boarding school over the summer. The conditions, Papa had said. So if he wanted to stay—to see Alexei and Ivan for more than just the Christmas holiday—he had to stay in bed.

He could do it. He could*. He was six now, almost seven. He'd be going into second grade next year. He wasn't a baby.*

But it really hurt. And the water cup by his bed was empty.

Sascha frowned at the empty cup. The stupid nanny had forgotten to fill it. Oh well, she'd be gone soon. Papa had seen her carrying him up the stairs earlier. Babying him. So bye-bye, nanny.

Sascha tried to smile, but it turned into a grimace as his tummy cramped again. He tossed his covers back and climbed gingerly out of bed.

Maybe he'd just check. Papa might be at the warehouse, anyway, and then Sascha could sneak into Ivan's room and ask if he knew where the medicine was.

He crept into the hallway. It was dark, but there were lights on downstairs. He went down the stairs, shivering as he went. Did he have a fever again? It felt like he did.

There was no one in the living room. No one in the kitchen either. There was light coming out from under the basement door though. Papa must have been down there.

Sascha wasn't supposed to go in the basement.

But he could hear voices down there, and one of them sounded like Ivan. If Ivan was down there, it couldn't be too bad, right?

Sascha opened the door as quietly as he could. He'd just take a peek. If it looked okay, he'd ask Papa for some medicine. Maybe he'd get the pink stuff that tasted like bubblegum.

He crept down the stairs. There was Papa's voice. And Sergei's. And one Sascha didn't recognize. A man's voice. He was kind of loud. And whiney.

Maybe his tummy hurt too.

Sascha made it to the bottom, the basement room now in view, and he suddenly couldn't be quiet anymore. He gasped.

There was Papa and Sergei and Ivan. Ivan was looking so grown up, standing next to Papa, his hands clasped behind his back.

And sitting in front of them—his back to Sascha—was a man. He was tied to a chair with rope, and he was...red. All over. Was that blood? Why would he be so bloody? It was dripping down the floor, onto a plastic sheet someone had laid down there.

Sascha swallowed hard, his tummy churning.

"Sascha."

He looked up to find Papa watching him. Sascha couldn't tell if he was mad. Papa always kind of looked mad. But he probably was, right? Sascha had disobeyed him, and now he was interrupting, and this strange man clearly had had some horrible accident, and Sascha was getting in the way.

"Come here," Papa ordered.

Sascha walked over to him, keeping as much distance between himself and the man in the chair as he could. Papa placed a heavy hand on his shoulder, turning him around. Facing the man in the chair.

Sascha kept his eyes on the basement floor. He didn't want to look at the man.

"I told you not to come down here, yes?" Papa's voice was flat and cold, thick with the accent of his homeland.

"I know, Papa. I don't—I don't feel so good though."

"Why are you looking at the ground, Sascha?"

Sascha didn't say anything. He somehow knew whatever answer he gave, it wouldn't be the right one. He kept hoping Ivan would say something. Offer to take him upstairs, maybe. Away from the man in the chair. Away from Papa.

But it was Papa's voice that rang out. "Look up, Sascha."

Sascha lifted his head. It was definitely blood the man was covered in. He had cuts and bruises everywhere, his face so swollen he almost didn't look human. And his hands...

There were fingers missing. More than one.

A burning sensation rose from Sascha's stomach to his throat. He was going to throw up. He was.

"You will not vomit, Sascha."

Sascha looked behind him. Papa was angry now.

It took everything in him, but Sascha swallowed the rising bile down. His mouth tasted like vomit in the end anyway. He wanted to cry. But if he did...

He knew Papa wouldn't hurt him, not like he'd hurt this man in the chair.

But what if Sascha was wrong about that?

He could hear the blood dripping onto the plastic. A steady, plopping sound.

Don't throw up. Don't throw up. Don't throw up.

When Papa saw he was keeping it down, he smiled at Sascha. Or his mouth smiled. Not his eyes though. "Good, Sascha. Now look again." *Sascha lifted his gaze, praying again everything in his tummy would stay where it belonged.* "This is what I protect you from, yes? Why I send you away to that fancy school with your weak, spoiled classmates. Aren't you grateful, Sascha?"

It was a long moment before Sascha could speak. "Yes, Papa."

"What do you say?"

The man in the chair was crying now.

"Thank you, Papa."

"What kind of sickness?" *Papa asked.*

"W-What?"

The man's cries were turning into sobs, loud and guttural. Sascha couldn't hear the blood dripping anymore.

"What brought you down here, Sascha?" *Impatience laced Papa's words for the first time.* "What kind of sickness?"

"My tum—my stomach. And my throat. And—and a fever?"

"All right." *That heavy hand lifted from Sascha's shoulders.* "Back upstairs. Sergei will bring you medicine."

"Thank you, Papa." *Sascha looked to Sergei. He was holding something that looked almost like a big gardening tool. It was covered in red.* "Thank—thank you, Sergei."

It was time to go back upstairs. But Sascha's feet wouldn't move. And his eyes kept returning to the man in the chair.

The man noticed him looking. His cries quieted. He opened his mouth, spitting out a large glob of blood.

And then the begging started.

And now Sascha was sick again.

It was the worst. Sickness always was. He always had to do it alone. Papa never let Sascha's nannies stay the night, even when he didn't feel good. And Alexei would be punished for coddling if he tried to sneak into Sascha's room.

But clearly this nanny must have disobeyed orders, because there was a cool, wet washcloth running across Sascha's forehead.

It felt like heaven.

He moaned weakly, the sound barely escaping his tortured throat. "Feels good," he mumbled.

"You're awake?"

Dang. This nanny had a deep voice. And they smelled like smoke and spice.

Sascha forced his lids open to find piercing blue eyes staring back at him. Right. He wasn't a child. There was no nanny.

Just him and his demon.

Kai was on the bed next to him in his demon form, his feet hanging off the end in order to fit, a small washcloth dwarfed by his large, clawed hand. His brows were furrowed, and his face looked pale, which Sascha hadn't been aware his blue skin tone was capable of.

Apparently Kai didn't find the twenty-four-hour flu very appealing.

Sascha frowned up at him. "I feel like crap." The words came out sulky, but Sascha was too weak to correct it.

"You told me you were dying," Kai said, his gaze weirdly intense, even for him.

Sascha attempted a laugh, but the sound quickly dissolved into a hacking cough. "Did I?" he managed once the fit stopped. "Sorry, I'm a drama queen when I'm sick."

Kai didn't laugh. He didn't even crack a smile. He just silently handed Sascha a glass of water.

Sascha licked dry lips and then chugged the whole thing down. The cool liquid did wonders for his throat.

He gave the glass back to an eerily quiet Kai. "Did I say something stupid when I was out?" Sascha asked. "How long *have* I been out?" Had Kai put him to bed at some point? Sascha could have sworn he was on the couch before.

He mustered up the strength to reach for his phone from the bedside table, but the screen was black, even after he tried to power it on. Dead. He waved a hand at Kai. "Give me that cord, will you?"

He plugged his phone into the charger and set it aside.

Kai was still staring hard enough to bore holes into his skull. "It's been a full night and day since you lost consciousness."

Sascha sat up, categorizing his aches and pains. His throat wasn't too bad now that he'd had some fluids. His limbs were feeling kind of weak, but that was probably just from dehydration. Same with his head full of fuzzy cotton. All in all, it could have been worse. "I didn't lose consciousness. I fell asleep."

"You would not wake," Kai insisted.

"I think I had a pretty bad fever." That would explain the weird dreams and Sascha thinking for that brief moment he was a child again.

Kai gave one decisive nod. "You clung to me, shivering, and then pushed me away, sweating. You wouldn't wake," he repeated.

Damn. His intensity sure wasn't lightening any. Sascha looked around hopefully for another water glass, pouting a bit when his search came up empty. "If you were so worried about me, why didn't you take me to the hospital?"

Kai let out a growl. "I've seen what human healers do. They would only speed your death."

Sascha waved a dismissive hand. "This is modern America. That only happens half the time nowadays."

Kai still didn't give him a smile. Real tough crowd. Instead, he cocked his head toward Sascha's phone, his expression unreadable. "I called for reinforcements. They have not yet arrived."

The words took longer than they should have to penetrate Sascha's fuzzy brain. "You...what?"

Like that had been its cue, his phone buzzed on the table, charged enough now to power back on.

Sascha picked it up. He had...twenty-seven text messages from Alexei? Plus quite a few voice mails. And almost as many texts from Ivan, but that was no surprise, considering how Sascha had left things the day before.

He gaped at Kai. "You called Alexei?"

The phone buzzed again, Alexei's name popping up on the screen.

Sascha answered it in a daze. "Hello?"

His brother's voice rang out, sounding harried and more than a little pissed. "Sascha? Thank fuck. Where are you? That asshole gave me the name of the town but not the goddamn address, then hung up and never answered again."

Sascha rattled off the address on autopilot, his head still too stuffed full of cotton to fully process what was happening. All he knew is that he'd kill for another glass or ten of water.

Alexei grunted his acknowledgment when he was done. "We'll be there in fifteen minutes."

Well, all right then. Apparently Sascha was now going to be hosting his brother. His brother he hadn't seen in two years. His brother who'd left—leaving Sascha behind—when he couldn't handle Ivan's shit anymore. His brother who still didn't know Sascha had been stabbed, or that he was technically in hiding.

Sascha set his phone in his lap, trying to figure out what emotion to feel. "You called Alexei," he said again.

Kai shrugged. "You said he was the better brother."

Sascha supposed it was preferable to Ivan showing up out of the blue and demanding to know who Sascha's new demonic bodyguard was.

He pushed the covers off him, giving Kai a pleading look. He wasn't sure his limbs would hold him. "Can you—I need to shower. I smell like death."

Kai's brow furrowed at the last word. Touchy, touchy.

But he helped Sascha into the bathroom.

And then made no move to leave.

Sascha started toeing off his sweatpants, one arm clinging to the sink for balance, feeling too crappy to be even slightly self-conscious about it. His entire body was covered in a thin film of dried sweat, and he needed it to be off him immediately. He cocked a brow at Kai, who was standing stubbornly in front of the door with his arms crossed. "This shower isn't big enough for the two of us, you behemoth."

Kai transitioned into human form in an instant, arching a brow in turn.

Touché. Sascha turned on the water. "Fine."

He watched Kai vanish his trousers while he waited for the water to heat. It honestly all had Sascha feeling a bit pouty. He had a superhot guy wanting to shower with him and was too sick to do anything about it.

Although, he did graciously allow himself to be bathed, instructing Kai on the right shampoo and conditioner, both of them pointedly ignoring Kai's growing erection.

Kai even dried him off once they were out, using one of the fluffy towels to dry him and another, fresh one to wrap him in, like Sascha was a little kid or something. He paused there, hands gripping the terry cloth. "You're healed now?" he asked Sascha, the words almost stilted.

Sascha assessed himself. He did feel worlds better after his shower. "The worst of the fever is over, I think," he reported. "And I have some meds I can take for anything lingering."

Kai nodded once, the weird tension he'd been holding seeming finally to melt, then led Sascha back to the bedroom. "Your brother didn't get here fast enough," he said, sounding decidedly unimpressed.

"Well, he lives in Colorado," Sascha explained. "Plus, you forgot to give him the address."

Kai stroked a lock of wet hair back from Sascha's face, his gaze soft. "I would have found you if it were me."

Oh. That was... Sascha cleared his throat, wincing at the lingering ache. "Yes, well, you're a magical demon, so..."

He sidestepped Kai and that alarming promise, throwing on fresh sweats and an oversize T-shirt. It wasn't the best outfit he'd ever constructed, but Kai had already seen him sweaty and incoherent and gross—he probably wasn't going to be scared away by Sascha's frump clothes.

Kai was still naked.

Sascha gave him a pointed look. "Can you clothe yourself please? Alexei's gonna be here any minute."

Kai hesitated for way too long. Was this some sort of demon power play? Greet Sascha's brother naked as a jaybird?

But eventually he let out a put-upon sigh, then waved his hand, black pants appearing once again on his form.

They made their way downstairs.

Sascha would have liked nothing more than to go back to bed again, but Alexei had probably been freaked out enough by Kai's vague phone call. He didn't need to see Sascha bedridden on top of it all.

There was a pile of packages at the entryway.

"Those were left on your doorstep," Kai explained.

Sascha's new clothing, most likely. "Um. Okay. Thanks for

bringing them in," Sascha said, patting Kai's arm and feeling more than a little awkward.

Why were things so awkward?

Kai shot him what was becoming his new trademark intense-as-all-hell look. "I left your side only to be sure it wasn't an intruder."

"Okay." Sascha held his breath as Kai stepped closer, towering over him even in human form. "You, um, stayed with me the whole time?"

No one had ever done that for him. Not ever. And sure, maybe it was just Kai making sure his bargain—his ticket back home—didn't break or whatever. But still. He'd stayed.

A knock on the door cut through the moment.

Sascha inhaled a shaky breath, letting out a laugh. "Time for you to meet the fam."

He opened the front door. He only got a flash of an image—Alexei's familiar face, eyes wide with surprise; the short, messy-haired man at his side—before he was thrown back, and then suddenly he found himself behind a wall of...black leather?

What. The. Fuck.

Sascha poked at the new barrier in front of him. "Kai...do you —do you have *wings*?"

There was no answer, only a lot of growling, seeming to come from every direction. And yes, those were definitely massive bat-like wings in front of Sascha's face. Not to mention the horns he could see poking out again from Kai's head.

Fuck, how was he going to explain this to Alexei?

But every time he tried to peer around the leathery wings obscuring his view, they would shift, blocking him further.

"Kai?" he prompted again. "You're kind of freaking me out."

Kai growled again. It was a distinctly different noise from his sex growl. Low and mean and threatening. "Bloodsuckers," he said.

Sascha nodded. Cool. That explained absolutely fucking nothing.

Then a chipper voice rang out. "Hello! I'm Jay. You must be the demon Sascha summoned." Kai growled again, and then there was an answering growl from the other side, but the voice rose in volume to be heard over the din. "Alexei didn't believe it, but I told him you never know. You're very large, and those wings are super impressive. But I think Alexei would like to see his brother now. We won't hurt him. We're very nice, I promise."

To Sascha's immense surprise, the wings blocking him slowly lowered, and he was able to peer around Kai's massive demon form to find Alexei, standing in front of his boyfriend, who was peering out behind him as best he could, an exact mirror of Sascha and Kai.

Jay—who Sascha had heard much about but never met—grinned broadly at him from around Alexei's side. He was a tiny thing, dwarfed by Alexei's height and muscles. "Hi! It's so nice to finally meet you."

"Um. Hi," Sascha greeted back, too confused to muster anything else.

Then he caught sight of Alexei's face.

It was a face he knew as well as any other, particularly Alexei's hazel eyes, so different from Sascha's or Ivan's icy-blue pairs.

Except now Alexei's eyes were black. And his teeth were bared at Kai, and those were *not* the teeth Sascha remembered.

His eyes widened, and he gasped, the sound quickly turning into another ragged cough. "Alexei," he managed to get out between coughs. "You've got—you've got *fangs*."

12

Sascha

Sascha hadn't expected his first time hosting in his new home to be filled with so much tension.

He cleared his throat, if only to make some sort of noise to cut through the silence. It was still mildly sore, but the ache was already easing every minute. It had just been a twenty-four-hour bug, probably.

And poor Kai had thought he was literally dying.

Kai who had lost all sense of reason and chill, and was acting like the living room they'd all settled in was a battleground and Sascha's brother was enemy number one. Kai's armor was back on—those shoulder plates that protected none of his vulnerable bits but did leave quite a lot of delicious chest on display.

Sascha steered his mind firmly away from that direction. It wasn't the time.

Alexei, for his part, was seated across from them on the couch —his boyfriend, Jay, tucked against him—alternating between eyeing Kai warily and staring with concern at Sascha. His fangs had disappeared, and his eyes were back to normal.

Even after his throat clearing, the silence was growing oppressive. Sascha caught Alexei's eye. "So. Your boyfriend's a vampire."

Alexei glanced down at Jay, who was staring at Kai in obvious fascination, and the fondness in his gaze as he looked at his petite partner was unmistakable. "Yes."

"And now you are too."

Alexei didn't answer that. He didn't have to though. Sascha had seen, hadn't he? Sascha let out a bitter laugh. "No wonder you never came home."

"I wouldn't have been welcome," Alexei said pointedly.

You would have been welcomed by me, Sascha thought. But he didn't let the words out. Alexei had stayed in New York longer than he ever should have, and Sascha knew well enough what his own role in that had been. Protect the baby, right? Even at Alexei's expense, even as Ivan had broken down his spirit year after year.

It was no wonder Alexei had grown tired of it.

Sascha glanced at Kai, who was still in demon form, standing halfway in front of the armchair Sascha had settled in. His wings were gone, but Sascha somehow knew if either Alexei or Jay even looked at him askance, they'd be back, blocking him from view. Protecting him from his own brother.

Would Kai get tired of it too?

It was a stupid fucking question. Kai wouldn't have a chance to get tired of anything. The contract would end, and he'd disappear.

As if sensing the pit of despair that thought opened up in Sascha's stomach, Kai settled the weight of his massive hand suddenly on Sascha's head, brushing at the strands there.

Another honest-to-God growl erupted from Alexei. "Don't touch him."

Kai looked back at him placidly, his hand still planted on Sascha's head. "I don't answer to you, bloodsucker."

Sascha cleared his throat again, wishing he had a glass of water. He grabbed Kai's arm and lowered the hand to his shoulder. "Let's all just relax, hm?"

Jay, who'd so far seemed happy enough to be tucked against Alexei's side—like this was any old family reunion and not a meeting of two different, not-supposed-to-be-real, supernatural entities—was apparently in agreement, because he laid a calming hand on Alexei's arm before straightening. "Oh! I know!" He reached down to rummage in the backpack he'd brought, ignoring Kai's warning rumble. After a moment of searching, he plopped a large ziplock baggie on the coffee table.

Sascha leaned around Kai—who'd stepped in further in front of him—to peer at it. "Are those...cookies?"

"Yes!" Jay beamed at him. "Peanut butter chocolate chip. Alexei said you liked those." He looked up to Alexei for reassurance, the only sign he might be nervous, before smiling widely again at Sascha. He looked a bit like a little doll, with his wide gray eyes, delicate features, and Cupid's-bow lips. "I wanted to make you something more fitting for a reunion, like a three-tiered cake! But Alexei pointed out that wouldn't travel so well. Your brother's very practical." He cocked his head, his eyes trailing over Sascha's face. "You really don't look at all alike."

They didn't. Where Sascha and Ivan had lean frames and the icy-blue eyes and white-blond hair of their father, Alexei was a different creature. Six foot five with a broad frame and rugged features, he had eyes of multicolored hazel, and his hair was a long dirty-blond mane he kept up in a bun.

Sascha was pretty sure the man-bun had started as an act of defiance against Ivan's desire for immaculate presentation from his brothers, but it suited him.

Jay turned his attention to Kai again. "May I see your wings again?" he asked politely.

"No."

"Okay." Jay nodded amiably before tucking himself up against Alexei again. He was wearing a highlighter-yellow sweatshirt with a tie-dye heart on the chest. It was disconcertingly hideous.

Alexei wrapped an arm around Jay's shoulder and stared at Sascha, an unreadable look on his face. "That one said you were dying," he said, his eyes darting to Kai and back again.

"I just had the flu. He misunderstood."

Alexei's lips twitched just the slightest bit. "So you really did summon a demon by accident?"

Did he think it was *funny*? After dismissing Sascha's phone call and treating him like a child? Sascha sniffed, crossing his arms. "I told you, didn't I?"

"Right. Guess you wouldn't call one on purpose." Now Alexei did smile. "Unless you were looking for a shopping buddy?"

It wasn't an unfair assessment. When they'd both still been in New York, Sascha had spent the majority of his time shopping or club-hopping. Alexei had even joined him every now and then. Still, Sascha couldn't hide his wince. Frivolous, spoiled Sascha.

Kai's fingers twitched on his shoulder. "He needs me to find the ones who had him stabbed," he said coolly.

Well, shit.

The color drained from Alexei's face. "What?" He rose from his seat. "You were *stabbed*? Where? Show me."

Sascha held up a hand, but it landed on Kai's back. He'd blocked Sascha again. Sascha pushed impatiently at his hip until the big lug stepped aside. "It's fine, Alexei. It's all good. Kai healed me. I don't even have a scar anymore."

Alexei looked no less stricken, although he hadn't come any closer. Jay was hanging onto his hand, keeping him from getting in Kai's face. "Why didn't you *call* me? I would have come."

"I know," Sascha said firmly. "I know you would have. But Ivan said not to."

Alexei's face turned thunderous. "Fucking Ivan."

Sascha shrugged. It was a familiar refrain between the two of them. "I didn't want to give him any reason to hurt you." He cocked his head. "*Can* you be hurt now?"

It was Jay who answered. "Not for long." He looked earnestly at Sascha. "So if you're stabbed again, please call."

Kai cut in, his voice harsh. "He won't be stabbed again."

Alexei gave him an appraising look. "You're going to find them?"

"Yes."

"Kill them?'

"Yes."

"Good." Alexei sat back on the couch, some of the tension in the room finally dissipating. He sighed heavily. "Ivan was supposed to be protecting you."

Sascha shrugged. "Well, he pissed someone off. He's been more careless than usual."

"He's not over it yet?"

Sascha knew the "it" Alexei referred to. Alexei leaving. Alexei costing Ivan millions. Alexei thwarting Ivan's plans and his iron grip over all of them.

Now it was Sascha's turn to sigh. "Are any of us over any of it?" He could only hope Alexei knew the "it" *he* referred to. Their father. Their childhood. The violence in their blood.

"Do you have a lot to get over?" Alexei asked him, not unkindly. "You were away for most of it."

And there was Kai growling again. "Are you that oblivious? Your brother is not without trauma."

Sascha's cheeks heated as Alexei narrowed his eyes. "It's fine, Kai."

Jay cut in then. "I think we should get Sascha some food. A human body needs food for healing. That's what Danny says, and he's a nurse. Why don't I make syrniki?"

Sascha blinked in surprise. "You know how to make syrniki?"

It was a Russian pancake dish their grandmother had made them, when they'd visited her in Russia. Sascha could barely remember; he'd been so young the last time. He wasn't actually sure he remembered at all or if he'd just heard Alexei tell the story so many times he'd convinced himself he did.

Jay smiled proudly. "Alexei taught me."

For the first time, Kai showed interest in their guests beyond suspicion and anger. "You know how to make human food?" he asked Jay. "Show me."

Sascha scoffed. "Why? You don't eat."

"But you do." Kai met his eye, something in his gaze Sascha couldn't quite read. Something heavy and...important.

Oh God, Sascha's cheeks were on fire. Maybe his fever was back. He could feel his brother's questioning gaze on him. But when he looked over, Alexei's expression was unreadable.

"You should have tea too, zaychik," Alexei told him. And him using the pet name Kai had taken over didn't do much for Sascha's blush. "Do you have any raspberry jam?"

Another of their grandmother's legacies. "No," Sascha said. "But I have some dusty chamomile bags from the previous owner in one of the cupboards."

Alexei nodded. "That'll have to do."

Jay patted Alexei's arm, planting a kiss on his shoulder. "Kai and I will cook. You two talk." He gave Sascha another one of his earnest looks. "Talking can be very helpful."

But Alexei grabbed Jay's hand when he tried to walk away. "Jay..."

"I'll be fine." Jay grinned up at Kai, who loomed a foot and a half above him, not including the horns. "You won't hurt me, will you, demon?"

Alexei's expression softened, and Sascha realized then how incredibly, deeply in love Alexei was. He would die for Jay, Sascha was certain of it.

A deep loneliness stabbed at Sascha's gut.

And then Kai's hand was in his hair again, brushing softly at the strands. "Talk with your brother. I'm only a room away."

Only a room away. That was a nice thought. Sascha wasn't alone, not yet. He still had someone in his corner.

The only question was, For how long?

Sascha and Alexei ended up talking late into the night.

Sascha wasn't sure what Jay and Kai got up to after cooking—Jay had handed Sascha a plate of pancakes with such sincere enthusiasm Sascha had worried for a minute he was going to watch him eat every bite, and then Jay had wandered off with three pancakes in each fist—but he could tell Alexei had an ear out for Jay and Kai. Every now and then, a bright laugh would erupt from elsewhere in the house, and a small smile would grace Alexei's lips.

So Sascha drank his tea and ate his pancakes, and they talked. Sascha told him all about the mess Ivan had created, and Alexei caught Sascha up more fully on what had happened to him in Hyde Park, and the life he'd made for himself there. It all might have stretched the limits of Sascha's credulity, if not for the fact that he'd summoned a literal demon into his living room just a few days before.

Eventually they were all up to speed—no more missed months to account for, no more easy (if unbelievable) topics to cover. An uncomfortable silence filled the room, full of too many things still left unspoken.

Alexei rubbed at the back of his neck, not quite meeting Sascha's eye. "So. Our childhood messed you up too, huh?"

Was Sascha really almost thirty and they'd never had this discussion? But it wasn't like their family was known for its heart-to-hearts. Even the two of them, in all their previous closeness, had been more action than talk—spending time together but not exactly plumbing the depths of their psyches. Sascha knew Alexei loved him, but he also knew Alexei thought of him as...careless. Care*free.*

Sascha hunched his shoulders up, fiddling with the tassels of the cushion in his lap. "I know what it was like for you. I—I remember Sergei breaking your finger that one time. For flinching." He winced. "You weren't even a teenager yet."

"Flinching." Alexei hummed. "Was that what it was for? I'd forgotten the reason."

Sascha gave a clipped nod. "So I know you had it worse. But just because I was sent away doesn't mean I wasn't *aware* of it. The danger. The violence. God, the way Papa's goons would look at me if I didn't act just right." Sascha shuddered, his stomach twisting.

"Our father wouldn't have let them hurt you. He was an asshole, but you were still his baby."

"I'm glad you're so certain." Sascha met Alexei's gaze resolutely. "*I* wasn't."

"Sascha..."

Sascha's hands clenched into fists on his pillow. "I've felt powerless my whole life. What else was I supposed to do but shop and party and—and dick around?" He let out a bitter laugh. "No one would let me do anything else. I have a business degree I've never even used."

"I'm sorry." Alexei's expression was pained. "I should have realized."

Sascha forced his tense muscles to relax. "I don't know if I wanted you to. I liked that we got to have fun together. And you had plenty of your own shit. I'm not saying mine equaled that. Just that I *did* have shit."

Alexei leaned back into the couch with a loud sigh. "Our family's legacy, huh? Complete and total shit."

"Ivan would disagree."

Alexei made a noncommittal noise. Then he cocked a brow at Sascha. "You know, there are legitimate branches of the family business you could take part in."

"Psh." Sascha waved a hand. "As if Ivan would let me."

Alexei leaned forward, looking surprisingly eager. "Then make him let you. So you've been powerless before? You're not anymore. You have an actual demon at your disposal, Sascha. One that looks at you like you're his precious fucking treasure."

Um. He did?

"Well, he has to look at me like that," Sascha said nonsensically, too taken aback by Alexei's assessment to use actual logic. "It's just, you know…the bargain."

"He learned to make syrniki for you tonight. Is that part of your bargain?" At Sascha's silence, Alexei gave a decisive nod. "You're not powerless anymore."

Sascha frowned down at his lap. "It's not my power though."

"It's power you've tamed. As far as I'm concerned, that makes it yours." Alexei glanced at the clock on the wall, some antique thing the previous owner had left behind. "It's late. You need to rest."

"I feel fine," Sascha argued with a pout. He did, actually. The tea had cleared up the last of the soreness in his throat, and the food had given him back some strength. Although, that didn't stop a yawn so wide it almost cracked his jaw from escaping him.

Alexei gave him a look.

Sascha huffed. "Fine. There's a guest bedroom made up for you and Jay. Kai's not using it." At Alexei's raised brow, Sascha flushed. "He likes to stay close," he mumbled.

"I bet he does."

Sascha stuck out his tongue. "Good night, Alyosha."

He flounced out of the living room to find Kai waiting for him right there, at the bottom of the stairs. Sascha glared at him, embarrassment making him peevish. "Have you just been lurking there the whole time?"

Kai smirked. "Not the whole time."

"Ugh. Come on, then."

And Kai did, just like that.

It's power you've tamed. As far as I'm concerned, that makes it yours.

Had Sascha really tamed this demon? He hadn't done much. Only exchanged orgasms and whined a lot and briefly made Kai believe he was dying. It wasn't like Kai was any less bossy or cocky.

But God, the heat in Sascha's cheeks just wouldn't go away. Whereas moments ago he'd been ready to drop from exhaustion, suddenly he was fully alert as he walked along with this monstrous beast from another realm who'd agreed to protect him.

Not by sending Sascha away. Not by ignoring him. But by standing *with* him (or, as he had earlier, deliberately in front of him). Blocking him from danger. Lending Sascha his power.

It was the kind of protection Sascha had never known.

Sascha's room was much more cluttered than when he'd left it. At some point during the night, Kai had apparently moved all his packages from the hallway in there. Sascha would go through them at some point, but it hardly seemed the time.

Instead, he went through the motions of getting ready for bed, incredibly aware of the demon waiting for him, perched on his bed and watching his every move.

"You're agitated," Kai eventually said, when Sascha came out of the bathroom after brushing his teeth.

Sascha frowned at him. Possibly it was more of a pout. "I'm not."

"I can feel it." Kai placed a taloned hand on his chest, over the swirling tattoos there. They should have been distracting, with that endless motion, but Sascha had gotten used to them. It was almost comforting to watch now.

"You can really feel me there? My soul?"

"Yes," Kai answered, staring intently, his eyes beginning to glow in the dim light of the room.

And because all Sascha's past easy flirtatiousness with men seemed to have fled his body, he blurted out with zero finesse, "Are you going to fuck me now?"

"Would you like me to?" Kai asked in a purr. He ran his tongue over sharp teeth, and Sascha noticed for the first time that it wasn't the light pink of a human's tongue but a dusky blue.

Of course it was.

Sascha shuffled his feet in place, suddenly unsure. "I don't know."

Kai cocked his head, a lock of silky black hair falling over his chest. Sascha wanted to touch it. The hair or the chest or both. "And why don't you know, zaychik?"

"When the contract's done, you'll be gone."

There was silence as Kai stared at him, his expression unreadable.

God, Sascha was stupid for bringing this up, wasn't he? This demon just wanted to get his dick wet, and Sascha was messing it all up with his stupid feelings.

Then Kai spoke. "I don't have to leave. There is a way."

Hope stole Sascha's breath, bottling it up in his chest. "What way?" he whispered.

"A permanent bond." A look of pure satisfaction crossed Kai's face, as if the thought pleased him. "A *mating* bond. I would no longer claim just a piece of your soul—I would be linked to all of it. Linked to this realm, and to you."

That was about as clear as mud. Sascha tried to make sense of it. "So you'd stay here for—for my lifespan?"

Kai shook his head. "*My* lifespan. You would be linked to me as well."

"And how long is that?"

"A very, very long time. Longer than you can fathom. Your aging would slow to the point of imperceptibility."

Cool. What an incredibly overwhelming proposal completely out of the blue. A breathless laugh escaped Sascha's lips. "Well, that's insane."

Kai didn't even flinch. "And why is that?"

"I mean..." Sascha lifted his hands in demonstration, trying to encompass everything. "We just met."

Kai scoffed. "What does that matter? I've tasted your essence. I know you better than anyone." His eyes narrowed. "You think perhaps you could not care for me?"

Now Sascha really laughed. "Not loving people isn't my problem. My father was cruel and cold, but I still loved him. Just like I still love Ivan, even when he's controlling and vicious. And Alexei, even though he left." He continued babbling, his brain apparently no longer in control of his mouth. "I'd have loved my mom, if she'd have let me. If she'd stayed even a few more years, like she did for my brothers, I would have loved her forever."

That was Sascha's real flaw, wasn't it? His horrible weakness. He couldn't help loving the people around him, even if they were terrible people. Even if they tortured men and pushed Sascha away and left him all alone.

Kai stood, and even after their days together, his height still took Sascha's breath away. "Then there's no issue. I'm not human, Sascha. I don't need your mortal reasoning to know what I want. I run on instinct." He stepped toward Sascha. "On desire." Another step and he was close enough that all Sascha could smell was that spicy, smoky scent. Kai's voice lowered almost to a whisper. "And what I *desire*...is you."

Sascha didn't know what to say. So of course he found himself blurting out, "You haven't even fucked me with that monstrous dick of yours yet."

Kai traced a finger down Sascha's neck, leaving a trail of fire in its wake. "Is that what needs to happen for you to decide?"

And then broad hands were wrapping around the backs of Sascha's thighs, and he was being lifted up with ease. "Very well, then. Let's get to it."

13

Kai

Kai picked Sascha up by the thighs—light as a feather, despite the solid muscle under Kai's hands—and carried him to the bed.

While it wasn't large enough for Kai's demon form to sleep comfortably, it was still well sized and elevated enough to serve his current purposes. He would make do.

Because if Kai couldn't be joined in a mating bond with Sascha —if his human wasn't ready to accept the permanence Kai craved —then Kai would take the next best thing. He would join their bodies instead, burying himself as deep inside Sascha as he could get.

No mortal man would do for Sascha after he tasted what Kai could offer him. He'd be begging to keep Kai close. To bond with him.

Because only a mating bond would do.

Sascha's illness had been…unacceptable, to say the least. It had instilled a fear in Kai he'd long thought himself incapable of, to see the vibrant man become so weak and listless.

And perhaps Kai had overreacted, calling the bloodsuckers forth to help (not that he'd known they were bloodsuckers at the time). But he'd seen many battles in the lifetime of his bargains and the illness that could follow. He'd seen fevers similar to Sascha's take men within days.

Humans were weak; Kai had always known that. With their fragile bodies and corrupted hearts. Too easily conquered by the world around them. And while Sascha's softness was part of his appeal—his tender emotions, his delicate features—it was becoming increasingly clear he could be taken from Kai at any moment.

Unacceptable.

Kai tightened his grip on Sascha's thighs, reveling in the little gasp his touch elicited.

Sascha was staring up at him through pale lashes, his pink tongue darting out to wet his lips. "We're going to…now?"

"Immediately."

"But…" Sascha's eyes trailed over Kai's form, down to where his groin rested against Kai's stomach. "I was serious before. That thing is not going to fit."

"It will fit," Kai insisted.

Sascha's plump lower lip jutted out into a pout. Kai bent his neck to catch it between his own, tasting the remnants of honey and herbal tea. Sweet. So sweet.

It was only a moment—a brief touch of lips—before Sascha leaned back, peering suspiciously at Kai's mouth. "How do I get in there without cutting my tongue?"

Kai grinned, flashing his sharp teeth. He knew how to bypass his own fangs. Sascha would just have to take it. "Open your mouth, pup."

He expected Sascha to object, if only to be difficult, but he opened his mouth obediently, and Kai pressed against him, eager for another taste. When Sascha's lips parted, Kai swept his tongue in, tangling with Sascha's, exploring every inch of what he had to offer.

Once Sascha was gasping, grinding his growing erection against Kai's stomach, Kai dropped him down on the bed, grinning at his indignant squawk.

"Strip," he ordered.

"Bossy," Sascha accused, not for the first time.

But Kai was unconcerned. Sascha *liked* him bossy. Every time Kai ordered him about, his pupils dilated, his breath hitching just slightly.

It made sense to Kai. He'd overheard much of Sascha's talk with his brother (the bloodsucker Jay had briefly scolded him for eavesdropping, then given up and wandered off to eat more pancakes). It wasn't just the violence of Sascha's childhood that had wounded him—it was the neglect. Abandoned by the mother, sent away by the father under the pretense of protection.

Was it any wonder Sascha wanted someone's full attention on him, even if that attention came with demands? He needed to be wanted.

And damned if Kai didn't want him.

His cock plumped as more of Sascha's skin was revealed with each item of clothing discarded. He was overwhelmed by the need to catalog every inch of Sascha's body, to map it and claim it for his own. The angles of his collarbone, the soft swell and then dip of his stomach. There was so much Kai wanted to explore.

But it would have to come later. For now, stretching Sascha would take his full dedication. Kai had a point to prove.

They *would* fit.

Once Sascha was sitting naked at the end of the bed, Kai tossed off his shoulder plates before undoing his belt and lowering his own trousers.

Sascha's light-blue eyes widened comically as he took in Kai's cock, which hung heavy and full between his thighs. He nibbled on his lower lip, which was slightly swollen from Kai's kisses. "You're *sure* it's going to fit?"

Kai cocked his chin. "Onto your stomach, zaychik."

Sascha rolled over onto his belly with a put-upon sigh, but he immediately tilted his ass up into the air accommodatingly, for all his protests.

And Kai hadn't missed the fact that Sascha hadn't asked him to change into human form.

He grabbed a pillow and tucked it under Sascha's hips, smiling to himself. Adventurous human, for one who claimed not to be brave.

An adventurous human with a plump bottom presented to Kai practically on a platter. He brought a knee up onto the bed for a better angle, then grasped it with both hands, squeezing hard enough for his claws to form little indents on the pale skin.

The sight was pleasing, but the talons wouldn't do for his purposes. Kai let out a breath, his sharp claws giving way to blunt nails more similar to a human's.

Sascha lifted his head from where he'd pillowed it on his hands to peer back at him. "I should have asked before—do we need protection?"

Kai frowned at him. Did Sascha think Kai had become careless? "My daggers are close at hand," he reassured.

"What? No—I meant..." Sascha let out a breathless laugh. "You can't give me diseases, can you?"

"My kind have no illnesses to spread to you."

Sascha turned back around with a nod, after giving Kai's daggers a sidelong glance. Kai softened his hold and parted Sascha's cheeks. He stared for a long moment, even as his fingers itched to caress. "Why are you smooth here? Don't human males have hair?" Sascha hadn't had any on his chest either, for that matter.

"I wax," Sascha told him with another little laugh. "Why, you don't like it?"

Kai let out a low rumble. "I like it very much."

He ran his fingers around the smooth skin of Sascha's cheeks before dipping them into the crease. Sascha shivered when Kai's fingers brushed over his entrance.

It wasn't enough. Kai leaned in close, his nose touching soft skin, and swiped his tongue straight up the furrow.

"Mm," Sascha hummed, craning his neck back again to smile at Kai. "How did you know? I love a good rimming. Nothing fingers can do that a tongue can't do better."

Did all humans talk so much when a demon was trying to seduce them? Kai gave him a stern look. "Hush, pup. Touch yourself."

"*You* hush." But Sascha turned back around, his hand slipping under his prone body, presumably toying with his cock.

Kai tongued all around that smooth, hairless cleft, drinking in each of Sascha's shivers and sighs, giving special attention to that puckered entrance. He softened it with his spit again and again before slipping the tip of his tongue inside.

"Oh!" Sascha jolted. "Your tongue's pointier than a human's."

Kai growled, squeezing Sascha's cheek in reprimand. "Don't compare me to the humans you've fucked."

Sascha giggled into his pillow. "Touchy, touchy."

He was too coherent by far. Kai speared him more aggressively, feasting on him the way he craved, sucking and licking and toying at his entrance with determination. Sascha's soft sighs turned to heavy panting, then to tortured moans, and finally to a rather high-pitched sort of squealing.

Eventually he thrust a hand back, batting at Kai's forehead. "'M gonna—gonna come if you don't stop."

"Come if you like," Kai told him smugly. "It will only be the first of many." But he paused to lean back and admire his work anyway. Sascha's hole was pink and puffy and open now. Even so, it wasn't nearly enough.

But this was where Kai's specific biology came in handy.

He stroked his own aching cock, gathering the slick precum on his fingers. He brought a digit to Sascha's entrance, massaging his fluids into the tender skin there.

"Wha—ohhh," Sascha moaned, his muscles tensing briefly before relaxing noticeably. "That feels…weird."

Kai grunted in acknowledgment, rubbing more of his precum into the skin. "But good?"

"Really good," Sascha sighed. "Really weird but really good."

"My coital fluids have slightly venomous properties," Kai informed him.

Sascha's muscles stiffened once again under Kai's hands. "Excuse me?"

Kai pressed in the tip of his finger, humming his pleasure when it slid in easily. "It works on the nerves, relaxing the muscles," he said, his tone conversational as he rubbed against Sascha's inner walls with more of his precum. "Like a mild paralytic. Was your mouth not numb when you sucked me?"

"I thought—" Sascha groaned as Kai crooked his finger. "Just—Spicy…"

Was his talkative bargain having trouble finding his words? Kai added a second finger. "Mm. It does have a spicy flavor, I've been told."

"Don't—Don't talk—Oh God! Don't talk about other people tasting your cum."

"As you wish, pup." Kai had a third finger in now, the glide smooth as silk. "How does it feel? Still good?"

Sascha's answer was a long, drawn-out wail.

Kai paused, cocking his head. "Did you come, zaychik?"

"Of fucking course I did!" Sascha's words were muffled, as he was now pressing his face firmly into the comforter. The tips of his ears were a bright pink.

"Good." Kai continued with his task.

But Sascha immediately let out a weak, strangled moan. Kai paused. "Is it too much? Should I stop?" Perhaps his human's fragile constitution couldn't handle multiple orgasms.

"Don't you fucking dare." Sascha's words came out in a slur this time.

Mm. So many new and interesting ways to trip up Sascha's tongue.

Kai slipped in a fourth finger, the squeeze enough to make his cock pulse with need. He stopped to assess. It would still be a tight fit. But it *would* fit. And there would be ample precum to ease the way.

He stayed where he was for another moment anyway. He'd never seen such an enticing sight as this—Sascha sucking his fingers in like he was made for it—and Kai's cock was acting accordingly, his ridges pulsing in a steady rhythm. He was eager to sheathe them in his human, to feel those inner muscles clench around them, milking him for all he was worth.

"Are you ready for me, zaychik?"

Sascha's voice was faint, but his words were firm. "Get on with it already."

Just as Kai had told him—he was a fierce creature at heart.

Kai took his cock in hand, gathering more of his natural lubricant. One last push of his fingers to coat Sascha's passage, and then he lined himself up. Even with the substantial height of the bed, he had to keep his knees slightly bent to get the right angle. It would perhaps have been more practical if he were to revert to human form, but for his first time claiming Sascha, it was—for some reason he could not name—important to be in his true state.

He notched the head against Sascha's entrance. "Relax, pup."

Sascha mumbled something about "*you* relax with a baseball bat trying to fuck you," but he did loosen his muscles.

Kai pressed in, excruciatingly slow, Sascha bearing down to take him in. His human was full of pants and grunts and muffled curses, but his bottom remained tilted up, pushing back against Kai, giving as good as he got. Kai stroked his lower back, soothing him as he'd once soothed riled horses during a siege.

He smiled to himself at the thought—Sascha would hate that comparison.

When he was fully sheathed, he took a moment to admire the sight—Sascha's hole a bright pink, bordering on red, stretched around the dusky blue of Kai's cock. It was a thing of beauty, really.

He pulled out in a tight but surprisingly smooth glide, the venom of his ejaculate having done its work quickly, relaxing Sascha's inner muscles.

Sascha turned his head to the side, revealing cheeks that matched the bright pink of his entrance. "Oh *fuck*. I can feel the ridges."

"Mm," Kai answered distractingly, his attention caught once more by the sight of his glistening cock sliding in and out of that stretched hole.

"I'm hard again. How am I hard again?"

Kai grinned wolfishly. "Because, sweet Sascha, my cock presses against all the right places. You'll come at least twice before I'm done with you."

Sascha managed to purse his slack lips into the semblance of a pout. "Don't sound so smug."

But Kai *was* smug. How could he not be? Sascha was taking him so well, his body accepting Kai's perfectly, as if made for it.

Kai had known it would be this way. He was going to get Sascha addicted to fucking a demon. To fucking *this* demon.

He grabbed at Sascha's hips, letting his talons grow, just to see the press of them into the soft, pale flesh there. Not enough to break the skin—not with Sascha's aversion to blood—but enough to tease at the idea.

He picked up the pace as best he could with the tight fit, setting a steady rhythm that had Sascha pressing his face into the bedding again.

It wasn't long before Sascha wailed once again, not quite as muffled as before. Kai growled his approval at another orgasm from his partner.

Sascha's body went limp. "Jesus," he sighed. "That was—"

"Was?" Kai wrapped an arm around Sascha's waist, hauling him up and back against him, before twisting until he was seated on the edge of the bed, Sascha in his lap with his back against him, still impaled on his cock. "What did I say before, zaychik?" He ran his tongue along the side of Sascha's neck. "That you'd come twice before I'm done. And I'm not done with you yet."

14

Sascha

Sascha blinked dazedly, trying to make his brain process the quick change of position. Were they really not done yet? He'd come twice already. And while it wasn't precisely unheard of for him, it was all usually a bit more...spaced out?

Kai shifted underneath him—shifted *inside* him—and Sascha let out a ragged moan.

He was so *full*.

He'd never been this full in his life, and he wasn't exactly virginal to begin with. It should have hurt, should have at the very least burned, but apparently Kai's venomous jizz really was magic, because there was no pain at all.

Just pressure and—

"Oh!" Sascha cried out as Kai lifted him by the hips, withdrawing almost completely, before dropping him back down in a slow glide.

Sascha's poor spent cock twitched, somehow filling with blood again.

It shouldn't have been possible, but those ridges were merciless, pressing against every inch of Sascha's inner walls, sending jolts of electricity up his spine. One would have thought the venom would numb the sensation as well as the pain, but no—it seemed to amplify it, if anything. A constant, heated tingling warming Sascha up from the inside out.

His head fell back against Kai's chest, his eyelids fluttering closed. He'd never had reason to be accused of being a pillow princess before, but in this case...all he could do was take it.

"Your dick should be illegal," he tried to say as Kai moved that massive cock in and out of him again. But it all just came out as another garbled groan.

"What was that?" Kai asked, amusement lacing his voice.

This fucking smug bastard. Just because he was a gorgeous giant beast with the cock of a god, he thought he had one over on Sascha?

Was he even affected by all this?

Sascha opened bleary eyes, tilting his head back against that smooth chest to peer up at him. Kai's eyes were glowing again, and his lips were parted, panting almost silently, his eyes locked on Sascha's hardening dick.

Not completely unaffected, then.

He was too beautiful by far though. Sascha needed to taste his mouth again. He just did.

"Kiss me?" he pleaded, somehow managing to form the words this time.

Kai growled, his head dipping down, that pointed tongue delving into Sascha's mouth. He tasted like the scent surrounding Sascha, like smoke and spice. He continued lifting and dropping Sascha on his cock while he plundered his mouth, determined to take every bit of Sascha hostage.

Eventually Sascha had to jerk his face away, gasping for air. His head was full of cotton, and his body was no better than a rag doll, but his cock was fully hard and leaking again, bouncing in the air with Kai's unforgiving rhythm.

"Oh God," he moaned, mortified to feel tears gathering in the corners of his eyes. "Again? Really?"

He'd at least had the friction of the bed and his hand to partially blame last time, but Kai wasn't even touching his dick at all.

"Yes," Kai growled, latching his mouth onto Sascha's shoulder. "*Again.*"

So fucking bossy.

But he was going to get what he wanted. Something was building in Sascha, low in his belly, so steady and insistent Sascha was almost afraid of the intensity.

Kai seemed to sense it. He didn't stop his movements, but he placed a hand on Sascha's stomach, petting the skin there. "Let it happen, zaychik. I have you."

And somehow, Sascha believed him.

So he let go, let that pressure build and build, let his orgasm crash over him like a tidal wave.

The third time should have been *less* intense, shouldn't it?

But Sascha could barely breathe as his inner muscles spasmed relentlessly. His vision whited out, and static hummed in his ears. He felt like he was holding on to consciousness by a thread.

He cried out. Or he tried to, but the sound that left his throat was weak and thready, overpowered by Kai's growling roar, the demon crushing Sascha against him as those ridges bulged and pulsed rapidly, filling Sascha with heat.

Like, literal heat, coating Sascha's insides, seemingly without end.

"How much did you *come*?" Sascha asked incredulously, about a million years later, when he was finally able to form words again.

Kai patted Sascha's belly, a pleased rumble emanating from his chest. "As much as is normal for my kind."

Sascha peered back at him suspiciously. "It felt like a lot."

"I'll help empty it from you," Kai offered. There was a weird gleam in his eyes, different from his creepy demon glow. Like that idea pleased him a whole lot.

Sascha was starting to think this demon was a bit of a perv.

Kai smiled at him, all sharp teeth. "You make many pleasing sounds when you're aroused, zaychik."

"Well, that's because—" Sascha paused, mortification running through him. "Oh fuck."

Kai stiffened underneath him, one hand already reaching for his daggers. "What's wrong?"

"My *brother's* here." Sascha covered his face with his hands. "I was supposed to be quiet. You—you hypnotized me or something, with that monster dick of yours. I forgot to be stealthy."

"You're a man grown," Kai said, his hand returning to pat at Sascha's belly. "What do we care if your brother heard?"

He sounded smug again. Had he done it on purpose? A perv with a voyeurism kink, perhaps?

Sascha didn't even have the energy to be indignant. Kai had apparently fucked it out of him. "Everything's filthy," he grumbled instead. "We need to shower. And change the sheets." He lifted one arm with heroic effort but plopped it back down immediately. "I can't move a muscle. You've broken me."

Kai nuzzled his cheek against the top of Sascha's head. "I'll bathe you. A demon cares for his mate."

"I haven't agreed to be your mate," Sascha reminded him, annoyed at himself for pressing into the touch.

"You will."

Kai lifted him off his cock slowly. Sascha could feel the cum sliding out of him, his hole probably gaping open. "Oh my God," he moaned. "You *have* broken me. It's never going to close back up again."

Kai's soft laugh was infuriating as he tucked Sascha against his chest. "The venom will wear off soon and you'll be back to normal. Let me wash you. I'll take great care."

"Fine," Sascha grumbled. "But it doesn't mean I'm your mate."

Kai only hummed, carrying Sascha bridal-style into the adjoining bathroom.

Smug bastard.

———

Time was moving strangely, Sascha's reality altered by too many orgasms.

One second, he was being carried by Kai; the next, he was in the shower, his hands propped up against the tiled wall, his legs shaking and his back arched while Kai fingered out his own cum with alarming thoroughness.

Sascha wasn't even sure how long it had been going on at this point, but he certainly didn't feel as full as before—besides the fingers stuffed inside him, that was.

He looked back at Kai—in human form again, presumably to fit under the showerhead—who was staring at Sascha's ass with focused intensity, watching his fingers move in and out.

"Um, I think we're good now," Sascha told him, amused in spite of himself.

He was also mildly concerned his dick was going to plump up again if Kai didn't start behaving. And Sascha wouldn't survive another orgasm. He really, really wouldn't.

And apparently he wouldn't have to, because Kai withdrew his fingers with a forlorn sigh, then placed a horridly (wonderfully) sweet kiss on Sascha's shoulder. "I'll draw us a bath, then."

He left the shower, reverting to demon form again while he toyed with the taps. The claw tub was some extra-large monstrosity, so he'd most likely fit. Maybe it was uncomfortable to be in human form too long.

Everything about him raised so many questions. So much strangeness. And yet he was fitting into Sascha's new life with such alarming ease.

Sascha turned off the water in the shower, shivering slightly without Kai's natural heat at his back. Kai was focused on the bath taps, testing the water temperature with a frown of concentration.

Caring for his mate.

No. Nuh-uh. Sascha couldn't go down that path. He couldn't contemplate forming a permanent bond with a demon he'd just met. That would go far beyond his usual impulsiveness. A whole realm beyond.

But you'd get to keep him.

Sascha shook the thought out of his head. "You knew they were vampires," he found himself saying, desperate to steer his mind in another direction. "When they were at the door."

"Mm. I know of bloodsuckers." Kai began opening various bottles by the tub and sniffing at them, eventually pouring some fancy bath oil Sascha had bought himself into the water. He seemed just as at ease nude as he was clothed. And why shouldn't he? His body was ridiculous, with or without the full seven feet of height. "Some of our kind believe them to be distant, weak traces of our own bloodline." He cocked a brow at Sascha. "*Very* weak. Perhaps descendants of a demon who found a way to this realm without a contract."

"I thought you said it couldn't happen."

Kai shrugged his tattooed shoulder. "It's not done. It's said to have terrible consequences. That's not to say it's impossible."

He stepped into the bath, making another one of those pleased rumbling sounds that did weird things to Sascha's insides. He held out a clawed hand. "Come, zaychik."

Unable to resist the pull of his charm, Sascha accepted the hand and stepped into the tub, finding himself immediately tucked against Kai's broad chest.

He relaxed back against him. "And what about your wings?" he asked. "Those were a fun surprise. Where are they now?"

Kai cupped the water between his hands and poured it over Sascha's chest, warming the parts of him the water didn't reach. "Sheathed until I have use of them."

"Does it hurt? When they come out?"

"No." Kai pressed a kiss on his head. "It's more like...a release."

Sascha hummed his acknowledgment, even though he had absolutely no basis for comparison, and they bathed for a while in comfortable silence. Kai smelled delicious, and the warm water soothed the lingering aches and tremors in Sascha's body.

Sascha's lids grew heavy, and he could only hope if he fell asleep like this, Kai would know to keep his head above water.

But apparently Kai had other ideas. "Tell me of the incident," he said softly. "The reason you faint when blood appears."

So much for sleeping. Every muscle in Sascha's body tensed, that comfy well-used feeling he'd been sinking into evaporating like smoke. "Why?"

"Because it haunts you." Taloned hands landed on his shoulders, cupping them gently. "And because it's part of you, and I wish to know all parts of you."

He'd found the perfect answer. Sascha couldn't resist. Who didn't want to be known? To be seen with all their flaws and hangups and still be wanted in the end?

He cleared his throat. He could feel panic hovering on the periphery, but it couldn't quite take hold, not with Kai's solid warmth surrounding him. "I was still a kid," he began. "Only six, I think. I went somewhere I wasn't supposed to. My father and his men were...torturing someone, I guess. There was blood everywhere."

Kai's grip on his shoulders tightened. "Too young for such a sight."

"Yeah, but I might've—maybe I still would have been okay," Sascha told him. "But when the guy saw me—when he realized someone new had arrived—he started...begging." Sascha struggled to swallow, to keep the panic at bay. Kai began stroking his upper arms in a steady rhythm. "Asking me to help him, to save him, telling me how much it hurt. I was so little— What was I supposed to do? I couldn't help. I couldn't do anything. My father sent me back upstairs eventually, but I could—I could hear him screaming as I left." He let out a harsh breath. "When I see blood, it's like I'm right back there. Helpless. Useless."

Kai's hands were a soothing balm. "Such pain you hold."

Sascha shook his head decisively. "No, I'm—I'm lucky. I'm spoiled," he said, repeating the familiar refrain. Spoiled Sascha who didn't have to work, who had a chauffeur and a maid and an entire apartment bought for him, who received a sizable allowance no matter how useless he was.

"We must have different definitions of the word," Kai murmured. "But no matter—*I* will spoil you." He started pouring palmfuls of water over Sascha's shoulders again. "A demon spoils its mate. And if we bonded, you could not be hurt. You could not fall ill."

He said the last part pointedly, like that was a huge selling point.

Sascha gave an incredulous laugh. "You want to permanently bond our souls together because you don't want me to get the flu again?"

"I want to permanently bond our souls because I wish to stay by your side," Kai said easily.

The words were so sweet, but after reliving his past, even for a moment, Sascha was one raw nerve. One raw nerve with serious trust issues. "But you're supposed to go home," he pointed out.

"You want me to?"

"It doesn't matter what I want!" Sascha half hissed, half yelled, anger rushing through him without cause. "You're going—you're going to *leave*. You told me yourself. Everyone leaves eventually, and you're included in everyone so…"

It was true. That was what happened when someone was weak and useless and stood still while everyone else moved on. People disappeared, no matter how attached to them someone got. Sascha's mother, all the nannies, Alexei.

The panic that had been hovering at the edge took hold, and he could only force breath into his lungs with heaving gasps.

Kai made soothing noises, wrapping his broad arms tightly around Sascha. His biceps were so large, so otherworldly, with the blue lines dancing on the skin of his right arm, that Sascha was taken out of his head in an instant.

"You're stupid big," he said dumbly.

Kai gave a soft laugh. Eventually, when Sascha's breaths had evened and his muscles had released their tension, Kai spoke again. "I can also protect you without staying," he said, holding Sascha more firmly when the words sent a jolt through him. "If you don't wish to keep me. You could use me to take control from your brother—I could give you that. You could have his power for yourself."

Sascha twisted in Kai's hold to glare at him. "Why the fuck would I want that? That isn't the bargain we made. I don't need his power; I just don't want to be stabbed again."

"I see." A broad smile graced Kai's lips. It should have been alarming, with all those sharp teeth. But it was only beautiful. "I would very much like a mate bond with you, Sascha," he purred, like Sascha had just given him a love confession.

Kai didn't get it. Didn't get that Sascha wasn't the catch he thought he was. "I don't want you to do something you'll regret," he told him.

Kai cocked his head. "And why would I regret it?"

"You just will." Sascha let out a bitter laugh. "I'm not that great, as humans go."

There was a long silence.

Sascha huffed, slapping at the water with his palm. "This is when you disagree with me."

Kai grabbed his hand, stilling his movements. "I'm gathering my words," he told him. After a moment, he spoke. "You asked why I entered my name and powers into the Book. There was the prestige and power, yes. But in truth..." Kai met his eyes, looking more serious than Sascha had ever seen him. "I have been a restless soul for as long as I can remember. It's why I attached myself to the Book. Why I looked to the human realm for diversion. But when I'm with you, Sascha, I am...soothed. Content. For perhaps the very first time in my existence. It's the way I would like to feel, going forward." He pressed a kiss to the back of Sascha's hand. "I will not regret."

Well, that was lovely. That was just so fucking lovely. What was Sascha supposed to do with that kind of loveliness? Fall in love and live happily ever after?

Was that even allowed, for someone like him?

"But we need to bond *before* we finish the contract," Kai told him, his voice gentle, as if sensing his declaration had shaken Sascha to his core.

"It's a big decision," Sascha murmured.

"It is. Be brave for me, zaychik."

"I'm not very good at that."

"Then, as I said. I will be brave enough for the both of us." Kai let out a breath, pulling the plug on the bath decisively. "But perhaps I place too much pressure on you. I'm not used to waiting for the things I want, unless forced to by outside circumstances." He planted a kiss on Sascha's shoulder. "I will stop pressing."

"I don't—I don't mind the pressing," Sascha said, watching the water swirl down the drain. "I just have a hard time believing it's real."

Kai lifted Sascha from the tub, once more carrying him bridal-style. "We'll let you sleep." He nuzzled Sascha's head. "Perhaps your credulity will improve with the morning."

15

Sascha

Sascha slept like the dead—no more fever dreams to mess with his head, not even lingering anxiety to force him awake two or three times over the course of the night, as had happened so often in the past.

He'd been soothed by demon sex, apparently. Or, more like, soothed by the big demon body pillow he was currently drooling all over.

Kai had changed to human form in order to fit in the bed when they'd gone to sleep, but at some point in the night, he'd reverted back, his feet now hanging over the edge.

Sascha would have to get something custom-made, if the big lug really was planning on sticking around.

He rose up on one elbow, wiping some of his drool off Kai's chest. The demon was sleeping, his gorgeous face as alluring as ever, even unconscious. Although, there was something about him awake—mischievous or demanding or arrogant in turn—that was even more attractive.

It was a bit annoying that his silky black hair wasn't even the slightest bit disheveled—Sascha could feel the unwieldy spikes his own blond locks had configured into over the night. Meanwhile, Kai's horns jutted elegantly out of the smooth surface of his hair, the tips brushing against the headboard.

Sascha slid up carefully under the covers, keeping an eye on Kai's closed lids. He got up to his knees at the head of the bed, peering closely at the horns. He couldn't quite see where the base of them began. He laid a finger on one. The texture was rough, like a goat's horn.

Or, at least, Sascha assumed. He'd never actually felt a goat's horn. Papa hadn't exactly been keen on taking his brats to petting zoos over the years.

Sascha began to stroke the horn more firmly, getting a better feel for the...consistency of the grain, maybe? What were the correct terms for horn qualities?

"You know, the base of a demon's horns are incredibly sensitive, zaychik."

Sascha pulled his hand back with a start. Kai's eyes were open now, and he was staring at him with amusement. "Oh! Sorry, I—"

Kai ran his tongue over a fanged incisor. "By all means, continue. But you might get more than you bargained for, hm?"

Sascha's gaze dropped down to where there was now a quite sizable bulge tenting up the bedcovers.

He scrambled off the bed, much more quickly than he usually moved in the morning. "Nope. No funny business," he scolded from a safe distance. "You broke me last night. And my ass is a national treasure. As such, it must be protected."

Kai's venom had definitely worked some sort of magic—Sascha probably wouldn't have been able to walk if it hadn't—but he was still a bit sore, and he didn't feel like testing his limits with Alexei in the house. His brother's eagle eyes would notice if Sascha came downstairs with a limp in his step.

Kai propped himself onto on elbow, smirking at him. "There are all kinds of ways to engage in 'funny business,' as you say. But all right." He tilted his head toward the pile of packages he'd left at the door the night before. "Why not open a few of those?" His grin widened. "A safe distance from the big, bad demon."

Smug bastard.

But Sascha did love a good unboxing. He glanced at the packages, the proof of his impulsive online shopping. Now that they were in front of him—with Kai watching him so closely—his cheeks were growing hot with embarrassment. He hadn't exactly held back when ordering. Would Kai think he was silly? Too frivolous to be worth his time? Not manly enough or something?

He could picture his father's face—or Ivan's for that matter—if he saw some of what Sascha had ordered. It wouldn't be a pretty sight.

Although, Sascha hadn't exactly been the pinnacle of masculinity in any of his and Kai's encounters. He'd summoned the guy with blue nail polish, for fuck's sake. And Kai wasn't some asshole mobster with outdated ideas on gender stereotypes. He was a demon from another realm who thought Sascha's soul was delicious and his yoga pants were cute.

So Sascha hustled over to the boxes, grabbing the first one within easy reach. He recognized the brand—some nightwear he'd ordered. He swallowed with a dry throat, then ripped the tape off and lifted out the first set.

Right. Some *pink* nightwear he'd ordered. Little satiny shorts with a matching short-sleeved button-down. The heat in Sascha's cheeks spread to the tips of his ears just from looking at them. So *pretty.*

Kai was staring intently, his eyes blazing. "That's for you to wear, zaychik?"

"Um...yes?" Sascha answered, his head suddenly filling once again with visions of his father scolding him for effeminate speech, his men murmuring among themselves whenever Sascha walked a certain way.

But it wasn't any sort of mocking condemnation that left Kai's mouth. It was a long, pleased rumble. "Perhaps you should see if they fit," he crooned. "And then come back to bed wearing them."

Oh. *Oh.* Kai was into it. Like, really into it, judging by the way he was looking at Sascha like he wanted to eat him alive.

Sascha shot him a mocking glare. "I'm not going anywhere near that monstrous dick of yours. Behave."

Kai grinned. "Open another," he urged.

Sascha ignored him, digging deeper into the box instead. There were two more pajama sets in there, as well as a pale-blue silk robe with a pattern of bright-orange and -yellow flowers.

He moved onto the next boxes after letting Kai admire each piece, which he did with slightly alarming intensity. There were some bright, tight shirts, some flowy pants similar to Kai's but in an array of colors. Business wear that was made to make a man actually look good, not just like an office drone. Nothing beige, nothing boring.

Every item received a grunt or rumble of approval from Kai, with a look in his eyes like he was imagining Sascha in each one. Or possibly taking Sascha *out* of each one.

When all but the last box had been opened, Sascha shot Kai a suspicious look. "Tell me, would you have fallen for any twinkish type you came across? Am I just the first?"

Kai looked surprised at the question. "Their soul would not have fit the same within my chest. It's not just your looks, pretty Sascha. Although, I do like them," he said with relish. "Very much."

Sascha frowned down at the package in his hands. "But how do you know? How do you know they wouldn't have fit the same?"

"I just do."

"But *how*?"

Kai cocked a brow. "Why do you continue to question it?" At Sascha's silence, a slow smirk graced his lips. "Ah. You wish to test me. Very well, zaychik. You may continue to do so. I will not falter or fail. I am strong enough for the both of us." He stretched languidly on the bed, ridiculously graceful for his large size. "Believe me when I tell you, no other 'twinkish type' would do."

Sascha searched for something to say in response to all that. All that he came up with was a petulant protest: "You think I'm sweet though. I'm not."

"You are," Kai insisted. "I can taste it."

"Hmph." Sascha turned to the last package to hide his blush. A padded envelope, without any logo to identify it. It was small, the size of a book maybe, but an irregular, lumpy shape. He couldn't think of what else he'd ordered. Some random accessory, maybe? He opened the flap and stuck his hand in.

"Oh!" Sascha pulled his hand back, flinching as he registered a sharp bite.

There was *blood* welling on his finger.

Sascha looked away immediately. Kai was already at his side, grabbing the package from his hand. He pulled out a knife, identical to the one that had stabbed Sascha two months ago.

A phantom pain throbbed in Sascha's upper arm.

The knife had dark rusting on the blade. Sascha swallowed hard. "Is that—is that dried blood?"

He did his best not to gag as Kai sniffed at it. "Animal," Kai told him. "Swine, I think."

"Oh. Okay." Sascha's head was starting to feel fuzzy. "So they know where I am. The—Ivan's mole must've..." he trailed off, trying to control his now labored breathing.

Then Kai's broad form was in front of him, his large hands weighty on Sascha's shoulders. "Listen to me, Sascha. You have me now. They cannot hurt you. We will wipe them out, zaychik. Every one of them who might wish you harm."

He kept repeating the words, "You have me now. They cannot hurt you," until Sascha's breath evened and the woozy feeling in his head evaporated.

Kai kissed his cut finger then, and Sascha felt the intense heat of his healing powers. Kai grinned at him. "All better?"

Sascha nodded mutely.

"Come. I will feed you. Your brother is already downstairs, making much noise."

ALEXEI WAS MAKING "MUCH NOISE," banging cabinets like it was his mission to destroy Sascha's kitchen or something.

Sascha shot a glare toward the back of his man-bunned head.

"What's up your ass?" he asked, annoyed that Alexei was acting pissy when it was *him* who'd received a threatening pig's-blood dagger in the mail.

Alexei whirled, casting a truly impressive scowl toward Kai, who'd made a beeline straight for the coffee pot. "Did your demon fail to tell you that vampires have *excellent* hearing?"

"What does that—?" The blood drained from Sascha's face, then rushed right back. "Oh." Right. The extremely thorough debauching he'd endured the night before, when he'd completely failed to muffle his voice.

Vampires or not, Alexei and Jay could have been half-deaf and they probably would have heard *something*.

He was pretty sure the heat in his cheeks could light the kitchen's ancient stove at his point.

"It was some very impressive sex!" Jay, beaming at him from the kitchen table, didn't seem to share Alexei's annoyance. "Alexei was afraid you were going to go for another round this morning. We were going to go out for breakfast if you did." He gave off every impression of being delighted by the idea. "I have to try a lobster roll while I'm here."

Sascha rubbed a hand over his face. "I don't think they serve lobster rolls at breakfast. And the best place for them in town is closed for the season, anyway."

"Oh."

Jay looked so instantly dejected that Sascha was opening his mouth again before he knew it. "But you two could come back and try one in the summer?"

What was he even saying? He wasn't going to still be here next summer, was he? He'd be back in New York, doing...

What *would* he be doing in New York? What exactly was waiting for him there?

He shot a despairing glance to Kai, only to find the demon mouthing the word *sweet* at him.

Sascha scowled back at him. Whatever. That didn't prove anything. Who wouldn't be sweet to Jay? He was one of the nicest people Sascha had ever met. What the hell he was doing with broody, tight-lipped Alexei was really anyone's guess.

The exchange between Sascha and Jay seemed to have deflated some of Alexei's ire though. He was looking at Sascha's chosen outfit with what on anyone else might have been a neutral expression but for Alexei might as well have been wide-eyed disbelief.

Oh, right. The colorful flower robe Sascha had put on over his underwear before heading downstairs. He fidgeted with the sash. "*Well?*" he asked Alexei pointedly, sounding snippier than he would have liked.

Alexei's gaze softened. "You look nice, Sascha. You always did like pretty things."

"Very pretty," Jay concurred, reaching a hand out to pet the hem. "And soft. Maybe I should get one? Although, I'm not sure when I'd wear it. Why have a robe when you can just be naked?"

Sascha coughed, choking on air. "Um...maybe for when you have guests?"

"Right." Jay nodded seriously. "Good point. So maybe I should—"

"Jay, sweetheart." Alexei came up to the kitchen table, stooping down to press a kiss to Jay's tousled hair. "Please don't buy a post-coital robe to match my brother's. I don't think I could take it."

"Oh." Jay's lips formed into a slight pout. "Okay, I'll choose my own, then."

Alexei gave him another kiss before straightening. "So your, uh, escapades aren't the only thing our ears overheard."

Sascha crossed his arms, glaring. "I'm a grown man, I can take a bath with whoever I want."

Alexei's lips twitched. "The knife, Sascha."

"Oh. Yes. The knife." Sascha's eyes darted to Kai, who'd dumped an entire bag of coffee grounds into the coffee pot and was adding what even Sascha knew was not nearly enough water.

"And you think Ivan has a leak? A mole?" Alexei pressed.

"That's what he says. But they still shouldn't have known. He hasn't told anyone or visited or..." Sascha remembered all the calls and texts from Ivan he'd been ignoring. "Oh fuck."

"What?" Alexei and Kai asked at the same time.

Sascha rubbed a hand over his eyes. "He's been trying to reach me while I was sick. I said something stupid to him before getting feverish. Let me..."

He ran upstairs to where he'd left his phone charging overnight before glancing at it as he hopped down the stairs. "You think he knew they'd figured it out? Or..."

There were a number of voice mails from Ivan, but Sascha didn't want to touch those. He looked at the texts instead.

Answer the phone, Sascha.

You're testing my patience.

You want to play games? I can play, baby brother. Get the guest room ready.

Oh fuck. Sascha checked to see when the last text had been sent. Yesterday.

He cleared his throat. "Um, Alexei, maybe you and Jay should be heading back to Colorado?"

"What? Why?" Jay looked back and forth between them. "Is it because I wanted to copy your robe? I don't have to get the exact same one."

And of course just then there was a knock on the front door.

Alexei gave him a small smile, seeming to already know what was on the other side. "It's fine, Sascha. It's a reunion long overdue." He put a hand on Jay's shoulder. "He can't hurt us. Not really."

Sascha's stomach twisted anyway. He was stuck in place for a long moment. He should change, shouldn't he? He looked to Kai. No, he wouldn't change. He was fine the way he was.

The knocking grew more insistent.

Sascha went to the front door, Kai right behind him, opening it to a face he knew better than his own. A face very similar to his own, although Sascha had never quite managed the icy cold of Ivan's eyes.

Ivan must have come straight from the office—he was wearing a tailored black suit, one he wore with the ease Sascha had always been incapable of. He wasn't glaring—he wouldn't, not when he could be equally terrifying with no expression, his face a smooth and forbidding mask. "About time," he said in a clipped voice. "What the fuck are you wearing?"

"A bathrobe." It took everything in Sascha not to fidget with the damned thing. "I'm surprised you don't have a key."

"I misplaced it." Ivan's eyes tracked behind Sascha's shoulder, and Sascha knew without looking that Kai was back in human form. "Who's this? You hired your own muscle? Is that what your hissy fit was about?"

"I sent you one text," Sascha sniped. "I don't think that counts as a hissy fit."

"You froze me out after. *That's* the hissy fit. Let me in, Sascha."

Sascha stepped back from the door with a sigh, Kai hovering over his shoulder like a forbidding guardian angel.

Ivan stepped inside, and his gaze flew immediately to the entrance of the kitchen, where Alexei was standing, Jay just behind him. For the briefest moment, pure shock crossed Ivan's face, making him look relatively human. Then the cold mask descended again. "Alexei," he said flatly. "You've returned."

"Sascha needed me."

"I see." Ivan glanced at Sascha, his expression unreadable. Sascha felt a complicated rush of shame and defiance. He knew his brothers were at odds, and always had been. And he knew they both loved him, in their own ways. That Ivan loved him as best as he was able, and it wasn't exactly his fault that his best had been stunted beyond belief by their upbringing.

And he knew, without a doubt, that Ivan would see this as a betrayal—Sascha turning to Alexei and away from him.

"Ivan, I—" Sascha started to say.

The slightest tensing of Ivan's shoulder was the only warning before his hand was in his suit jacket and he was pulling out a gun, firing two shots into Alexei with no hesitation.

And then, for the second time in twenty-four hours, Sascha found himself behind a wall of leather.

16

Kai

Kai was in front of Sascha in an instant, his wings blocking his human from view. Blocking him from *harm*.

Kai's heart was in his throat. What if this brother had aimed the gun at Sascha instead? It didn't matter that Kai knew deep down he would have been fast enough to stop it. The thought of it —the what-if of it—had his hackles raising.

What he wouldn't give to snap Ivan's neck.

But it seemed he would have to wait in line. Because the bloodsucker Jay—who had, the night before, been distressed by the violence of Kai cracking an egg too hard when making pancakes—had Ivan on his back on the floor and was crouched atop his chest, two small hands wrapped around his throat.

Jay's true vampire face was out—the all-black eyes and snarling fangs—but with his diminutive size and delicate features, the effect was slightly muted. Still, Kai knew he was stronger than he looked.

Much stronger.

"You do *not* hurt Alexei," Jay was telling Ivan, his sweet voice as close to a growl as was possible. "You've hurt him enough already."

Ivan, for his part, looked remarkably unfazed for someone a hair's breadth away from death's fangs. "I was told he was a monster now," he said, not even attempting to fight Jay's hold. "That you both are. It seems I was correctly informed. I didn't kill him, did I?"

"That's doesn't mean it didn't fucking *hurt*." Alexei was still upright, two dark splotches of blood growing on his chest and stomach. "What if you'd been wrong?"

Ivan cocked a blond brow at his brother. "You'd deserve it."

"I don't hurt humans, and I don't like violence," Jay said evenly, some of the tension having left his frame after Alexei had spoken. "But I think you could be my exception."

But he was already removing his hands from Ivan's neck—he hadn't even been holding him hard enough to leave a bruise on his skin—his face returning to its human visage as he crawled off him.

Ivan suddenly turned his head, meeting Kai's eyes.

Kai had known what the eldest looked like from his photo, but it was still odd to see a face so similar to Sascha's without any of his warmth, or enthusiasm, or sulky charm.

"And it seems our baby brother has acquired his own monster," Ivan drawled as he rose to a seated position, looking surprisingly put together sitting there on the floor in his suit. "A conspiracy, is it?"

Sascha, who'd been mumbling something about "big fucking bat wings," yelled out from behind Kai, "Stop being so paranoid, Ivan! There's no conspiracy. I summoned him on accident." He tapped at Kai's shoulder, lowering this voice. "I'd like to come out now, please."

"Not until the little bloodsucker grabs the weapon," Kai insisted, keeping his wings exactly where they were.

Jay had knocked the gun out of Ivan's hand when he'd tackled him, and it was lying on the hardwood floor between him and Alexei.

Jay—already back at Alexei's side, fussing over wounds that were surely healed by now—shook his head. "Oh, no thank you. I don't like guns."

"I've got it," Alexei told them, bending down to grab the thing. He nodded at Kai. "You can let Sascha out now."

"No. Change your shirt first." At Alexei's glare, Kai arched a brow. "Sascha doesn't like blood."

"Oh." Alexei's glare dropped in an instant. "Right. Sweetheart, would you grab me one? I don't want to leave these three alone."

At the pointed look Alexei gave him, Kai realized he was brandishing two of his daggers. Did he think Kai would kill Ivan in his absence?

It was tempting. Unbearably tempting. But Kai hadn't forgotten Sascha's words.

I still love Ivan, even when he's controlling and vicious.

Sascha wasn't the kind of human who wanted vengeance, who yearned for violence to answer violence. It wasn't just blood Sascha hated—it was suffering. That was the part of the story from his childhood he'd told Kai that clearly hurt him the most— the man's suffering, and his inability to do anything to help.

And Sacha claimed his soul wasn't sweet.

But it was. *He* was. Sascha didn't want either of his brothers to hurt, however much they themselves may have hurt him in the past, intentional or not. Kai was certain if this rival Mafia family weren't an active threat, Sascha wouldn't want them hurt either, no matter the past stabbing. He didn't want power or carnage or to have Kai wreak havoc in his name. He wanted to exist in peace. He wanted someone by his side while he did so.

So Kai put his daggers back in their sheaths with a nod to

Alexei as Jay bounded up the stairs and back down again, fresh shirt in hand.

Ivan stood slowly from the floor, dusting off his suit, as if being threatened by a vampire had been no more than a minor inconvenience.

There was a cleared throat from behind Kai.

Right.

Kai lowered his wings, and Sascha stepped out from behind him.

But Ivan, for the moment, seemed to have eyes only for Alexei. His lips quirked in a cold smile. "Tell me, Alyosha. Are you going to shoot *me* now?"

Alexei studied the gun in his hand. "I'm thinking about it."

Sascha made an exasperated noise. "No one's shooting anyone. Jesus, Vanya, what were you thinking? Alexei, are you really all right?"

Ivan took his eyes off Alexei to narrow them at Sascha. "Don't call me that in mixed company."

Sascha's lower lip pushed out into a pout, and he rolled his eyes. "You *just* called Alexei Alyosha. Plus, it's not mixed company. They're like your brothers-in-law."

Both Alexei and Ivan stared at Sascha incredulously.

Kai grinned. He'd known Sascha was softening to the idea of the mate bond.

Ivan shook off his surprise first, turning to Jay, who was looking a little sheepish at Alexei's side, then to Kai, whose wings were folded but not yet returned to their hiding place. "And what species, pray tell, are these brothers-in-law of mine?"

Sascha pointed to Jay. "Vampire." Then to Kai. "Demon."

Ivan nodded slowly. "The text you sent. Your summoning."

"See?" Sascha smiled winningly at him. "I even tried to tell you. There's no conspiracy."

Ivan cocked a brow. "That singular text was your attempt to inform me?"

Sascha put his hands on his hips. "It's not my fault you don't take me seriously! You wrote me off like a dick."

Was this what having brothers was like? It seemed exhausting at best. Kai was newly grateful to be the sole member of his brood.

"And how did you accidentally summon a demon?" Ivan asked.

"I found a book. I'll show you." Sascha looked to Alexei and immediately threw up his hands. "Alyosha! Put down the gun!"

Instead, Alexei used it to point at Ivan's face. "I don't trust him."

"I can vanish it," Kai offered, if only to stop the bickering.

"He has more than one on him," Alexei told him. "He always does."

"Then he may leave." Kai would allow no more gunshots near Sascha. There was no bond in place yet, and his human was too fragile to risk it, even with Kai's supernatural reflexes.

But a soft hand landed on his bicep. "Kai, it's fine," Sascha told him. "He won't hurt me. He just needs to feel protected."

Kai sneered in Ivan's direction. "As if a mere pistol could protect him from the likes of me."

He didn't miss Sascha's eye roll. "Yes, yes. Everyone here is very tough and scary, except for me."

And yet it was Sascha herding them all into the living room like wayward children, keeping his older brothers on separate sides of the room. And while he may have thought he loved too easily, it was clear that love was returned. Even Ivan's cold mask slipped for an instant when Sascha sat him down with a pat on his shoulder, a look of unmistakable fondness there and gone in a flash.

Perhaps he truly had been worried by Sascha's silence.

But Kai wasn't letting down his guard. Ivan looked to Kai to be the exact sort of man who would have summoned him in the past. Power-hungry, paranoid, determined to be an army of one against the world.

His only saving grace was that his soul didn't yet have the stench of rot. There were humans for whom it was too late, whose actions had corrupted them past a point of no return. It was useless making bargains with them—their souls provided no sustenance.

Ivan wasn't there, at least not yet. But Kai was sure he had the potential for it.

Kai would need to keep an eye on him.

Kai had sat in on war councils with less tension than this reunion of brothers.

There was nothing but barbed jabs and hostile silence passed continuously back and forth between the two elder brothers—all while they refused to speak directly to each other—and, for his part, Sascha repeatedly attempted to break the tension with silly remarks about silly subjects.

Kai was beginning to understand where Sascha's spoiled reputation came from in the family—he seemed to brandish his own foolishness like a sword, hacking down the others' aggression when it grew too potent.

Eventually Ivan insisted on a full recounting of Kai's summoning, and Sascha obliged, in much more specific detail than Kai would have preferred.

Finally Ivan addressed Alexei directly for the first time since they'd entered the living room. "And your own monster?" he asked, head tilted toward the bloodsucker Jay, who'd remained uncharacteristically quiet since his mate had been shot. "How did that come to pass?"

"Don't call him that," Alexei said, the words escaping through clenched teeth. There was another prolonged silence, but before Sascha could interject with another aside about wealthy television housewives or the latest in New York socialite drama, Alexei spoke again. "You were supposed to protect him."

"And I have," Ivan told him coolly.

"He was *stabbed*."

Ivan shrugged. "Not by me." He sneered at his brother. "You're the one who left, Alyosha. Leave me out of your guilt."

The callousness with which Ivan treated Sascha's attack had Kai's shoulder blades aching, his wings itching to come out again. The horrible, violent things he could do to this human, if only Sascha would let him.

But Sascha had already leaped up from the couch, asking far too loudly, "Who wants to come see the attic?" At the ensuing silence, he let out a strange half cough, half giggle. "It's where I found Kai's Book."

"We'll pass," Alexei answered, his hard stare still focused on Ivan.

It was a fair enough answer, considering the offer was a clear attempt to cut through the hostilities, although Kai himself was curious about where his Book had been hiding.

Surprisingly, Ivan stood from his chair. "All right. Show me, then."

Sascha led the way, and Kai inserted himself between him and his brother, reverting to human form before climbing the ladder in order to fit into the smaller space.

The small, dirty, nondescript space. Such an odd location for a demon's binding Book to be found. It was all ordinary cardboard boxes and a few dust-covered pieces of furniture.

Sascha waved a hand, encompassing the mess. "So this is it."

Ivan opened the nearest box, mouth pinched as a small cloud of dust erupted in front of his face. "And how would we know if anything else of consequence was up here?"

Kai reached out with his demon senses. He wouldn't be notified of absolutely everything, but that which pertained to demons would trigger a certain awareness. Like his Book, downstairs on the coffee table—he could sense the presence of demonic energy in its pages.

"There's nothing else of note here," he surmised after a moment. "I'd be able to feel it."

Ivan arched a brow. "Neat trick."

They fell into silence.

Ivan brushed his fingers against another box. "You called Alexei," he murmured.

Sascha shrugged, avoiding his brother's eye. "Technically, Kai did."

Ivan did not seem to find that reassuring. "And do you share our dear brother's belief that I failed to protect you?"

"*I* do," Kai told him.

He was ignored.

Sascha fidgeted with the sash of his robe, his eyes on his twitchy fingers. "I think... Well, Alexei has always thought...even growing up, you know?"

It was a nonsense jumble of words as far as Kai was concerned, but Ivan seemed to catch their meaning. His affect grew even frostier, if possible. "I should have done more? Been *nicer*? Forced our *father* to be nicer? What was I to do? A boy in a roomful of guns. The only way to protect us all was to learn how to be just as ruthless."

"Mission accomplished...," Sascha mumbled.

"Yes," Ivan agreed, voice like ice. "And here we all are. Still alive."

For some reason beyond Kai's understanding, that seemed to be enough for Sascha, and his gaze softened, his hand reaching out toward his brother. "Vanya..."

Ivan turned away before the hand could reach him. "But I may have a solution to your problem. That's why I'm here. The Caruso family wants a trade."

Sascha's arm dropped. "A...trade?"

"They'd like the use of our docks for a new venture. One I've refused in the past."

Sascha seemed to take a moment to translate his brother's words, then his eyes widened. "Ivan, no. Not—not *people*."

"It would put an end to the price on your head," Ivan told him, peering out the small attic window, as if he didn't care one way or another.

Sascha was trembling, the soul piece in Kai's chest roiling with confusion and sadness and anger. "You said we'd never do that. You said *never*."

"And we wouldn't, would we? We'd be looking the other way while someone else did."

Sascha's hands clenched into fists. "*No*."

"And what would you have me do instead?" Ivan straightened from the window, cocking his head at Sascha. "Start a war between our families? You and Alexei have no idea the cost of business," he hissed. "You never have."

"That's not fair."

Ivan's voice grew cutting. "I'm not interested in *fair*. You have a new protector now, don't you?" he asked, cold eyes moving to Kai. "Fix the problem yourself, then, Sascha. I'll be going now. This was a waste of time, and I have business to attend to."

He made his way out of the attic, ignoring Sascha's protests.

Kai did nothing to stop him. He wanted the eldest out of the house. Preferably permanently, or at least until he could learn to stop distressing Kai's human.

Sascha was staring around the attic, looking dazed. "He's talking about human trafficking. He's never— He said he'd *never*..."

Kai tugged Sascha to him, running a soothing hand down his back. "And he isn't now, zaychik," he reassured.

"What?"

"He's using us," Kai told him. "You have a weapon at your disposal now." Kai placed a hand on his own chest. "One he wishes he possessed. He's manipulating you so you use it."

Sascha might not have been used to having power to wield, and the complications that arose from it, but Kai was. He'd marked Ivan's game from the beginning: hit Sascha where it hurt —innocents being harmed—then guilt him until he acted himself.

Some of the tension in Sascha's frame relaxed. "You think so?"

It was like a dagger to the chest, the hope in Sascha's voice. Like he would rather be ruthlessly manipulated by someone he loved than believe his brother capable of evil.

Sascha pulled back, peering up into Kai's eyes. "You think he's lying about the Caruso family completely?"

Kai thought it over. "I think it's highly possible the proposal is real. The question is whether Ivan actually intends to take it."

Sascha's brow furrowed as he considered. "He wants *us* to act. So he doesn't have to."

"Perhaps it's time, pup." Kai cupped Sascha's cheek, keeping his voice low and soothing. He didn't want to alarm him, but they had realities to face. "They know where you are now."

But Sascha surprised him. He didn't panic, didn't lose himself to strangled breaths. "So...we need to bond now?" he asked, looking at Kai with clear eyes. "Before we deal with it and end the bargain?"

Kai tried to tamp down the rush of greed that arose with Sascha's words. He should by all accounts say something measured. *If you're ready*, or, *Take your time*.

But what came out was a fervent "*Yes.* Yes, Sascha. Now."

Sascha narrowed his eyes. "And you won't change your mind down the road?" he asked.

"I won't."

"And you won't regret it?"

"No." Kai tilted Sascha's head up with a finger under his chin, searching his face. "And what of your regret, zaychik?"

"Who, me?" Sascha gave him a cheeky grin. "I'd never let future regret stand in the way of an impulsive decision. How do we do it?"

Kai had been told long, long ago. He gave silent thanks he still remembered. "There's a ritual at the end of the Book."

"Okay." Sascha let out a slow breath, then cocked a brow at Kai. "This is when you ask me if I'm sure."

Kai cupped his cheeks with both hands. "I will be sure enough for the both of us," he promised.

"You're very arrogant."

"Yes," Kai agreed.

Sascha bit down on his lower lip. "God, why do I like that so much?"

Kai grinned down at him. "Because our souls are matched, my zaychik. A perfect fit."

"They'd better be." But Sascha's eyes were on Kai's mouth now. "Can I try kissing you without the fangs?" he asked.

In answer, Kai grabbed Sascha under his thighs and lifted him, wrapping his legs around his waist, the silken robe bunching up under Kai's fingers. He claimed Sascha's lips, and Sascha met him greedily halfway, licking into Kai's mouth like he'd been dying for it.

He was easier to reach with a half foot less of distance between them. There could be many benefits to fucking him in human form, for that matter. Kai could go harder, not need to stretch him quite so thoroughly.

He used his hold to press Sascha down against his hardening cock, and Sascha gyrated against him accommodatingly, moaning into Kai's mouth.

Perhaps they should practice now.

But a throat clearing pointedly had Sascha pulling away from Kai's lips, gasping for breath.

Alexei's head had popped up from the attic opening, and he was frowning at them both. "I hate to break up this display, but—"

Sascha glared at him. "Fuck *off*, Alexei. I'm busy here."

"I thought you'd want to know—"

"There's nothing—"

Alexei raised his voice to be heard over Sascha's protest "—that Ivan's run off with your Book."

17

Sascha

It took Sascha more than a moment to reorient to reality, heaving gasping breaths as he stared at Alexei.

He'd just agreed to the most impulsive decision of his life, and with Kai's mouth on him and his bulge pressed so nicely against Sascha's dick, Sascha had honestly been gearing up to consummate that decision in this...gross, dusty attic.

On second thought, maybe it was for the best that they'd been interrupted.

Kai's teeth were bared, and his talons were digging into Sascha's hips almost painfully. If Sascha hadn't known any better, he might assume Kai was just turned on. But he could read Kai better now—Sascha's demon was furious, and maybe a bit panicked. It was enough to have Sascha's stomach twisting into knots as well.

"He can't have taken it," Kai growled, setting Sascha back down on the floor as Alexei's head disappeared back down the ladder. "I can still sense it in the house."

But he was already climbing down after Alexei, and Sascha rushed to follow.

Alexei explained as they hurried to the living room, "Jay and I went out into the backyard. I was worried if I stayed inside any longer, I'd shoot Ivan with his own gun. When I heard the front door slam, we came back in. Jay noticed right away that the Book wasn't in the living room."

"Then why can I—" Kai's words cut off as he stopped in front of the coffee table so abruptly Sascha almost slammed into his back.

Sascha peered around him to see what had caught his attention: a single piece of thick paper. It had an eerie design in black ink etched on its surface, one that sent a shiver down Sascha's spine for some reason.

"Nightmare's mark," Kai murmured, reaching out a hand, his fingers stopping just before they would have touched the page. "That's what I can sense." He frowned down at it. "I didn't think the pages could come out."

Sascha's brow furrowed as he looked at the creepy mark. It wasn't one he would have traced in nail polish for fun; that was for sure. "Isn't the Book, like, ancient? Of course it's coming apart."

"It's not an ordinary book, pup." Kai sighed, lowering his arm. "But I suppose it's for the best. We wouldn't want to see your brother with Nightmare at his disposal." His frown deepened. "Although, I suppose Chaos could still do quite a bit of damage..."

Sascha almost laughed. "That's what you're so worried about? Ivan summoning a demon?" He tried to picture it, but it was a challenge to even imagine. It was just so strange to think of his cold, rigid brother dabbling in the paranormal.

Then again, Ivan *did* love consolidating his power.

But Kai was looking as distressed as ever. "We need the Book to bond," he reminded Sascha. He closed his eyes for a moment, then shook his head. "I can't sense its location. It's moving too fast."

He could sense that thing even when it wasn't in the building? Would Sascha ever learn the extent of Kai's powers? He supposed, if they had close to an eternity together, he eventually would. Maybe every bonding anniversary, Kai would reveal another neat little demon trick.

Focus, Sascha.

"I'm sure he's driving straight back to New York," he reassured Kai. "The paranoid dummy probably isn't even stopping for bathroom breaks."

"Then we'll find him there," Kai said, his tone decisive. "That's where your Caruso family is, anyway, correct?"

"And we'll help!" Jay offered from where he'd joined them, tucked under Alexei's arm.

Alexei frowned down at him. "Jay..."

Jay bit at his lower lip, his brow furrowing. "I know, but..."

Sascha looked between them. "What's going on?"

"Jay's animal shelter is opening in Hyde Park Monday," Alexei explained, rubbing Jay's arm, somehow looking both concerned and proud. "He's been working really hard on it."

Jay was frowning down at the floor now. "Your brother needs help though."

"And he has it," Alexei looked to Kai. "After you're bonded, can Sascha be hurt?"

"By a human weapon?" Kai shook his head. "No."

"And does the Caruso family pose a threat you can't handle?"

Kai scoffed, folding his arms against his chest, biceps bulging. "Hardly."

Alexei nodded, then sent a tender look toward Jay. "Sweetheart, I don't want you to miss this."

His voice was gentle, his concern clear as day. And it hit Sascha like a bolt of lightning how much their lives had changed. Alexei's priorities had shifted in a monumental way after running to Hyde Park—he lived now for this man beside him. And that was beautiful, really.

Sascha's brother really did have a completely new life.

Sascha swallowed a hard lump in his throat.

Alexei seemed to catch it. He gave Sascha a slight smile. "I wouldn't go if I thought you were in any danger, Sascha." He jerked his chin toward Kai. "I'm choosing to trust him."

Sascha cleared his throat, then put his hands on his hips with exaggerated sass. "And you're okay with me bonding to a demon I just met? Where are your overprotective older-brother instincts?"

Alexei smirked at him. "I've found logic doesn't really come into play when it comes to the paranormal. It's better to trust your gut. How you feel rather than what you think."

Sascha looked up at Kai. His stupidly beautiful face, staring at Alexei with the first modicum of respect he'd shown since they'd met. "I feel safe," Sascha found himself saying. "And I'm realizing I've maybe never felt that way before."

Jay sighed, his hands clasped in front of his chest. "Oh, that's lovely."

"Not that it's any of either of your business," Kai grumbled, seeming to remember he didn't care for anyone else's opinion. "He'd already agreed."

Sascha coughed, patting Kai's arm in reassurance. "So you're leaving?" he asked Alexei.

"It's only Friday. We can stay one more night." An almost playful look entered Alexei's eyes. "For old time's sake."

Sascha grinned. "Old time's sake" was their code. Alexei and Sascha used to go clubbing together back home, picking their... entertainment for the evening. It had been their thing, at least when Alexei had been able to escape Ivan's demands for a night.

Although, now they were both spoken for.

How boring of them.

"You want to go out?" Sascha hated how hopeful he sounded. But he'd missed his brother. He'd missed having fun together, in the pockets of space they'd made for themselves within their family's oppressive legacy.

Alexei cocked a brow. "I've heard this town has a gay bar. Think they have any decent music?"

Sascha bounced up on his toes. "Really? You want to go dancing?"

Alexei didn't usually dance, but he would stand in the corner with a drink in his hand while Sascha did his thing in the crowd.

Kai frowned down at him. "It's a delay, zaychik."

"Just a little one. Please?" Sascha got up on tiptoes, whispering in Kai's ear, "I'll wear one of the new pretty things I bought. You can take it off me afterward."

A low rumble left Kai's chest. Sascha grinned.

They were going out.

A FAMILIAR HIMBO was standing inside the bar's entrance with a little black light.

Buff Dude grinned at Sascha like an old friend. "Hey, man. You didn't drop your coat tonight." He raised his fist for a bump.

Sascha couldn't help it—he grinned back, ignoring Kai's rumbling growl, and bumped fists like an idiot. "I didn't drop it," he agreed. "So where's your coat check?"

Buff Dude just laughed easily, like Sascha had told some sort of joke, and waved them on. All of them except Jay, that was, who he halted with a raised palm. "Gotta check that ID, little dude."

Jay beamed at him. "I have one of those!"

Buff Dude nodded, holding his fist up yet again. "Right on."

He cleared Jay after a flash of his blacklight, and their party walked further into the bar, surrounded by the familiar, comforting sound of 2000s pop divas.

There was a surprising number of people there, a smaller core group already gyrating on the dance floor.

It was promising. Very promising.

Sascha turned to Alexei, raising his voice to be heard over the music. "Grab us drinks? Something easy." He still didn't trust this place with any sort of real cocktail.

Alexei nodded, grabbing Jay by the hand and leading him to the bar.

Sascha debated getting a head start on the dance floor, but then a familiar voice cried out from the crowd. "Sascha!"

And there was Seth, his full cheeks flushed in the heat of the bar, light-brown curls artfully tousled, with some sort of sparkling shadow on his eyelids. "You came out!" He gave Sascha a quick hug, nodding his greeting to Kai, who was lurking behind Sascha, a warm presence at his back. "You picked a good night too. First Friday has dancing. People come from two towns over, when the roads are good."

Unsure as ever what to do with such wholesome friendliness, Sascha blurted out, "There's no coat check."

Seth rolled his eyes. "Dude. Just toss it in the corner. No one's taking your coat."

"It's designer," Sascha muttered with a huff. But he did as Seth suggested, revealing the tight bright-pink tank top he'd put on.

Seth's eyes lit up. "Ooh. That's a great color on you."

Sascha was annoyed to feel his cheeks heat at the compliment. But Seth didn't seem to notice, holding up a finger as he rummaged through the small cross-body bag he had over his own tight T-shirt. "Wait just a sec. I've got the perfect eye shadow in my bag."

"You walk around carrying bright-pink eye shadow in your bag?" Sascha asked doubtfully.

"Pale pink," Seth corrected. "But it'll do." He found what he was looking for, holding up a small makeup pallet in the dim light of the bar with a raised brow.

Sascha glanced back at Kai, who was watching them with curiosity but no censure. Sascha turned back to Seth and nodded, closing his eyes so Seth could smear some of the creamy shadow on his lids.

Seth finished with a gleeful, "Ta-dah!" and then his eyes widened as Alexei and Jay returned with their drinks. "Another Viking, huh?"

Sascha scowled. "Don't ogle him. That's my brother, and you're a child."

Seth only looked amused, raising his brows at Sascha. "How old do you think I am exactly?"

Sascha hazarded a guess. "Sixteen?"

"The curse of the baby face," Seth mused, although he didn't seem all that put out. "I'm twenty."

"Still too young for a bar," Sascha pointed out.

Seth shrugged. "I know a guy. Speaking of." He nodded at Alexei, who was entering the dance floor with Jay. "Has Benny tried to recruit him to his fitness empire yet?"

"Who the fuck's Benny?" Sascha asked.

"The 'bouncer,'" Seth said, using air quotes around the word. "My cousin. People give him odd jobs around town."

"Oh. I've just been calling him Buff Dude in my head."

"That works too." Someone called to Seth from across the bar, and he shot them a wave. "Gotta go. See you on the dance floor."

He made his way to the other side through the crowd, and Sascha and Kai were left alone.

People were staring, as they seemed to do no matter what when Kai was around. Although, an almost equal number were staring at Jay and Alexei, which could either have been due to

Alexei's size and looks or the....unique dance moves Jay was busting out.

"It's like a robot having a seizure," Sascha murmured, watching in awe.

The heat at Sascha's back intensified. He looked over his shoulder to find Kai gazing intently at him. "You want to dance?" Sascha asked.

Kai traced a finger down his cheek. "You look pretty with paint on your eyes, zaychik."

Sascha found himself lifting his chin so Kai could continue his trail down Sascha's neck. "Thank you," he said quietly, his pulse beginning to race.

Kai wrapped his hand around the back of Sascha's neck, leaning down to bite at his ear. "I wish to have you again," he murmured.

Sascha's blood rushed south so fast he grew light-headed. "Well, we're in public," he reminded Kai. And himself for that matter.

Kai's sultry expression shifted into something suspiciously close to a pout. "If we were going to delay bonding, we should have spent the delay in bed, with my cock inside you."

Jesus. Sascha swallowed hard. In public. He was in public. *No fucking the demon in public.* He did his best to change the subject away from beds and cocks. "What, you don't like dancing?" he asked.

There was a long pause.

"Oh my God." Sascha grinned. "You've never danced before, have you?" He turned to face Kai, smirking up at him. "Well, lucky for you, you're a giant hunk of man meat, so you can get away with just standing there, mostly. I, as your sexy twink accessory, will do the heavy lifting."

Kai looked at him like he was speaking gibberish.

"Come, come." Sascha pulled him out onto the dance floor,

well away from Alexei and Jay's writhing, then backed up into him until his ass was pressed nicely against Kai's crotch. He grabbed Kai's hands and placed them on his hips. "Think you can manage a sway?" he asked.

He didn't wait for an answer, just started rocking his hips, raising his hands in the air, getting a feel for the beat. It wasn't the most graceful dancing of his life, but it did have the bonus of brushing him against Kai's growing erection again and again.

Kai seemed to enjoy that part very much. He moved his hands from Sascha's hips to his waist, caressed his chest, trailed them back down again. Sascha let his arms wrap around Kai's neck, leaning back into the touch.

"I had a thought earlier," Kai murmured eventually, his breath hot against Sascha's ear.

"Mm. Did it hurt?"

Kai's grip tightened. "I thought it would be pleasing to fuck you in my human form."

All the air left Sascha's lungs. "Would it?" he managed to gasp.

"Mm." Kai hummed against his cheek, holding Sascha firmly against him. "I wouldn't have to hold back, would I? You take me so well as it is. I could fuck you as hard as I wish." He gave a low chuckle when Sascha couldn't respond. "You'd like that, hm?"

Fuck. Sascha turned, leaping into Kai's arms and slamming his mouth against him. Kai responded perfectly, holding Sascha up with firm hands on his ass, kissing him like it was his only purpose.

Someone let out a wolf whistle.

Kai released Sascha's mouth, smirking down at him. "I like dancing."

"This isn't dancing," Sascha corrected, panting. "This is dry humping."

Kai let out a low rumble, then claimed Sascha's mouth again.

Sascha was just considering luring him into a dark corner and seeing what they could get away with before they got arrested when Kai stiffened.

Sascha leaned back. "What's wrong?"

Kai was staring intently across the bar. "That man in the corner. He reeks of ill intent."

Sascha followed his gaze to a nondescript dude wearing black, nursing a beer at one of the standing tables. "He does?"

He was watching them, but then, so were quite a few people. Sascha and Kai had been putting on a bit of a show, after all.

Kai lowered Sascha to the floor carefully, his muscles tight with tension. "Do you recognize him?"

Sascha studied the stranger again. "No, but I wouldn't necessarily." He caught Alexei's eye and motioned him and Jay over.

Alexei frowned at him. "What's wrong?"

Kai pointed out the problem, and Alexei nodded slowly. "He does look the type. Could definitely be one of the Carusos."

"Why's he just staring?" Sascha asked, a chill running down his spine.

"He wouldn't make a move in a place so crowded. They want you to know you're being watched." Alexei's gaze slid to Kai. "Or maybe they didn't expect you to have a bodyguard."

Sascha nibbled at his lower lip, trying to push the growing anxiety down. "They wouldn't. Ivan didn't even know at first. Ivan's mole would think I'm unprotected."

And Sascha would have been, if not for accidentally summoning Kai. He would have been in this town without any backup. Defenseless. Alone.

His stomach twisted.

Kai's eyes darkened, as if he sensed Sascha's dark thoughts. "Shall I dispose of him for you?"

"No." Sascha looked around the bar. At Seth, laughing on the dance floor. At Benny, chatting with some equally muscled dude at the entrance, most likely about gym routines of some kind.

Sascha might still not know them very well, but he wasn't going to risk these people getting hurt in the cross fire of his baggage. Sascha had brought evil here, to this town that was accepting him so easily. And it wasn't the demon at his side.

Anger replaced the unease swirling in his gut. Hot and fierce and strangely satisfying.

"We need to deal with this," he told Kai firmly. "At the source. The delay's over. Time to clean up our mess."

18

Sascha

It felt like an entire lifetime had passed since the last time Sascha had walked up to Ivan's office building.

Just the sight of the hulking structure should have been enough to send Sascha into a panic—considering his last visit had ended with an ambulance—but he couldn't muster up the appropriate anxiety with Kai at his back. His soothing warmth, the steady presence that in such a short time had come to mean safety to Sascha.

Sascha had meant what he'd told Alexei: he couldn't ever remember feeling this way, safe and cared for. It wasn't that there hadn't been any love in his childhood. Papa had loved him—Sascha knew that—but always there'd been that threat of violence, of consequences for disobeyed orders.

Maybe Sascha had felt that safety with his mother, when he was a baby? But he'd been too young to remember now. And she'd left when Sascha was barely a year old, so how safe could he really have been with her?

What kind of mother left her baby with mobsters?

But Kai wasn't going to leave. And he wasn't going to send Sascha away. And he wasn't going to let anyone or anything hurt him.

So Sascha wasn't even fazed when the new security guard sneered at the outfit peeking out from Sascha's black wool coat. His new version of business attire: loose-fitting white trousers and a matching white tank, with a short-sleeved baby-blue overshirt tucked in. He'd even accessorized with a few gold necklaces.

He looked fucking amazing, but he knew it wasn't what these mobsters were used to. They wouldn't know fashion if it bitch-slapped them in their judgmental faces.

The man's sneer didn't last long though. Not after he caught a look at Kai over Sascha's shoulder. Kai, who looked equally amazing, if intimidating as hell, his human form dressed all in black and his long hair swept over his shoulders, placing his neck tattoos on full display.

Sascha waltzed up to the guard's desk, leaning over it with a bright smile. "I'm here to see Ivan."

"He's not in," the guard mumbled after another wary look at Kai.

Sascha glanced over his shoulder, and Kai nodded with a wicked little grin—he sensed the Book here. Sascha turned back to the guard. "I think you must be confused. He's here, and he'll see me."

He didn't wait for any acknowledgment, just swept past the desk, leaving Kai to deal with the guard's protest. By the time Sascha rounded the corner to the elevator, Kai was already back at his side, a strange whimpering sound coming from the security guard's desk.

Sascha hit the button for the top floor in the elevator, sending a wink to the security camera in the corner. He hoped Ivan was watching, the dick.

And he must have been, because the door to his office was open.

Sascha took a deep breath before entering, fortified by the heavy warmth of Kai's hand on his lower back. He wasn't alone. He wasn't powerless.

He could do this.

Ivan was seated behind his desk. He looked...oddly flustered, in a way Sascha had never seen. His tie was loosened and the top two buttons of his shirt undone. His short blond hair was mussed, like he'd been running his hands through it.

But his expression was as cold and placid as ever. "Sascha," he greeted, ignoring Kai's presence entirely. "I expected you hours ago."

Sascha got right to it. "We need the Book, Ivan."

"Why?" Ivan asked, as if he had a right to. As if he hadn't stolen the thing right off Sascha's coffee table and fled. "To summon more demons, perhaps? Maybe give one to Alexei? Then the two of you can really fuck me over."

Of all the ridiculous bullshit.

Sascha threw up his hands, all his poise leaving him in an instant. "God, Ivan, what the fuck? You really think we're conspiring against you? When have I *ever* wanted even a piece of your empire? You're such a lunatic."

"Am I?" Ivan asked quietly. "I had two brothers who were supposed to be at my side. Now I have none."

"Well, maybe you should take a long, hard look at the way you *treat* people."

Ivan sighed, like Sascha was being unbelievably taxing. "I don't have time for this, Sascha."

Heat flushed through Sascha's body. "You never do!" he yelled. "What would it take for you to just chill out for a few seconds and act like a real brother and not a controlling asshole?"

An unfamiliar, sultry male voice echoed out from the back

corner of Ivan's office, where a door to an inner room had opened at some point during their argument. "Personally I think he needs to get laid, but that's just me. I could be biased."

Sascha found himself speechless as the personification of walking sex on a stick sauntered out of that adjoining office door.

Like, *damn*. The dude was all long limbs, decked in skintight black leather pants and an equally tight purple shirt sheer enough to reveal that he was rocking some nipple piercings and unbuttoned low enough to display an abstract tattoo in his chest. His long, wavy red hair was up in a high ponytail, and his eyes were hidden by designer sunglasses.

Before Sascha could wonder what the hell this porn star was doing in his brother's office, he found himself pulled back against Kai, his arm like a steel band across Sascha's chest.

"Incubus," Kai growled.

The redhead lifted his glasses as he grinned at the two of them, revealing lushly lashed purple eyes, like Elizabeth Taylor. "Kaisyir!" he greeted. "And here I thought we'd never meet again. Well, if we're among friends..." He cocked a hip, shooting a wink at Sascha.

And then he was transforming, quick as a blink. He didn't grow in size, not like Kai did, but his skin took on an almost lavender tint, his ears growing pointed, with two short dark-red horns curling out from his hair. Sascha blinked in surprise as something that looked suspiciously like a tail flicked out from behind his legs.

Another demon. An incredibly pretty demon. Drop-dead gorgeous, really.

Ivan somehow didn't look the least bit shocked by any of this. Only exasperated. "I told you they were coming. Why act surprised?"

The newcomer—the new *demon*—shrugged. "For the drama."

Those purple eyes latched back onto Sascha, sweeping over his form. "And is this baby bro? Love the outfit. Very chic."

Sascha felt his cheeks go hot, and Kai's arm around him tightened even more. "Incubus," he growled for the second time.

The incubus threw his head back and laughed. "This guy. You'd think the rest of us don't have names." He tossed Kai an alluring pout. "It's not like I go around calling you 'big, hulking warrior demon.'" He rolled his eyes at Sascha, like they were sharing some secret joke. "You can call me Nix, baby."

"Sascha," Sascha found himself saying, oddly entranced. Nix was so beautiful it was like talking to a demonic supermodel.

Kai grunted his disapproval. "Don't speak to him."

Sascha wasn't sure which one of them he was talking to.

Nix huffed. "I'm not going to seduce your bargain. That would be poor form. Besides, I have one of my own now." He shot an exaggerated adoring look at Ivan.

Sascha let out a breathless laugh. "You summoned an incubus?" he asked Ivan. "*Why?*" Weren't they like...sex demons? What the fuck was Ivan going to do with a male sex demon? He was straight as all hell.

"I did not *intend* to summon an incubus," Ivan ground out. "I thought to summon one like him," he explained, referring to Kai.

"Ouch." Nix settled on top of Ivan's desk, crossing his long legs and ignoring Ivan's glare. "You wound me, Vanya."

What. The. Fuck. Never in his life had Sascha heard anyone outside the immediate family—besides Sergei, that was—call Ivan his diminutive, Vanya, and live to tell the tale.

But Ivan only pinched the bridge of his nose with a long-suffering sigh.

The incubus's lips quirked into a catlike grin, and then he was turning back to Sascha. "Oh! Nail polish on the one hand. Is that a new trend?"

He shook his own right hand, and bright-red polish appeared on his talons.

"As I said," Ivan said through clenched teeth. "I don't have time, Sascha."

Sascha fought to clear his head. He couldn't get distracted by this incubus side quest, not when he and Kai were on a time crunch. "Well, make time," he snapped. "We need the Book to bond."

"A bond," Nix murmured, eyes widening in surprise. He hopped off the desk and crept closer with alarming speed, only stopping when Kai released Sascha and shoved him behind his back, grabbing Nix by the throat instead.

"Keep your distance," he ordered.

"Get your hands off my demon," Ivan snapped at the same time, rising to his feet.

Nix only grinned, as if Kai threatening to choke the life out of him was a joke. "But Kai," he crooned. "We're family."

"We are *not* family," Kai growled. "And you will keep your distance from my mate."

God. They were never going to get anywhere like this, were they?

Sascha tapped Kai on the arm. "Um, maybe the two of you should go into the other room for your reunion? I think Ivan and I need a moment."

"Perfect!" And just like that, Nix was out of Kai's hold, somehow already at the door to the inner office. "Kaisyir and I can catch up. We have *much* to discuss, don't we?"

Sascha gave Kai a pleading look, and after a long moment, Kai released a heavy sigh, stomping to the inner door to join his demon friend.

Leaving Sascha with his brother.

The room seemed bigger—and much quieter—with Kai and Nix sequestered in the inner office.

Sascha took a deep breath and pulled out the chair across from Ivan's desk. "Should we sit?"

Ivan didn't answer, just sat in his own black leather chair, his eyes still on the door the two demons had left through.

Sascha watched him for a moment, unsure where to begin. The massive wooden desk seemed like an uncrossable ocean between them.

Or maybe that was just the emotional distance Ivan had spent a lifetime creating.

"You know I love you, right?" Sascha asked. The question succeeded in taking Ivan's attention off the door. A muscle in his jaw twitched, and Sascha smiled sadly. "It's okay if you can't say it back. But I didn't summon Kai to hurt you."

"I'm aware," Ivan conceded stiffly.

"Then why did you steal the Book and summon your own demon ten seconds after discovering him?"

Ivan ran a hand through his mussed hair. "I have a mole in my organization, a mob war on the horizon, a loose cannon of a middle brother, and an oblivious younger one."

"I'm not oblivious." At Ivan's look, Sascha shrugged. "Okay, sometimes. But that's the way you and Papa molded me. I have a business degree, you know. I could be an asset, if you'd let me."

Ivan continued to stare at him impassively.

It was like pulling fucking teeth. Sascha sighed. "I know our family messed you up. Papa...being Papa. Mom leaving."

Ivan's gaze shifted away. "Our mother didn't leave."

At Sascha's confused expression, Ivan let out a bitter laugh. "I thought Alexei would have told you by now. Our mother didn't leave. Our father had her killed."

"Wh-What?" It was like ice water rushed through Sascha's

core. He struggled to take a choked breath, all the air having left the room.

"She intended to leave," Ivan explained coolly. "She was going to take you and Alexei with her." Another bitter laugh. "Not me. I suppose she thought at eleven years old, I was already a lost cause. And while our father might have been willing to let *her* go, he wasn't willing to lose his sons. He ordered a hit."

As Sascha tried to get some sort of oxygen through his closed throat, he thought maybe this was a necessary reminder: there were some types of pain Kai couldn't protect him from. Some wounds that hit too quickly to block, struck too deep to heal with magic.

It took the better part of a minute, but Sascha finally got himself breathing relatively normally. He blinked watery eyes. Nothing in Ivan's expression gave any indication whether he'd told Sascha to help or harm. "And Alexei knows this?" Sascha asked.

"I always assumed he did." Ivan shrugged, like he didn't care one way or another. "Maybe I assumed wrong."

So they'd never discussed it. Ivan had been keeping the secret to himself all this time, holding it close. Sascha realized there was a third option why Ivan might have told him: not to help or to harm but to let some of the poison out.

He let himself process for a few long minutes, let the tears stream as they would while Ivan looked on.

"Okay," Sascha said eventually, letting out a long breath. "Okay. So I guess the question is, How like our father are you going to be, Ivan?"

He was met with stony silence. That might have cowed him in the past, but Sascha wasn't going to be intimidated this time. He straightened in his chair, wiping at his wet cheeks. "I'm staying in Maine, Ivan. And I'm keeping that house. I'll take one of our legitimate businesses to run, working remotely. My salary will reflect my current allowance. If I run it all into the ground, we can reassess. You may visit when—or if, I suppose—you can find it in yourself to be a human and not a mobster."

Ivan tapped his finger against the desk, lips twitching into a small smile. "Any other demands?"

"Yes, actually. I need the address for the Carusos'...offices? Headquarters? Evil lair? Whatever you want to call it. You won't be taking that deal with them."

"There's a meeting scheduled," Ivan told him immediately. "Tomorrow night. The main higher-ups of the family will be there."

Kai was right, Sascha realized. He almost laughed. "You planned this, didn't you? For me to bring Kai and fix it for you."

Ivan kept tapping his finger. "Maybe I've grown tired of cleaning up our family's messes all on my own."

"*Your* messes," Sascha corrected.

Ivan shrugged. "Alexei started it."

"Alexei just wanted out," Sascha told him for the hundredth time. "That's all he ever wanted. To have his own life."

Ivan's gaze grew distant. "Some of us don't have that luxury."

Sascha wasn't sure if Ivan meant their mother or himself. But Ivan would have to figure that one out on his own. Sascha didn't have it in him to dig into Ivan's trauma for him. He was just...tired. And unbearably sad. For his mother. For his brothers. For himself. He wanted to get to his apartment and regroup. To be held by someone bigger and stronger until he didn't feel so fragile anymore.

"I need the Book now, Ivan," he said wearily.

Ivan bent his head, unlocking the top drawer of his desk. He removed the Book from it, pushing it toward Sascha across the desk. "You'll return it to me when you're done."

"So you can summon more demons?" Sascha asked.

"A human may only participate in one bargain. So that one tells me," Ivan said, tilting his head toward the inner office door.

"Then why do you want it back?"

"Call it security."

He was still paranoid, then. Still thought Alexei would summon one of his own, to have one more monster than Ivan at his disposal.

Because it was what Ivan would have done in his place.

"Whatever," Sascha sighed, not caring one way or another anymore. It didn't matter if Ivan was lying. Let him summon a thousand demons, if it made him feel better. Sascha just wanted to be…away. "I'll bring it back."

19

Kai

Kai stood at the door, not precisely eavesdropping but listening for tone. Should even a harsh word be spoken between Sascha and his brother, he'd be there. He didn't trust Ivan with Sascha, not fully.

He didn't trust anyone in that cursed family with his soon-to-be mate.

The damned incubus—seemingly not at all concerned with the goings-on in the larger office—sauntered over to the window, looking down at the busy street below. "It's changed an awful lot, hasn't it? The human realm."

Kai glared at his back, not in the mood for niceties. "What are you doing here?"

The incubus turned, a false expression of innocence on his face. "Why, Kai. A bargain, same as you."

Kai scoffed. "And what possible use could a mobster have for an incubus?"

Nix's specialty was, as he would put it, desire. Kai called it lust, plain and simple. There were a myriad of ways he could be used—igniting passion between those who lacked it; creating intricate, realistic fantasies brought to life for his summoners; or, occasionally, serving as the object of desire himself.

None of which seemed particularly helpful for a power-hungry mobster.

"Oh, I can think of a myriad of ways our dear Vanya could use me," Nix told him with a sly smile, licking his lips for good measure.

Always evading the point, and never with a single ounce of subtlety. Kai pressed, "What was the bargain for exactly?"

His only answer was another sly smile.

But Kai had spent centuries with this creature. He might have laughed, if it were any other human they were discussing. "You tricked him, didn't you?"

"Ah, ah." Nix wagged his painted talon at him. "You know how it works. It was a bargain, fair and square."

"And why not wait for someone who could use your real...services?"

Nix shrugged, studying his nails. "I only have three contracts left. Maybe I'm eager to be finished."

"You hate the demon realm. You're in no hurry to—" Realization came swift and sudden. "Ah," Kai murmured. "You plan to draw this one out? Stay in the human world as long as possible?"

Nix's purple eyes flashed, then darted away. "A bargain's a bargain," he said easily. "Plus, he has a deliciously complex soul. Very tasty."

"Rotten, more like." Kai knew that wasn't true, exactly. But it was damn close.

Nix pursed plush lips. "Not rotten. More...twisted." He shimmied his shoulders. "Gives me the chills. In a good way," he said with a wink.

"From what I've gathered, he doesn't dally with men."

Nix stood to his full height, cocking a hip in a practiced pose. "But I'm more than a mere man, aren't I?" he purred.

Pain.

Kai stiffened, the frustrating conversation immediately forgotten. Sascha was hurting. Not physically—he hadn't been harmed, or Kai would have smelled the blood. But his soul piece felt...wounded.

Kai put a shoulder to the door to the office, but before he could open it, there was the incubus in his way. "Now, now," Nix scolded, ignoring Kai's warning growl and the hand upon his throat. "Your bargain's safe. Vanya's not going to hurt him. Let them talk. Humans need to air their trauma. Let it breathe, as it were."

Kai squeezed. "What do you know about what humans need?"

"Babycakes, my entire existence is about what humans need." Nix wrapped a hand around Kai's wrist, and Kai allowed him to lower his arm from his throat. "Let them talk," he repeated.

The insufferable creature had a point. So Kai held off, standing there at the door, tense and miserable, his ear keyed into the soft murmur of voices. He ignored Nix's many attempts to start another conversation.

After an eternity, Sascha's voice rang out clearly. "You can come back in now."

Kai was at his side in an instant, hands on either side of his lovely face. Sascha's eyes were red-rimmed, his cheeks pale.

"You're hurting," Kai murmured, running his thumbs along the soft skin of his cheekbones.

"I'm okay," Sascha told him. But the tone was all wrong, dull and lifeless, with none of his usual saucy spitfire, or even a demanding pout. "I'll tell you on the way to the apartment."

"We can leave now?"

"We can leave. And look what I've got." A shadow of a smile graced Sascha's lips as he lifted the Book.

Kai grabbed Sascha's other hand, tugging him out of the office.

He wanted out of this poisonous place with this poisonous brother.

The incubus's voice followed them out. "Leaving without a goodbye? Does this mean you don't want to spend another eternity together? I'm hurt, Kai!"

Kai hit the button for the elevator with more force than necessary, furious they had to wait for the contraption to arrive. Sascha was quiet at his side.

"What did he say to you?" Kai asked, half expecting him not to answer.

"He told me my father killed my mother."

Ah. Kai felt only a small measure of surprise—he was sure, if he'd been able to taste their father's soul, it would have been rotten to the core—but the small amount of shock was quickly overshadowed by rage. He'd never met this mother, could hardly care about her fate, except that the news had upset Sascha, had wounded him deeper than Kai had yet seen.

If Kai could resurrect Sascha's father and kill him all over again, he would.

"Zaychik," Kai murmured, keeping his voice soft, tugging Sascha into his arms.

He was stiff in Kai's hold. "I come from evil stock," he said woodenly. "Half of me...half of where I came from...it's corrupt. Rotten."

"I've tasted your soul," Kai reminded him, stroking a hand down his spine as they entered the elevator. "There's no evil there."

Sascha tucked his head into Kai's chest, his next words muffled by the fabric. "Maybe your taste buds are faulty."

They weren't, but easy reassurances didn't seem to be enough for Sascha at the moment. "What do you need?" Kai asked.

"I need to go to my apartment," Sascha murmured. "And I

need you to help me forget." He lifted his chin, meeting Kai's gaze. "Can you do that, demon? Can you help me forget?"

Kai could do absolutely anything, if it meant lessening Sascha's pain. "I'm at your command," he told him. "Always."

Sascha's New York apartment wasn't at all like the house in Maine. It was...cold. That was the only word Kai could think of to describe it. Large and modern and technically beautiful, but cold, with its white couch and white walls and white appliances.

Kai shot a questioning look at Sascha after the brief tour. Sascha only shrugged. "I went out a lot, when I lived here," he explained, voice still listless. "Watched TV in my bedroom when I stayed in. I didn't really make it a home, I guess."

He led Kai to the bedroom. There was a bit more of Sascha's essence here: a colorful bedspread and an overflowing closet, for example. Although, the clothing was all wrong—black and gray and beige.

Sascha flopped face down on the bed, then turned his head to the side to speak clearly. "My mother didn't leave me."

"No, she didn't." Kai sat gingerly on the edge of the bed, not sure how best to comfort. He knew nothing about families. Demon parents—if one could call them that—didn't stay with their spawn. They raised them to self-sufficiency and moved on.

"But I lost her anyway." Sascha rolled onto his back. His limbs were limp, but his gaze was suddenly fierce. "Promise I won't lose you," he ordered Kai. "Promise that you'll never, *ever* leave."

"Never," Kai swore. He could give Sascha that, easy as breathing.

Sascha smiled weakly. "The fact that I'm asking you—after we've just met, really—that's all wrong, you know. It's just evidence that I'm too fucked up for a relationship. Too codependent, given the chance."

"I care not." It was the opposite, in fact. Kai *wanted* Sascha to need him, to demand for him to stay. Kai had found exactly what he'd never known he was waiting for—nothing could make him leave now. If that made him codependent, so be it. What did that matter to him?

Sascha kept eyeing him, like he was looking for an answer to something. There was a brittle edge to him now. He was all sharp edges, but it was like he'd crack to pieces at one wrong word. One wrong answer.

"You said you wanted to fuck me in your human form," he eventually said, almost conversationally. "So you could fuck me as hard as you wanted."

"Yes." Heat flashed through Kai at the reminder of their time on the dance floor, Sascha pressed against him, swaying so enticingly.

"Well?" Sascha cocked a brow.

Kai hesitated. "You don't wish to...talk?"

"I do *not* wish," Sascha said firmly. "I want to forget, for a little while. Who I am and where I come from. I don't want to know anything except the feel of your cock inside me. Can you do that?" He smiled meanly. "Or do I need to call in another stud?"

Kai growled, no matter that he knew Sascha was only pushing at him, making sure he wouldn't break under pressure. "You think to toy with me?" he asked, his voice soft and dangerous.

Sascha's eyes flashed. "I'm asking you to toy with *me*."

His anger at the mention of another man aside, Kai's cock was filling rapidly with Sascha's demands. Perhaps Kai should offer soothing words, should tell Sascha fucking could wait for another time. Perhaps that was what a human man would have done, one who knew what the pain of losing a loved one was like.

But Kai was not a human man.

"Take off your clothes, then," he ordered, standing from the bed.

"No," Sascha countered, his tone petulant. "You do it."

Kai bared his teeth. "Gladly."

He tugged Sascha to the edge of the bed by his ankles and swiftly removed his clothing, until Sascha was bare before him, looking defiant and wounded and unbearably beautiful.

Sascha drew his legs up and let his knees fall open, revealing all of himself to Kai's stare. He was half-hard already, eyeing Kai like he was starved. "And you?" he asked.

Kai waved a hand, his clothes disappearing.

A small hitch of breath escaped Sascha's mouth. He rose onto his elbows. "You're very attractive, you know."

"Yes," Kai acknowledged. He knew he had a fine form.

Sascha's lips twitched. "Arrogant as well."

"I am."

"Possessive?" Sascha asked, cocking his head.

"Very."

"Would you let me leave you?"

"No," Kai answered, without hesitation. A mating bond was permanent and sacred. They would stay at each other's side always. He would make sure of it.

"Would you kill me to keep me?"

"If I killed you, I would not have you. It's an illogical choice." Humans were so stupid that way. Sascha's father had been stupid. Cruel and stupid, a wretched combination Kai had seen too often in his time in this realm.

Some inner tension seemed to leave Sascha. His gaze trailed down to Kai's cock, his questioning taking a different direction. "Is your precum still venomous in that form?"

Kai gave himself a lazy stroke. "Yes."

Sascha fell back on the bed. "Open me up, then," he demanded.

Kai climbed onto the bed on his knees, draping himself over Sascha. He gathered his precum and brought a finger to Sascha's entrance, breathing in Sascha's soft sigh of relief at the touch.

Kai kept it light at first, softening the muscle there with gentle, thorough circles, watching Sascha's face all the while.

His human kept up the brittle front for an admirably long time, but eventually he cracked. His features slackened, his eyes shut as if in pain. "Kai," he pleaded, vulnerability in his voice for the first time since that cursed office.

"Yes, zaychik," Kai crooned.

"Kiss me."

Kai captured Sascha's mouth. Without his fangs in the way, Sascha met him furiously, as he had in the dance club, battling Kai's tongue, trying to devour Kai from the inside out. He was writhing against the tip of Kai's finger, wordlessly begging Kai to give him more.

Kai leaned back, grabbing Sascha's hips, lifting them off the bed and folding him in half.

"Oh," Sascha gasped, his eyes widening at the new position he found himself in.

Kai draped himself back over him, pressing in one digit, then another. He scissored them, reveling in this close-up view. He didn't realize how lost he was in it until Sascha gave a breathless laugh. "You really have—have a thing for fingering me, don't you?"

"You're so small," Kai murmured, pressing in a third finger, watching Sascha take it. "It's fascinating."

Sascha pouted. "You're supposed to be fucking me into the mattress already."

"Am I?"

But Kai shuffled his knees closer, letting Sascha's thighs fall into the crook of his elbows. He pressed the head of his cock against Sascha's hole, but without his hand to guide it, it slid away at the slightest pressure. He did this again and again, rubbing his leaking head against Sascha's entrance, teasing them both.

"Kai," Sascha pleaded.

"Guide me, then," Kai demanded. "Get your hand on my cock and place me inside you."

Sascha reached for him immediately, bending his torso in half to get a hand on Kai's cock, notching it against his entrance and bearing down to let him in.

"Oh fuck," Sascha gasped, releasing his hold and dropping his head back onto the bed. "I thought you'd be manageable like this. But you're still fucking huge."

Kai pressed a hand down onto Sascha's lower abdomen, smirking when it made him keen. "You can take me, zaychik. You were made for it."

Sascha huffed, then moaned again. "Of—of course I can."

And he did, his body making way, his inner muscles sucking Kai in until he was bottomed out. It was still a tight fit—Sascha wasn't wrong about that—but there was more give than when Kai was in his demon form. A smooth glide out and a quick press back in had Sascha gasping, his hands clenching on the bedspread.

This was real. This was truth. Sascha's rotten Mafia legacy meant nothing in the grand scheme of things. He'd been born to be claimed by Kai, as Kai had been born to be at his side. Destined to be his mate.

Kai knew it as well as he knew anything.

"Better?" he asked, his hips pressed flush against Sascha's pert bottom once again.

Sascha clenched around him experimentally. "So much better," he sighed.

"You no longer wish to call another stud?" Kai asked, smirking down at him.

Sascha smiled to himself. "Well..."

Kai growled and started moving, snapping his hips at a brutal pace, and Sascha's head bent back with a strangled yelp.

"You will have no one else," Kai demanded.

It took Sascha a long moment to find his words, his throat too busy creating high-pitched moans with each of Kai's thrusts. "N-No one else."

"You will be mine alone."

"Yes. Oh *God*. Yes, Kai."

Kai halted his movements, ignoring Sascha's mewling protest. He leaned in close, every word deliberate. "I will care for you and spoil you and claim you as my mate. And in return you will give me your soul." He ran a hand up Sascha's stomach, caressing his chest. "Not a taste, Sascha. Not a mere morsel. All of it. Every bit."

Sascha pressed down against Kai's hand on his chest, arching his back up into his touch. "Yes, Kai."

Kai wrapped his hand around Sascha's leaking cock, stroking him without mercy. He moved his hips again, knowing just the right angle to hit that bundle of nerves unerringly. "And now you will come for me," he ordered.

"Yes, Kai," Sascha sighed. And he did, with a gasp and a weak moan, his legs trembling in Kai's hold, his cock dripping cum all over his stomach.

Kai went hard and fast after that, chasing his own release relentlessly, until Sascha's bones were loose as jelly in his hold and Kai had filled him to the brim with his cum.

If this was what Sascha needed to forget the sorrows of his life, Kai would oblige him. All day, every day for the rest of eternity, if need be. He would give Sascha anything he asked for.

His Sascha. His mate.

20

Sascha

Sascha was mush. A puddle of mush.

Kai dropped his thighs and made as if to pull out, and it took everything in Sascha to lift his limbs and lock them around him. "Don't you dare," he warned.

They'd put in all that hard work to get him to this point of mind-melty goodness, chasing all his tragic thoughts away, and Sascha wasn't ready for it to be undone.

Kai's heavy-lidded eyes lit up with new interest. "You wish for another round?" he asked, reaching for Sascha's spent cock.

"No, I—" Sascha squirmed, weirdly irritated to have to spell out his need for continued contact.

But it turned out he didn't have to spell it out at all. Kai nodded with a grin, his hands caressing Sascha's thighs instead. "Ah. You wish for me to remain inside."

And then he was switching into his demon form, growing in size not just around Sascha but *inside* him.

Sascha squirmed again, this time experimentally. "Oh," he

gasped. Kai was very much staying firmly inside him. "That's...convenient."

He smiled his pleasure up at Kai, and the demon's own smile softened, gazing back at him. Sascha couldn't help it—he traced his fingertips first around that smile, then up to Kai's cheekbones, then began petting the silken strands falling around his face. He stretched his arms to reach Kai's horns, stroking around the base.

Kai let out a rumble. "I'll swell again if you continue," he warned.

It was tempting, but Kai had gone hard—as promised—and Sascha was feeling too well used for another round. Plus, he was sore. Not his entrance—the venom was still delightfully helpful in that department—but his heart.

His soul.

He wondered if Kai could feel it.

So Sascha left the horns alone, stroking at Kai's hair again. He could feel the angry, heartbroken thoughts at the edge of his consciousness, trying to break through, but he wasn't ready to let them back in. He needed a distraction.

"How do you fight with all this hair?" he asked. "Doesn't it get in the way?"

"I braid the front portions back for battle."

"You do?" Sascha asked with surprise. He'd expected something more like, *I'm a badass demon warrior, mere strands of hair could never impede my wrath.*

"Mm," Kai hummed, his eyes almost completely closed now, like a cat being pet.

"Can I do it for you?"

Kai's eyes opened in a flash, subjecting Sascha to a weirdly intense look. "You wish to braid my hair for battle?" The rumble emanating from his chest grew louder.

"Yes?" Sascha answered. Or asked. Had he just offered up something completely taboo?

But Kai gave him a smug smile. "Mating behavior," he murmured.

Something twitched inside Sascha. He gasped, pushing at Kai's shoulder. "Hey! You're getting hard again. Take it out."

Sascha hadn't been prepped for the monstrosity that was Kai's demon dick in full, erect glory. What if that thing got stuck in there?

Kai withdrew his now half-hard cock with a pout, mumbling something about "stroking horns and teasing with mating promises."

But his sulk didn't last long.

Sascha shrieked as Kai turned them both without warning, rolling until Sascha was perched on his stomach, gazing down at him.

Which was all well and good, but there was too much space between them. It was allowing too much cool air to touch Sascha's sweaty skin. He lowered his torso, curling his body into Kai, pressing his cheek against Kai's broad chest.

Kai began rubbing his back in long, soothing strokes.

There. That was much better. Warm and cozy. Safe.

Just enough safety, really, to allow those dreaded thoughts to return. Sascha's father hadn't just murdered bad men, thugs already entrenched in the Mafia world. He'd murdered Sascha's mother, someone who—if Alexei's memories were to be believed—had been kind and decent and loving, if a bit sad and distant.

Sascha let out a long breath. "I don't know what to think right now," he admitted. "Or how to feel."

"Should you?" Kai asked, his voice a soothing rumble against Sascha's cheek. "Truths such as these can take years to process."

"I just...I wish I could hate him completely."

"Your father?"

Sascha folded his hands on Kai's chest and propped his chin on top, meeting Kai's eyes. "He used to sit me on his lap when he was doing paperwork," he recalled. "Before he sent me away to boarding school. He'd let me stay up past my bedtime like that, if I was quiet. Sometimes I'd fall asleep there. He always smelled like cigarettes and milky tea."

Kai brushed a strand of hair back from Sascha's face. "Hatred and love can coexist, zaychik. Even if it hurts for them to do so."

"But I don't like pain." It was easy to admit to Kai. He didn't care that Sascha wasn't some badass warrior or hardened mobster. He didn't mind that Sascha was soft.

"Most don't," Kai told him. "What do you do when you're hurting? What dulls the pain?"

Sascha thought it over. "Sex, I suppose. Shopping."

"Mm. What else?"

"Oh!" Sascha sat up with a start, ignoring Kai's disgruntled noise when he kneed him in the chest with his movements. "You're gonna like this one."

Kai peered up at him suspiciously. "Why do I doubt that?"

Within ten minutes—after a cursory clean and changing into silky sleep shorts—Sascha had them both settled in the living room, his duvet from the bedroom draped over his shoulders, Kai sitting cross-legged in front of him on the hardwood floor.

Sascha had "Viking braid tutorials" pulled up on his phone next to him on the couch, but Kai's eyes were fixed on the TV screen. "I don't understand," he said, frustration in his voice. "If these housewives are so wealthy and pampered and famous, why do they yell so much?"

"The yelling is *why* they're famous," Sascha explained for the third time. "It's all about drama."

"I hate it," Kai grumbled.

But two episodes later, Kai's eyes were still on the screen. "The blonde woman should apologize. She has greatly wronged the brunette."

"Don't hold your breath," Sascha warned him, putting the last braids into place. "Apologies are rare." He patted his handiwork. "There, all done. But don't get up!"

He hopped off the couch and ran to grab his compact from his vanity. He handed it to Kai, smiling at the way the thing looked so ridiculously minuscule in his hand.

But Kai held it with great care, bringing it up to his face and eyeing Sascha's efforts. When he turned back to Sascha, he was grinning. "These are very fine braids, zaychik. I'm lucky to have you as a mate."

Sascha's cheeks heated. He leaned down, placing a chaste kiss on Kai's lips.

Kai's smile grew even wider.

Sascha cleared his throat, willing himself to be brave. "Speaking of mates. Is it a whole to-do? Like candles and robes and whatnot?"

Kai's grin dropped, his expression taking on a new intensity. "No props. Only words, to be spoken by each of us with intent."

"Oh." Sascha shifted on his feet. "Okay."

Kai cocked his head. "Now?"

Sascha took a deep breath. "Now," he confirmed. "Except, wait." He grabbed the remote, turning off the TV. "I can't get demon-married with *The Real Housewives* playing in the background. It's too tacky, even for me."

ONCE THEY'D COLLECTED the Book and returned to Sascha's bedroom—Kai had declared his living room "too sterile" for bonding—Sascha could only giggle.

While Kai looked fairly regal (Sascha had done, he had to admit, a fucking fantastic job on his braids), Sascha was apparently going to bond his soul to his mate while wearing a pink silk pajama set.

Kai cocked a brow. "What amuses you?"

"Just…we're going to have to have a real wedding, you know?" Sascha told him, surprising himself in the process. He waved a hand to encompass his whole ensemble. "I can look much better than this, I promise."

Kai's eyes gleamed at he looked him over. "But you look good enough to eat, zaychik."

Sascha considered Kai's sharp teeth. "I'm a little worried you mean that literally."

Kai huffed at that, and Sascha giggled again, his nerves making him a little loopy. "I'm just saying, we're both too hot not to have professional photos of us in our matrimony finest. It could be small and still be fabulous."

It would *have* to be small, actually. Kai came from another dimension, and Sascha didn't have any real friends back in New York. It had been too difficult, with his family, to befriend normal people, and the other Mafia sons had all terrified him.

Oh God, he was almost thirty and he didn't have friends. That was pathetic. *He* was pathetic.

Kai was in his face in an instant. "What happened?" he asked, brow furrowed in concern. "Why are you sad? We may have a wedding," he rushed to say. "Whenever you like."

"No, just—" Sascha couldn't help his pout. "I don't have friends."

"You desire friends?" Kai asked with surprise. "Then we'll procure some for you."

Sascha let out a helpless laugh. "I don't think that's how it works. It's not like coffee, we can't just order a delivery with an app."

"What of the round-cheeked fellow with the painted nails?" Kai mused. "He's been friendly."

"Seth? He's just being nice."

"And friends aren't nice?"

"They are. But it's—it's complicated." Even as the word left his mouth, Sascha suddenly wasn't so sure they were true. Maybe it *was* that simple. He was starting a new life in a new place, with a new partner by his side. Maybe easy niceness was how it all began. Maybe people just...kept being nice to each other over a period of time, and then it became friendship?

Was there a YouTube demonstration he could watch about this?

Kai laid a warm hand on Sascha's cheek. "We will procure you friends," he promised again, apparently deciding to ignore Sascha's explanation on why that wasn't a thing. "And, in the meantime, *I* will be your friend."

"You will?" Sascha asked, his voice coming out thick. He was unaccountably moved by the offer, which was ridiculous. They were about to bond souls, but Kai promising to be his friend had him on the verge of tears.

"I've never had a friend before either," Kai told him.

"What about Nix?"

"Ach." Kai made an irritated noise. "A pest. And soon to return to the Void."

"Not back to the demon realm?"

Kai shook his head. "This is not his final contract."

"What if he bonds with my brother?"

They stared at each other for a long moment, and then both burst into laughter at the thought.

When they'd caught their breaths, Kai grinned at him tenderly. "Enough jesting, zaychik. I'm making you mine tonight. My own, sweet Sascha Kozlov."

"And you won't regret it," Sascha reminded him.

"And I won't regret it," Kai vowed.

Sascha let out a breath. "So what do we do?"

"You'll repeat the words after me. With *intent*." Kai gave him a look, as if to bring that point home.

"With intent," Sascha repeated dutifully.

Kai released his hold on Sascha's face, turning toward the bed. But his words still came out perfectly clear, if very fast. "And then just the exchange of blood and we're done."

Sascha froze in place. "*What?*"

Kai sat down cross-legged on the floor at the foot of Sascha's bed, his expression serene. "It will be just like the contract. A mere nibble."

Sascha pointed a finger at him. "You said 'exchange.'"

"You may keep your eyes closed."

"*Obviously,*" Sascha snapped.

"It will be but a moment," Kai promised.

Sascha was tempted to throw a fit, but he knew Kai wouldn't have said it in the first place if it weren't completely necessary. And Sascha was doing this. He was bonding to this arrogant-ass demon. Not even his distaste for blood was going to get in his way.

He plopped down across from Kai, crossing his legs to match, the Book in his hands. He opened it to the last page, where Kai had told him there was a final poem, not connected to any demon mark.

"What do the words mean?" Sascha asked Kai. "If I'm supposed to say them with intent."

Kai hummed in thought. "A direct translation is difficult. But, in essence: I bind myself to you, body, heart, and soul. To be parted from each other only by death, and that parting merely temporary. My soul for my mate, and my mate's soul for me in turn."

"Oh," Sascha sighed, tracing the poem with his finger. "That's kind of nice."

Kai began saying the words, the strange language coming much more naturally out of his mouth than it had Sascha's during the summoning. Sascha repeated it all as best he could.

With each word spoken, Kai's eyes gleamed brighter, and blue smoke began filling the room. Sascha was tempted to ask if all this was going to set off his apartment's smoke alarm, but he wasn't sure he was allowed to say anything non-demony during the bonding.

Eventually Kai went silent, and Sascha did as well.

Kai's glowing eyes met his. "Turn around now."

Sascha turned in place, closing his eyes in preparation for pain. There was the hot blow of Kai's breath on the back of his neck, then a sharp pinch. "*Oh.*"

But it lasted only a moment. Then there was a warm wetness at Sascha's lips, pressing against them. "Open your mouth, Sascha."

Oh God. What if Sascha threw up during the ritual? But he did as Kai asked, choosing to trust his judgment. He realized it was Kai's finger pressing into his mouth. And it didn't taste like coppery grossness—it tasted smoky and spicy, like Kai's scent. Rich.

Maybe it wasn't his blood at all?

But it must have been, because suddenly Sascha's every nerve was alight, his whole body shaking.

"Easy," Kai murmured, in front of Sascha now.

Sascha's eyes flew open. Kai's body was trembling as well. "What's happening?"

Kai might have been shaking, but his voice was firm. "The bond is taking effect."

"Oh. It's— It's—"

"Overwhelming," Kai finished for him. "It will pass. I promise."

"H-How?" Sascha asked, teeth chattering. "W-When?"

Kai somehow managed a sly grin. "Consummation eases it, I'm told."

Of course. This pervy fucking demon. But Sascha needed… something. And he realized he was hard in his silk shorts. Which was weird in and of itself. Sascha didn't even remember getting turned on in the first place, but now his whole being suddenly felt like it was on the edge of something.

That something might as well be an orgasm.

"Take off your pants," he ordered, sliding out of his shorts with trembling fingers.

Kai was blessedly hard as well, and Sascha didn't waste any time on foreplay or moving them onto the bed. He was still stretched from earlier, and the floor was as good as anyplace else.

He clambered over Kai's thighs, wrapping his arms around Kai's neck and burying his face in his smoky skin. Sascha lowered onto his cock, Kai's precum easing the way.

It was still a tight fit, but that didn't matter. Because as soon as they were joined, it was like pure magic. The jittering energy that had invaded Sascha's body faded, and all that was left was Kai.

Kai.

Sascha could feel him. Kai's soul, it must have been. A solid, warm weight in Sascha's chest that screamed *safety*.

"Your soul is lovely," Sascha whispered against Kai's neck.

He leaned back. Kai was grinning as wide as Sascha had ever seen. "And yours is perfect," he told Sascha. "But I already knew."

Sascha highly doubted that. He was pretty sure his soul was worn and ragged, bruised all over by proximity to violence and a lack of care. But maybe it was perfect for Kai. Maybe his soul felt just as comforting in Kai's chest as Kai's did in his.

"You still like the taste of it?" he asked anyway.

Kai stroked Sascha's cheek. "My precious mate. I'm going to take such good care of you."

Sascha smiled, tucking his head back against Kai's neck. Mates. They were mated.

Their consummation was slow and sweet. Kai lifted and lowered Sascha over his cock almost leisurely. He kept murmuring all the while, about all the ways he was going to ensure Sascha remained certain of his choice.

He didn't have to, not really. The feel of Kai's soul was confirmation enough. It felt right, like it had always belonged there. Like Sascha had been incomplete before, walking around without that reassuring presence.

See? He'd known he was codependent.

Sascha's orgasm built with a sure, steady pressure, and he came with a sigh, Kai following close behind.

Afterward, Kai lifted them both from the floor with ease, keeping Sascha in his hold. "Now I will bathe you," he told Sascha. "A tub is not a river in the demon realm, but it will have to do."

21

Kai

Kai was slow to rise.

After he'd bathed Sascha, cleansing him of any lingering evidence of their consummation, the new bond had taken it out of them both. Kai had slept more than he was used to needing, wrapped tightly around his mate.

Now his mate was wrapped around him, with his lovely face pressed into Kai's chest.

Which was all well and good, but Kai had a horrid crick in his neck. He tried to stretch it out but got caught halfway through the motion.

He tried once more before realizing what the issue was.

His horn point was lodged into the wall.

Cursed human bedrooms with their cursed human-sized furniture.

Kai tugged himself free with effort and scooted lower on the bed, until his feet were dangling off the end. It wasn't ideal, but it was better than having a horn trapped in plaster.

The movement had Sascha turning in his hold with a sigh, his back now to Kai's chest. He grabbed Kai's arm and wrapped it tightly around his middle, forcing Kai onto his side. "Wull haff one custom-made," he slurred before closing his eyes again.

Kai tucked his face against Sascha's hair, smiling into it. His sweet, perfect mate. Kai could feel him, secure within his chest.

What he'd been able to feel before had been just a piece. A mere morsel. Now Kai was *filled* with Sascha, the weight of him settling Kai's own restless soul for the first time in...perhaps ever. It was like he'd spent his long life only partially tethered to his own existence, and now here he was, fully secured. He'd never known anything like it.

Even after having found Sascha, after knowing he wanted to bond with the human, Kai had still been...antsy. Anxious for the bonding ceremony to take place, haunted by that one last incomplete step. What if they didn't bond in time? What if he was forced away?

But now it was done. Their souls were linked, inextricably. Now Kai could just...be.

The thought was almost overwhelming, the freedom of it too much to bear. No Book to bind him, no human's commands to tend to.

But Kai didn't need those things, not anymore. He had the sweet warmth of Sascha in his arms to anchor him. His human had long been under a different yolk—the vicious father and controlling brother. They would explore their newfound freedom together.

Kai pressed a kiss to Sascha's shoulder. The rest of Sascha's bare upper arm was peeking out from under the cover, revealing the spot where his stab wound had once been. The spot that was now unbroken, unblemished skin.

A reminder that there was indeed one more step, beyond their bonding. Kai needed to do as he'd promised—he needed to vanquish Sascha's enemies. To make sure they could never harm him again.

Not that they had a chance of killing him anymore, not with Kai's demon strength and healing simmering in Sascha's veins, waiting to be unleashed in case of illness or injury. But the Carusos could still cause him immense displeasure. Could upset his tender stomach with their threats. And Sascha had been most distressed at the mention of human trafficking.

As his mate, it was Kai's responsibility to rectify that.

The leaders of the Caruso family had to go.

And the meeting tonight would be the perfect opportunity. Which left the rest of the day for...other pursuits.

Kai unwrapped his arm from Sascha's middle and leaned back a bit to admire his sleeping form, fingering the soft silken shorts Sascha slept in. He'd changed into a different pair after their bath—these were not pink but a dark royal blue. A perfect match for Kai's skin markings.

They were fascinating—the slightest movement from Sascha and the silken material would shift, revealing glimpses of his pale, tender flesh.

Like now. When Sascha had turned, he'd sprawled his leg over to the side, and one globe of his bottom was almost completely bare. Kai's cock began filling at the tempting sight. There was hardly a barrier between them at all, since Kai slept in the nude himself. He would only have to nudge forward the slightest bit, and his cockhead would be pressed against him. He could slide himself back and forth, caught between smooth skin and smooth silk. Perhaps Sascha wouldn't even wake. Perhaps...

A loud rumbling filled the room, startling Kai out of his musings.

Sascha's eyes were open now, his cheeks pink.

Kai laughed in disbelief. "Did that come from...your stomach, *zaychik*?"

"I'm hungry," Sascha muttered with a frown, embarrassment still coloring his cheeks. "We didn't have dinner last night. So you'll have to stow your pervy thoughts."

"What do you know of my thoughts?" Kai asked, running a finger along the bare skin of Sascha's upper thigh.

"You think them very loudly," Sascha told him snippily, rising from his reclined position and dislodging Kai's hand.

"Mm. What if I told you—"

The rumbling sound rang out again.

Right. What was Kai thinking? His mate was hungry. Starved, even, by the sound of it. They were newly bonded, and he'd allowed such a thing to happen.

He was a disgraceful excuse for a demon.

He leaped from the bed, summoning his trousers to his body as he strode to the kitchen ahead of his mate. Once there, he took stock.

It was an unmitigated disaster.

He turned to Sascha, who was blinking blearily at the edge of the kitchen. "You have nothing to eat in here," Kai complained.

"Riiight," Sascha said slowly, as if Kai were being foolish. "Because I've been living in Maine? Not that I would have had anything anyway. You can have literally anything delivered here, you know. I'll order us some bagels."

"No!" Kai closed the distance between them, grabbing Sascha's phone from his hand before he could press any buttons. "*I* will do it."

He *would* feed his mate, lack of resources be damned.

He stared down at the little device, unsure where to begin. Should he just goggle it? He tried painstakingly typing out "need bagels for mate," but nothing useful came up.

A strangled sound came from his left. Sascha was peering over Kai's arm at the phone screen.

Was he laughing at Kai?

Kai huffed. "It's not amusing. How am I to be a mate to you if I can't feed you?"

Sascha grabbed the phone back, rolling his eyes. "Then let me show you, you loon."

He walked Kai through the many buttons—the "apps," he called them—and had soon ordered bagels and coffee to be delivered to them.

But not even the thought of imminent coffee could lessen Kai's despair. He muttered to himself the many failings of this realm, "No hot rivers. No fine oils. No fresh kills…"

He was halted by Sascha grabbing his face with both hands, tugging Kai's head down to bring them eye to eye. "Look, I know you've got a lot of feelings about how your mate should be treated," Sascha said. "But we don't need hot demonic rivers—we have bathtubs. And if you want to anoint me with oils or whatever, we can order some to be delivered by tomorrow. And fresh kills frankly sounds….disgusting. I'll teach you about human food."

"How?" Kai frowned at him. "You seem to know less about preparing human food than I do."

Sascha shrugged, his hands still keeping Kai's head in place. "Then we'll watch the Food Network. We'll learn together."

"The TV can teach us how to cook?"

Sascha sighed before pressing a kiss to Kai's lips. "Never underestimate the power of television, Kai. Never."

That was strangely reassuring. Kai gave him a smug smile, his despair forgotten. "See how sweet you are to me?" he crooned. "My perfect mate."

"Ugh." Sascha released his face with a groan. "It's too early in the day to be calling me sweet."

"It's almost midday," Kai pointed out.

"Exactly. Way too early. So here's the plan." Sascha started pacing through the kitchen, his bare feet smacking the tile. "We're going to eat our bagels. You're going to tell me all about those pervy thoughts of yours. If they please me, you may perform them. And then..." He let out a harsh breath, stopping in his tracks. "Then we'll get ready for tonight."

Kai cocked his head. "You're nervous."

"I know they can't kill me, now that we're bonded," Sascha told him, resuming his pacing. "But men like that still scare me." His shoulders shook in a shudder. "They've always scared me."

"You don't have to come with me, if you don't wish to," Kai reminded him. "I can take care of them on my own."

"No." Sascha shook his head decisively. "I need to be there. I need to see it through."

"Then I'll be at your side." Kai snagged Sascha by the waist, halting his pointless marching and tugging him in close. "You won't be facing them alone, zaychik. You won't be left alone ever again."

Sascha collapsed against him, all his restless energy leaving him in an instant. "I think my codependent heart just skipped a beat," he murmured.

Kai frowned down at him. "It shouldn't be doing that. You should be fully healthy after the ceremony."

Sascha only laughed at him.

THE DIRTY WAREHOUSE they arrived at was a far cry from the sleek chrome fortress Sascha's older brother did his business in.

Sascha sniffed the air as they approached. "Mm. Smells like my childhood."

Kai wrinkled his nose. "It smells of mold, zaychik."

"Exactly," Sascha told him with a bitter laugh. "Mafia life's not always glamorous, especially when your father is still building his empire."

They stopped at the entrance to the warehouse, not yet

announcing their arrival. Sascha looked formidable, dressed in an elegant, formfitting suit, with his pretty hair slicked back out of his face. His hand drifting to his stomach now and then—as if it pained him, but he didn't want to say—was the only tell his nerves were strained.

Kai rumbled his displeasure at his mate's fear. "You're certain you want to do it this way?" he asked.

"Yes," Sascha said firmly, bringing his arm to his side. "I need to be sure."

Kai already was. He could smell the fetid stench of the souls inside. The intention to buy and sell humans as property was without a doubt one of the acts that could taint a soul beyond repair, could rot someone from the inside out.

The souls inside the warehouse were ones Kai—or any of his kind, if they knew what was good for them—would refuse a bargain with. Souls that would provide him no sustenance or power, that would only serve as a constant source of ache and itch within his chest.

He would be happy to take them off this realm.

But if Sascha wanted his turn at the helm first, to air some of that rage he kept bottled up so tightly inside, Kai would oblige.

"I'll be right here," he promised, planting a swift kiss to Sascha's lips and winking at the camera monitoring the door before slipping into the shadows.

It was a bit of an uncomfortable fit. Shadow work didn't come naturally to Kai—he wasn't like Nightmare, slipping in and out with ease. But with a concentrated effort of power, he could hide in them well enough. It wasn't true invisibility; if someone knew where to look, they would see him. But the average human's gaze would skirt around him, only registering a vague sense of unease.

Sascha knocked on the door. A large man with dark hair shorn close to his skull opened the door. He glanced behind Sascha pointedly. "What happened to the bodyguard?"

"He went back to the car," Sascha said easily. "Ivan was told to come alone."

"And he sent you instead," the henchman said, looking Sascha up and down with a sneer.

Kai would be happy to rip those eyes out of his skull.

In time.

The henchman led Sascha inside, and Kai followed, passing from shadow to shadow. There were nine men in the warehouse, with nine rotten souls. Hardly the entirety of the Caruso operation, but Ivan had assured them the head of the family and a few key right-hand men would be there, enough to strike a crippling blow to their dealings.

And seated in a chair in the middle of the room, surrounded by three men on each side with conspicuous guns, his legs crossed casually as he watched Sascha approach, was Luca Caruso, presumably. The acting head of the family. He was the only man in the room with his dark strands grown out—all the rest had it shaved down, like it was part of their uniform.

Kai was pleased that Sascha's spine stayed straight, his steps even. The mate bond between them didn't allow Kai to feel every little emotion—only the extremes would break through—but Kai could scent Sascha's fear and unease on the air as they grew in strength.

But none of it showed on his face. Nothing these enemies could latch onto.

Kai was so proud of his mate.

"Sascha Kozlov," Luca Caruso announced, a faint Italian accent softening his vowels. "So I see you are alive still."

Sascha smiled sweetly at him. "Oh, I think you knew that already, Luca. I saw one of your men recently, all the way in Maine."

"Did you? How odd." Luca smirked. "He must have been on vacation."

Sascha tucked his hands in his pockets, rocking back on his heels, the picture of ease. "Ivan says there's a way to end this. He authorized me to make the deal."

Luca cocked a brow. "Straight to business, hm? It's very simple. A blind eye at the docks for some ongoing special shipments."

"You have them ready to go?" Sascha asked, his tone light, as if it didn't matter much either way. But this was the reason Sascha had insisted on showing his face—they needed to know whether the Caruso family already had people ready for shipment. If they did, it complicated their immediate future immensely. They would need to find out where, need to figure out how to free them.

But Luca shook his head. "It's an expensive business. We needed to be sure your brother would play ball before investing. You know how it is." He gave a tight smile. "Ivan has been a thorn in our side for a very long time."

"I do know how it is," Sascha agreed, his shoulders slumping briefly in relief before he straightened again. "And I just want you to know it's nothing personal."

Luca's brow furrowed in confusion, and his bodyguards shifted in place.

"You wanted to get at my brother, so you came at me." Sascha smiled again, the look full of tender understanding. Kai had no idea his mate was such an excellent actor. "I get it. I'm not even that mad, not at you. And maybe grasping at power is just one of those innate human traits. I can't be mad about that either. But when you use that power to hurt innocents?" The smile dropped from Sascha's face. "When you want to 'invest,' as you say, in pure evil? Well, I just don't think that can be excused."

In the shadows behind him, Kai licked his lips. The rage Sascha held so deep in his chest—rage at his father, at the brutality he'd always been surrounded by and never been strong enough to stop—was spilling into the air, a steady stream of glorious anger. Kai drank it in.

It was as delicious as he'd known it would be.

Luca uncrossed his legs, motioning to his men with two fingers. "I hope you realize how outnumbered you are, Sascha. I know you haven't been very active in the business, but I'd hoped you were capable of simple mathematics. Ivan is going to be so put out when I send him back your corpse."

Sascha shrugged. "I'm outnumbered, sure. And if it were just me, that would be an issue. But, unfortunately for you, I'm not alone anymore."

That was Kai's cue.

He pressed a kiss against the back of Sascha's neck, whispering, "Close your eyes, zaychik."

And then he stepped into the light.

There was the clamoring of voices, guns being taken out of their holsters. Kai let his wings burst out, spreading them wide to shield his mate. Sascha couldn't be killed so easily—not by pests like these—but neither would Kai let him be inconvenienced by stray bullets.

There was more yelling. Shots fired. Everything was chaos. Mayhem.

Havoc.

Kai grinned, baring his sharp teeth.

And then he got to work.

It was so easy, slicing through the bodyguards. It almost made Kai nostalgic for the old battlefields, when swords and daggers had been the norm, rather than these silly toy guns.

He was careful not to let any of the blood spray hit Sascha, even as he took the head off Luca Caruso, who wasn't looking nearly so casual as he met his end, his eyes wide with horror, his fingers grasping his gun with shaking fingers.

It was disappointingly quick work—in mere moments, there was silence all around. Silence but for a few harsh, panting breaths.

But neither Sascha nor Kai were panting.

"Can I open my eyes yet?" Sascha asked, the faintest tremble in his words.

Kai pressed a hand to his arm. "Not yet, zaychik."

There was one more soul here in the warehouse, so timid and fearful Kai had missed it among the others' rot. He stalked over to one of the cement pillars and ducked behind it, snatching at a collar.

He brought forward his prize, ignoring its startled squeak.

"What do we have here, then?"

22

Sascha

Sascha kept his eyes closed tight, using all his inner strength to keep his breaths steady and even, to not let a whimper or yelp escape his lips.

It wasn't that he didn't trust Kai to keep him safe—Sascha trusted him with every ounce of his being—but the familiar sounds of violence still put him on edge.

Luckily, his demon seemed to be efficient—any screams were brief, and there was not even one word of begging to set off Sascha's horrible memories.

These are bad men, he reminded himself. *Evil men.*

But it didn't matter the justification. It didn't matter what they'd planned to do, or the fact that this one over-the-top act would act as a deterrent against a longer, more brutal mob war between the two families.

Sascha was never going to like violence. He was never going to revel in other men's lives being taken. It wasn't in his nature. He let the anger that had built within him for years dissolve with every second that passed.

After not too long at all, there was silence. Sascha swallowed hard. "Can I open my eyes yet?"

Kai's hand landed on his arm with reassuring warmth. "Not yet, zaychik."

There was more silence, and then a startled, squeaky yelp, followed by Kai murmuring, "What do we have here, then?"

Had Kai missed one?

Despite his curiosity, Sascha kept his eyes shut tight. Eventually a firm, warm weight landed on his shoulder, a familiar smoky scent surrounding him.

Kai.

"I'm going to turn you to the wall, zaychik," Kai murmured softly. "You'll keep your eyes there. No looking around."

"Bossy," Sascha chided, even as he let himself be pivoted.

But Kai wasn't accepting half answers. "You'll keep your eyes where I tell you, yes?"

Sascha huffed. "Yes, yes." While he had no objections to the way Kai bridal-carried him whenever Sascha pulled off the damsel act, he didn't actually feel like fainting today.

"I have a surprise for you," Kai told him, an alarming amount of mischievous glee in his voice.

"If I open my eyes to you holding up a severed head, I swear to God—"

There was that startled squeak again.

Unable to hold in his curiosity any more, Sascha opened his eyes.

Huh.

Kai—looking for all the world like an owner wrangling a wayward pup—was holding a boy by his shirt collar,

Or not a boy. A young man? Probably early twenties, but it was hard to tell. He was short and way too thin, small by anyone's standards but even more so compared to Kai's massive size.

His dark hair was shorn close to his scalp like the other Mafia drones, but where on them it had looked vaguely intimidating, on him—with his enormous dark eyes and dazed expression, visibly shaking in Kai's hold—it reminded Sascha more than anything of a fuzzy baby chick.

"Who—?" Sascha started to ask.

But Kai interrupted, grinning smugly, shaking the guy lightly. "You wanted a friend, zaychik. I told you I'd procure one for you."

There was so much wrong with that statement that Sascha didn't even know where to begin.

But then Kai's captive spoke for the first time. "Y-You're not going to kill me?" he asked, wide eyes darting between them.

Kai made a disgusted noise. "Why would we?"

"Because you killed all of them?" the guy pointed out, not unreasonably. "And Mr. Caruso, he's m-m-my—"

"Boss?" Sascha guessed, after it didn't seem like Kai's captive would finish.

The little chick shook his head furiously. "Stepdad," he corrected.

Sascha didn't remember hearing that Luca Caruso was married. "What about your mom?" he asked.

The chick shook his head again.

"Well then, um, I guess Mr. Caruso *was* your stepdad?" Jesus, what was Sascha supposed to say here? *Your father figure was an evil dick and we had to do away with him*? He didn't have any experience with this. Papa had died suddenly of an aneurysm, no Mafia violence required. "Are you going to want vengeance or something?" he asked.

That brought out a low growl from Kai.

The little chick gave another terrified squeak, staring at Kai like he was the devil incarnate. As far as this poor guy was concerned, he probably was. "N-No!" He looked over Sascha's shoulder at something, his voice taking on a firmer note. "*No. But...*" To Sascha's horror, tears filled his big brown eyes. "They all know I was here, and now... They'll come for me. They'll kill me. I have nowhere to go. No one to help. You should just kill me now and get it over with." He closed his eyes tight, like he was already waiting for the fatal blow.

And here Sascha had thought *he* was the one with all the Mafia dad trauma.

He supposed he had to be the grown-up in this situation. "Did you have anything to do with this trafficking plan?" he asked.

The guy opened his eyes the tiniest bit, shaking his head warily. "But I didn't—I couldn't—couldn't stop it."

Well, then. Sascha knew a little bit about feeling powerless in the face of mean men with big guns.

"I don't smell any soul rot on him," Kai pointed out gruffly.

Sascha honestly wasn't sure what that meant, other than Kai hadn't deemed this guy evil enough to do away with.

"No one's killing you," Sascha said, gently as he could. He could feel the swell of another massively impulsive decision bubbling out of his chest. "You can come with us," he offered before he could stop himself. "The house is definitely big enough. No one will think to come for you there. What's your name?"

The little chick opened his watery eyes more fully. "Matteo."

"All right, Matteo. How do you feel about Maine?"

Kai grinned, looking all smug again. "See? All settled." He let go of the little chick's collar and gave him a push. "Go wait outside now."

Sascha wasn't so sure about "settled." Matteo hadn't even technically agreed. But it seemed like they were going to be adding kidnapping to their list of charges today, because they sure as hell couldn't leave him here.

Matteo scuttled out of the warehouse obligingly—presumably

not running away, but who the hell knew—leaving Sascha to assess Kai. He must have worked his demon magic, because there wasn't even a spot of blood on him.

"Did I do well?" Kai asked, a smirk on his lips.

Arrogant bastard.

"The vanquishing of my enemies, or the extremely traumatized boy you just foisted on us?" Sascha asked.

"Both."

"You know that's not how human friendships work?"

Kai gestured to the warehouse behind them. "Shall we leave him here, then?"

"What?" Sascha asked, startled. "*No.* We just took out nine men and left him the only survivor. And if he really doesn't have anyone..." He shook his head. "We're taking him with us."

Kai caressed his cheek with a talon, his smirk turning into a tender smile. "My sweet Sascha," he murmured.

"I'm not being *sweet*," Sascha told him haughtily. "I'm being impulsive. It's different."

"Of course." Kai leaned in for a kiss but stopped halfway there. He grabbed Sascha's hand, sticking Sascha's pinky finger in his mouth instead.

"Um..."

Was Kai really trying to start hanky-panky in the middle of their murder zone?

But he only sucked once perfunctorily, then dropped Sascha's hand. Sascha realized—he must have had a drop of blood on his finger. Kai had been making sure he didn't see it.

It was too much. Kai had just taken care of the threat against Sascha—the threat that had hounded him for months—with complete ease, lending Sascha his strength and his power and asking for nothing in return but Sascha's affection. Finding what he believed—in his misguided way—was a new friend for him in the process. And now he was treating Sascha with such delicate care, no matter the corpses waiting behind them.

"I love you," Sascha blurted out, horrified at himself but unable to stop the words. "I know we haven't known each other very long and it's too soon to say, but I do."

Kai cocked his head. "We're already bonded for eternity, but you're worried it's too soon to say those words?"

"Yes?"

"Sweet Sascha," Kai crooned.

"Now you say it back," Sascha told him.

Kai laughed, grabbing Sascha's hand and leading him to the front doors of the warehouse. "Humans are so strange."

"Yeah, but now you say it."

"So very strange," Kai mused.

"Kai. Now you *say* it."

WALKING into Ivan's office building felt different this time. *Sascha* felt different.

Even without backup, Sascha only gave the guard a little ironic salute before making his way to the elevators, ignoring his huffing protest.

It hadn't been as difficult as he'd thought it would be to convince Kai to stay in the car. That could have been because they had Matteo there as well, and Kai thought he needed more babysitting than Sascha. Or, more likely, it was Kai's faith in Sascha's new, convenient imperviousness to harm.

Which, actually, Sascha should at some point get the details of. But it didn't seem incredibly urgent at the moment. It wasn't like he was going to be throwing himself off a building to test it anytime soon.

He found Ivan sitting predictably in his desk chair, looking a bit more put together than their last meeting—his shirt was buttoned, his tie in an immaculate knot, his hair neat as ever. Except...

"Is that a *hickey* on your neck?" Sascha asked in disbelief, flopping down in the seat across from him.

It wasn't like Sascha thought Ivan didn't get laid—he'd seen him canoodling one too many times with the tacky, brash women who frequented their family's clubs to be under that impression—but Ivan had never let them leave *marks* before.

Sascha wasn't even sure Ivan let them kiss him on the mouth, for that matter. He was half-convinced his older brother had some sort of *Pretty Woman* agreement with his conquests.

But it didn't seem like any answers were going to be forthcoming, since Ivan only glared at him, holding out a hand. "The Book?"

"Yeah, yeah." Sascha handed it over, trying and failing not to stare at the conspicuous hickey-shaped bruise on Ivan's neck, just above his shirt collar.

"You've done it, then?" Ivan asked, after tucking the Book safely away in his desk drawer.

"The Carusos are taken care of," Sascha told him. "You're very welcome, by the way. I'm sure the family will be scrambling for some time to get new leadership established."

Ivan waved a hand. "Not that. The bond. You've done it?"

Sascha tried to hide his surprise that Ivan was asking a personal question over business. "I have."

Ivan only nodded, looking distracted.

"And we maybe picked up a stray," Sascha mumbled, hoping Ivan's new chill would extend to kidnapped Mafia members.

Ivan gave him a sharp glance. So maybe not. "What the fuck does that mean?"

"Do you know anything about Matteo Caruso?"

"Enough to know he's not a Caruso by blood." When Sascha

made a *go on* gesture with his hand, Ivan tipped his head back against his chair, gazing up at the ceiling. "Let's see. Luca Caruso's stepchild from a since-dissolved marriage. He was being raised to be a successor, then next I heard, he was the family's whipping boy. Possibly literally."

Sascha flinched. Fuck. If he'd been having any second guesses about his course of action, that did away with all of them. "We're offering him sanctuary," he told Ivan firmly.

He was proud of himself for coming up with something that sounded like official Mafia speak. Better than, *We've semi-kidnapped him because he looked too emotionally wounded to be let out into the real world.*

He raised a brow at Ivan. "Is that going to be problem?"

Ivan was still staring at the ceiling. "They'll think he's on the run, I'm sure. And a rival family wouldn't be anyone's first guess." He waved a hand again. "You should be fine."

"Well...good," Sascha said slowly, a little concerned by the lack of pushback.

"I have a club for you," Ivan told him abruptly. "One that's clean. You should be able to manage the back end of things remotely. If you do well, we can add on others." He lowered his gaze to meet Sascha's eyes again. "You'll need to make visits every now and again."

"That's fine. I can show Kai more of New York."

Ivan's lips twitched. "Yes, play tourist with your demon husband. That's exactly what I meant."

Sascha held back his eye roll. "Anything else?"

Ivan's fingers tapped on the desk in a steady rhythm. "Your demon is going to need paperwork to exist in the modern world. Identification at the very least."

"I guess so." That wasn't something Sascha had thought much about. Those were the types of things that were just...taken care of in his life.

"I can have Cooper arrange it," Ivan offered.

Sascha knew his brother well enough to recognize the offer for what it was: the closest thing to an olive branch he was ever going to get.

"Thank you," he said, meaning it. He looked around for the first time. "Where's *your* demon?"

Ivan's tapping stopped abruptly. "My apartment," he answered shortly.

"And are you going to be...okay with all that?"

Anything that could have been construed as warmth in Ivan's expression dissipated immediately. "Everything is under control," he said tightly.

"I meant what I said yesterday," Sascha told him, a little concerned by what—for Ivan—might as well have been a whiplash of conflicting emotions. "You can come visit if you want a break from all this." He paused, then couldn't help but add, "You kind of seem to be falling apart at the seams a bit."

Ivan's tapping started up again, his face blank. "My seams are just fine, Sascha."

"And the mole in your organization?"

A vein in Ivan's temple pulsed. "Everything's under control."

"All right." Sascha knew that was the best he was going to get. He rose from his chair. "I'm going now. I love you," he added.

Because if Ivan was extending olive branches, Sascha could too.

He received a stilted nod in return.

Back in the car, Kai was waiting in the passenger seat in human form, poised in a way that suggested he was willing to leap out of the car and avenge Sascha's honor if Ivan had slighted him in any way.

Sascha leaned across the dash to kiss him. "We're all good."

He caught Matteo's eye in the rearview mirror. He was hunched in the back seat in an oversize sweatshirt Kai had plucked out of thin air for him, chewing on his nails like they were his last meal. "Ivan doesn't think we'll run into any trouble bringing you with us," Sascha told him.

Matteo nodded jerkily, his eyes flitting away again in the next moment.

Yeah, definitely the start of a beautiful friendship.

But maybe there really was some secret sweetness hidden somewhere in Sascha, because he still only wanted to take this traumatized kid back with them and tuck him under a million blankets, keep him safe until he stopped flinching at every word.

Sascha turned to Kai. "Let's go home, shall we?"

23

Sascha

Compared to the chaos that had been Sascha's life lately, the next few weeks were almost a dream.

Even with a new human roommate who jumped at every other noise.

There'd been a nagging fear in Sascha's mind that they'd return to Maine and Kai would realize how small Sascha's world was. Would realize that he was free to move on. To explore. To roam. He'd been stuck in one place for so long before this; how could he bear to settle down?

But if anything, Kai seemed delighted to stay put. He'd taken to... Well, Sascha could only describe it as nesting, like he and Sascha were newlyweds and Matteo their new baby.

Sascha hadn't put much effort into making the Maine house a home during his two months in Seacliff—he'd made do with what was already there or the little Ivan had let him bring with him. It might not have been as impersonal as his New York apartment, but it was lacking a certain level of comfort.

Kai's first act had been ordering Sascha to drive them into one of the bigger towns to buy better bedding—soft blankets and sheets with a thread count comparable to Kai's age. He'd insisted they couldn't order it online, that he'd needed to feel it all himself. Sascha had thought *he* was the one with expensive taste, but apparently it was nothing compared to a demon making a home for his mate. He supposed it was Kai's human-world version of draping him in the finest furs of the demon realm or whatever.

Sascha had time before he was supposed to start officially working for his brother—the first real job of his life—but it was still Kai who deep cleaned and straightened and did away with the extra boxes in the attic.

Apparently Sascha didn't need a maid service anymore—he had a house husband instead.

Kai liked to tuck Sascha under the new blankets on the couch, plop Matteo next to him ("for friendship bonding"), and turn on trash TV for the both of them while he made the house suitable. Although, he could never resist the pull for very long—Kai would hardly make it an hour before he was joining them, hoisting Sascha onto his lap and tucking the blankets around both of them.

Matteo, for all his twitchiness, was a decent housemate. He didn't seem to mind the PDA (although Sascha didn't miss the wistful looks he sent their way every now and again). And the little traumatized chick had endeared himself forever to Kai by knowing how to correctly use the coffee maker Sascha had been pointedly neglecting even since his first disastrous effort. Now Kai liked to have a brew going at all hours of the day and night.

He still sneered at human food though.

Like this morning.

Sascha and Matteo were having toaster waffles, as that was currently the extent of anyone in the home's cooking abilities (although Kai claimed he would be learning any day now, once the TV taught him). Matteo had poured an ungodly amount of syrup on his plate, and Sascha was teasing him gently. "A secret sweet tooth, Matty?"

Matteo flushed, ducking his head into the oversize hoodie he wore pretty much every day.

Kai looked curiously at Matteo's plate over his mug of coffee. "Is your waffle sauce sweet, then?"

"You've never had syrup?" Matteo asked, peering at him shyly from underneath his hood.

"He's never had anything good," Sascha told him, rolling his eyes. "Except coffee. But he drinks it black, so even that doesn't count."

"I've tasted sugar," Kai insisted, almost haughty. But Sascha supposed that would have been impressive a billion years ago or however long it had been when Kai last roamed the earth.

"Syrup's different," Sascha said around a bite of waffle. "Maple-y."

"Like the tree," Kai mused.

"Exactly like the tree," Sascha told him solemnly, gratified by Matteo's quiet giggle.

"I'll try it," Kai declared, before tucking a pinky finger into the bottle's small handle and upending it into his mouth, chugging half the bottle in one go.

He set it down a moment later, smacking his lips. "Passable," he deemed. "It would be better hot."

He went back to his coffee, ignoring Sascha's horrified stare. Matteo's giggles grew in volume until he was laughing for real, the loudest sound he'd made by far since coming to stay.

Out of nowhere, it hit Sascha like a freight train. This was working, the new life he and Kai were making together. A life where Sascha could be not only safe but happy.

He *was* happy, in a fierce, bright way he'd never experienced before. So much of his life before now had been spent just... passing time, engaging in whatever activity would cause the least boredom from one moment to the next, trying to walk the fine balance between entertaining himself and not pissing his family off.

But now he had a home, one that was truly his, one where he was free to explore all its corners without fear of retribution. He had a partner who accepted him just as he was, who considered Sascha's faults nothing more than extra delicious seasoning on his soul. And he had maybe the beginning of friendship, with someone from whom Sascha didn't need to hide any of his family's baggage—Matteo got it, better than most ever could.

Sascha's gaze caught on Kai, who was leaning against the counter, looking incredibly pleased with himself after his syrup stunt. Kai, who'd made a home for Sascha but had nothing of his own.

"We need to get you things," he found himself saying.

Kai sipped his coffee. "What things?"

"Um..." Sascha didn't know. He just suddenly felt like he needed Kai to have something in the house. Something all his own. Something that proved he belonged there—that the home belonged to them both. "What about clothes?"

Kai wore pretty much the same summoned outfit every single day.

"But you have plenty of clothes." Kai's eyes gleamed, and his voice lowered. "So many pretty clothes, zaychik."

Sascha flushed, hoping Matteo wouldn't notice. But he was not going to be distracted by Kai's pervy thoughts. "Those are *my* clothes," he pointed out. "What about you?"

Kai waved a hand. "We're bonded. There's no distinction. What's yours is mine."

That was all well and good, but Sascha couldn't exactly see Kai fitting into Sascha's newest pair of hot pants.

Although, it was an intriguing thought...

Eventually Kai agreed the house could use a few more decorations. On a mission now, Sascha took him into town after breakfast, leaving Matteo curled up on the couch. The main touristy shops were closed for the season, and there were only a few small knickknacks for sale in the grocery store and diner. But Kai seemed delighted anyway. Sascha had to forcibly steer him away from a lobster sticker with "What's crackin'?" on it. Instead, Kai chose a remarkably ugly sailboat ornament and a small frame holding an embroidered lighthouse.

"You have terrible taste," Sascha told him later, when they were walking along the trail on the cliffs.

"It was your idea," Kai pointed out. He had a suspiciously self-satisfied grin on his face. "You wanted trinkets for your mate."

Sascha narrowed his eyes. "Is that a demon thing? Did I accidentally stumble into some demon courting?"

"You're not as skilled at it as I am." Kai wrapped an arm around Sascha's shoulders, tucking him close. "But you don't need to be. Your sweetness is enough for me."

"Gross."

Kai was undeterred. He pulled Sascha closer to the cliffs. "Come stare at the ocean with me, sweet Sascha."

Sascha settled against him, unable to keep the stupid smile off his face. "I love you," he murmured. "Even with your terrible taste. I'm very...very happy, with you."

Kai pressed a kiss against his head. "As I am with you. I have never known contentment such as this, zaychik."

SASCHA LAY on his side on the bed, his hands propped over the bedside table, half his attention on the TV and half on his nails.

Seth had lent him some pale-pink polish to replace the extremely chipped blue mess he still had on, and Sascha was determined to get both hands done this time—no unexpected demonic interruptions to get in his way.

Except there was a demon in his bed, sliding his fingers up under the hem of Sascha's ruffled sleep shorts where he'd sprawled his leg to the side. It was another silky set he'd ordered, one with a camisole top with thin straps, much too flimsy for the season. He'd felt a little ridiculous picking it out.

But then Kai had looked about ready to drop dead the first time Sascha had worn it, and Sascha had decided it was a fine purchase after all.

Sascha shot Kai a suspicious glance now, but his eyes were on the TV, intent on the boring reality show about blacksmiths he'd put on, his touch on Sascha's skin an absent-minded petting.

They'd moved a TV into the bedroom in an effort to give Matteo some space from them, if he wanted. Sascha wasn't sure he *did* want that—the poor kid seemed pretty reluctant to be left alone most times. But he most certainly didn't want to see them engaging in their more illicit activities, so sometimes a little space was necessary.

And sometimes Kai apparently wanted to watch his weird blacksmith show, and Sascha wasn't so cruel as to subject another person to that.

But speaking of.

"Hey," Sascha said, spreading polish on his pinky. "Do you think Matteo is doing okay?"

The fingers on Sascha's upper thigh paused for a brief moment, then started their circling again. "I think there's someone out there he still fears," Kai mused. "I think he jumps at every shadow."

Sascha frowned down at his nails. He'd finished the left hand now. "So...no?"

Was Sascha not doing enough for him? They'd given him a place to stay, but should they be, like...talking about things? He'd been following Matteo's lead, but maybe he should be pushing harder?

Kai tugged on the bottom hem of Sascha's shorts, bringing him out of this thoughts. "Zaychik. I think he's healing as best he's able, because you've provided him a safe space to do so."

Sascha turned away from his nails to cock a brow at Kai. "So what, you're all wise now or something?"

Kai ignored the dig, humming thoughtfully. "You know, if he has enemies in need of vanquishing…"

"No," Sascha said quickly. They were not getting involved in any more mob business, even for sweet Matteo.

"It wouldn't have to be me. We have Nightmare's pa—"

"No. Nuh-uh. I take it back—you're severely lacking wisdom. You think that scared little chickadee can handle a deal with a demon?"

"Not like you handled it," Kai told him, a new gleam in his eyes. His wandering fingers traveled up at the crease where Sascha's thigh met his ass, stroking more deliberately. A pleased rumble left his chest. "You wear nothing underneath."

Sascha fluttered his lashes. "I never do." He arched into the touch, then remembered he was in the middle of something and shot Kai a glare. "I'm painting my nails, you know."

"You lie like this on purpose." Kai's lower lip pushed into a pout. Possibly he'd been picking up bad habits from Sascha. "To entice me."

Sascha laughed, setting down the bottle of polish. "It doesn't take much to entice you." Still, he propped his head on his unpolished hand, watching for what Kai would do next.

Kai had one hand down his own sleep shorts now, a much less scandalous pair he wore around the house. When he was actually sleeping, he chose to lie in the nude, but Sascha had insisted he have something to lounge in. Kai had seemed to think, initially, that now that the house was his home, he could parade around with his dick out whenever he wanted. Sascha had needed to pointedly remind him there was another person living there, one who didn't want to see Kai's demon cock every time he turned a corner.

Kai's hand returned to Sascha's skin, pushing his shorts up and to the side. Something slick teased at Sascha's entrance.

"And my nails?" Sascha asked, trying to ignore the way his breath caught at the touch.

"Keep painting yourself, pretty Sascha," Kai murmured. "I'll be careful."

"Arrogant," Sascha huffed, blowing on his painted hand. But he hitched his leg further to the left, sighing with pleasure as Kai stroked his hole with his precum.

Sascha was destined to only ever have one hand painted, wasn't he?

But he couldn't complain, not when Kai's thick finger nudged more insistently at his entrance, sliding in easily with the combination of the venom and the fact that they'd already fucked only that morning.

Sascha did his best to pretend to focus on his drying nails—stifling his little gasps and hitches of breath as best he could—while Kai opened him up with the intense focus he always brought to the task. Sascha knew if he looked over again, Kai would be staring, glowing eyes locked onto the fingers working inside his mate.

Which was all well and good. Because if he looked elsewhere, he'd realize Sascha was already hard and leaking, a damp spot forming on the front of his pretty silk shorts.

Maybe Kai already realized.

Sascha yelped as his lower half was suddenly lifted off the bed, only his shoulders remaining on the mattress, his legs still twisted to the left, toward his bedside table. Kai was kneeling upright on the bed now, holding Sascha's bottom level to his now naked hips.

His cock looked enormous, pulsing blue and purple, his viscous precum leaking from the tip.

Sascha's shorts were bunched up and around to leave his ass bare. But the elastic digging into his skin wasn't wholly unpleasant. Not with the way Kai was eyeing the sight. "You aren't going to undress me?" Sascha asked coyly. Or as coyly as he could when he was being manhandled by a brute.

"No." Kai fingered the soft fabric. "I like your pretty clothes."

"You're going to get them dirty."

"Yes." Kai smirked down at him, lining the head of his cock up with Sascha's hole.

He pressed in slowly, always cautious and careful with Sascha's size. But he still pushed all the air out of Sascha's lungs with his girth, his ridges merciless as ever.

"You take me so well, zaychik," Kai murmured, his talons digging into Sascha's hips. "You always do."

He didn't wait after bottoming out, just began sliding Sascha over his dick again and again, his movements torturously slow and steady.

Sascha let his lower half be puppeteered like a rag doll, his whole focus on the immense feeling of fullness, the way his body shivered and trembled with the effort of keeping Kai inside.

He loved this so fucking much.

He loved every time Kai filled him, in whichever form he chose. Sascha had Kai's demon cock when he wanted to be stuffed so full he couldn't think, his human cock when he wanted to be fucked so hard he couldn't think, and the occasional bout of tenderness when he wanted to be fucked so sweetly all he could do was think, *God, I love this demon.*

Kai took advantage of Sascha's limp complacency, dragging him halfway down the bed, presumably so Sascha's head didn't bump the headboard.

I'm going to get nail polish on the sheets, Sascha thought dazedly.

Or maybe his nails were dry already. Who the fuck knew? Who the fuck knew anything except the feel of Kai's cock inside him, the pulsing of his ridges and the harsh edge to his breaths the only sign he was nearly as affected as Sascha.

Kai straightened Sascha's hips, turning him fully onto his back, his shoulders pressed firmly into the mattress. He pushed forward, folding Sascha in half, his smoky scent surrounding him.

Sascha moaned at the new angle, heat swirling in his belly and shooting down his spine. He let his body go limp, giving in to the helplessness of the position. It didn't matter if he was helpless. Kai had him.

Kai always had him.

"My mate," Kai growled, his eyes roaming over every inch of Sascha now. He gave a quick snap of his hips, eyes blazing when Sascha keened.

It was too much already. Sascha grasped his own cock, thumbing at the head. He needed to come, needed to release some of this pressure.

"Yes, zaychik," Kai murmured, thrusting his hips again. "Touch yourself for me."

Kai kept moving steadily, the heat in Sascha's core building and building until Sascha was arching back with a scream, coming all over his own stomach, all the way up to his chest.

Kai rumbled his approval, fucking Sascha through his orgasm, dragging those ridges back and forth all over Sascha's hidden places.

Sascha whined, oversensitive and wrecked already. But Kai was relentless.

He was going to make Sascha come a second time, wasn't he?

Sascha gave in to it, his body going lax again, secure in Kai's hold.

Except for Sascha's traitorous dick, which was already twitching, trying to rally for their unrelenting mate.

When Sascha came for the second time, it was with Kai's hand wrapped around his cock, his strokes as slow and methodical as the push of his hips. Sascha twitched and moaned, his legs shaking with the force of it. Kai growled, beyond words now, picking up his rhythm until Sascha was filling with a familiar heat, his spasming muscles milking Kai for all he was worth.

They sprawled out on the bed, Sascha a pile of useless jelly. Kai lay on his side next to him, nuzzling in close. He picked up Sascha's left hand. "No smudges," he reported, immense satisfaction in his voice.

Sascha made some sort of gurgling sound of agreement. Kai's other hand was tracing over the skin of Sascha's thigh. Not tantalizing, not anymore. More proprietary. Comforting.

Sascha had his eyes closed. He was under the impression Kai was watching his show again until Kai spoke suddenly, "I've never understood the human concept of love."

Well, then.

Sascha opened his eyes, trying to get his wayward brain cells to focus. Kai was staring at Sascha's chest with a deep frown. "When I was summoned, all those times...I saw humans hurt those they claimed to love, if it helped to grow their power."

Sascha thought of his father, his brothers, his mother. "It can be...complicated."

"The love you have for your brothers isn't complicated," Kai insisted. "It's pure."

Sascha considered that. It was true there were complicated feelings surrounding that love—their upbringing, the ways they'd hurt one another, intentional or not—but he supposed the love itself *was* pure. Sascha was never going to screw his brothers over, for power or for anything else.

"As is the love you have for me," Kai told him smugly.

Sascha narrowed his eyes. "Cocky."

"You're my mate," Kai said, suddenly insistent. "The bondmate of my soul. It is beyond words. Beyond human love."

"Sometimes words are nice." Sascha shrugged, too relaxed and well fucked to get worked up. "I like them. The words."

"You do?" Kai asked with surprise. And then he smiled, as if that was all he'd needed—to know Sascha liked something. "Then I love you, my sweet Sascha," he crooned. "Better and more deeply than any human could."

Sascha almost wanted to tease him, to make another remark about Kai's arrogance. But he couldn't. It was true—Sascha had never felt so cared for, so understood, protected against the cruelty of the world by the strength of Kai's body and the warmth of his soul. He'd never met a human man who could have made him feel this way.

"I know you do," he said simply.

Kai grinned at him, then gathered Sascha into his lap, facing the TV again. "Now come, watch how the swords are made."

So Sascha did. It was silly and a little boring, and he'd never in his life loved anything more.

EPILOGUE

Kai

Kai sat on the beach, watching the gentle waves rocking the boats moored close to the coast. There was one in particular that looked just like Kai's ornament, the one Sascha claimed was proof of his terrible taste.

But how could Kai's ornament be terrible when it was a reflection of the same view Kai had seen that first time he'd laid his hands on Sascha? Wringing an orgasm out of him on this very beach, planting the seed in his mind on how he would mate this human.

It seemed to Kai he had excellent taste, actually.

Although, now the weather had warmed and their little beach was full of other people. As was the town itself. Tourists, Sascha said. People who came from other parts of the world to admire their home.

Kai couldn't blame them. Their home was beautiful.

He knew Sascha worried, on the days he let his insecurity get the best of him, that Kai would grow bored. That the life they led here couldn't possibly be enough for him. But Kai had spent centuries in the Void, with only three unlikely companions for company. Here he had Sascha. Just that alone made it infinitely better.

And in truth, the human world was quite pleasant when one was not being ordered around by some power-hungry bargain.

Like this ocean. Kai enjoyed the rhythm of it, the soothing sounds the waves made, as steady as Sascha's heartbeat in slumber. He came to stare at it quite often.

They hadn't had oceans where he came from.

No oceans and no Sascha.

So why would he ever want to return to the demon realm?

A familiar form sat down next to him in the sand. Young Seth in a tank top, the tops of his shoulders reddened from the sun. "Hey, Kai. What's up?"

It was a nonsense question, so Kai ignored it. What was he supposed to say? The sky above them? The single fluffy cloud on the horizon?

Seth knew him well at this point and was unoffended by his silence. "You and Sascha coming out on Friday?"

That was a question Kai could answer. "Yes. For the dancing."

Kai had become very, very fond of dancing. Especially as the warmer weather meant Sascha wore smaller and smaller bits of clothing as they went out. Seth had also taught Sascha how to paint his eyes, how to mark them so the pale-blue color stood out even more.

Between that and the coffee from the bakery, Kai was very tolerant of this human. He was a suitable friend for Sascha, even if he hadn't been procured by Kai like their Matteo.

But it was time to return home. Kai grabbed the bag next to him and nodded his goodbye to Seth, who smiled in return, and hurried back on the path.

He found Matteo curled up on the living room couch. It was

where Kai often found him. Eight months later and Matteo still didn't leave the house without one of them to accompany him. And he didn't always leave *with* them either. He'd come dancing only the once, and the night had ended with him panicking and needing to be brought home.

Sascha thought he needed therapy.

Kai thought he needed something else.

"Hello, Kai," Matteo greeted, smiling openly. A movie with a screaming woman was on the TV. For someone as jumpy as Matteo, he watched an awful lot of movies with screaming and monsters.

Humans were odd.

But at least there was that—the smiling. Matteo had grown more comfortable around the two of them over the months. When he wasn't frightened, he was all smiles and quiet laughter. His soul would probably be sweet. Too sweet, most likely, without Sascha's interesting pockets of sour and bitter to even him out. Not to Kai's taste.

But perhaps to someone else's.

"There's a paper, hidden between the books on that shelf," Kai told him, pointing across the living room.

Matteo took his eyes off the TV. "Um, okay?"

"You copy the symbol. Say the words. Spill a drop or two of blood."

Matteo stared blankly at him, and then his eyes widened. "And then one of you comes out?"

Kai waved a hand. "Different from me but still strong. You can make your bargain for protection. Or vengeance, if that's your preference. And then be done with it," Kai warned him. "The owner of that mark is not someone anyone wants to keep."

He left it at that, climbing the stairs and making his way to the spare room Sascha had turned into his office.

And there was Kai's mate, in a pale-blue button-down and

tight underwear, on a video call that showed him from the waist up only, speaking haughtily into the laptop. "And when I say I don't want a repeat of last month's ordering fiasco, I mean it. Run the numbers by me first if you're unsure."

"Yes, Sascha," said the man on the other end.

"Good." Sascha caught sight of Kai, a brilliant smile lighting up his face. "Lunch break!" he said into the screen. "Got to go. Ta-ta."

He shut his laptop with a snap, twirling his chair to face Kai.

Sascha had taken to working quite well. He seemed to thrive on a chance to use his mind and natural charm for something with a bit of challenge.

But, Kai thought smugly, he liked Kai even more.

"What did you bring me?" Sascha asked, opening his hands.

"A rolled-up lobster."

"Lobster roll! Gimme."

Instead, Kai picked him up from the chair and sat, placing Sascha back on his lap. He kissed Sascha's neck while Sascha opened the bag he'd brought. Kai would like to do more than kissing, but Sascha needed nourishment on his break, as he often had to remind Kai.

Kai's poor, neglected cock (they'd had sex that morning but just the once) would have to wait.

He busied himself kissing along all the spare skin he could find, enjoying the way Sascha writhed while eating his sandwich.

"I told Matteo to summon a demon," Kai murmured when he'd covered all that he could.

Sascha rolled his eyes, his cheek bulging with his last bite. "Of course you did."

"Are you angry with me?"

Sascha sighed. "No. In some ways, it might be better than asking Ivan to babysit when we leave." He immediately gave Kai a stern look. "I don't really mean that. Two demons on the East Coast in more than enough. I'll talk to him."

Now that Kai had identification from their computer cousin, he and Sascha were going to travel for a bit, as Sascha could work from anywhere. They'd be visiting the brother in Colorado first, and then Kai planned to take Sascha to the places he'd been summoned before, to see how they'd changed over the centuries. And to give Sascha a chance to experience somewhere new.

Sascha wasn't ready to explore his own past yet—to visit Russia and the remnants of his family there—but perhaps they'd get there someday.

Kai didn't mind waiting.

He'd spent so long waiting for his mate, though he hadn't known what he was doing at the time. So many decades of restlessness and boredom.

But now that he knew—now that Kai had him, his Sascha—he could say with every ounce of truth that it had been worth the wait.

Every moment of it.

AUTHOR'S NOTE

Thank you so much for reading Wreaking Havoc! I hope you enjoyed this first installment in the Demon Bound series.

Oooh these two! I was more than a little nervous starting a new series after spending so long immersed in my vampire boys, but I had SO MUCH FUN with Sascha and Kai. It was a thrill to do something a little different while keeping all the possessive, growly, paranormal bits I can't get enough of (and while keeping a few familiar faces around). Kai is such a mix of cocky and caring, and Sascha such a mix of salty and sweet, and I love the way they blended together.

What's Next

As some may have guessed, next up is Ivan and Nix! Ivan may not be everyone's favorite brother at the moment, but you all know I can't resist a villain redemption for the life of me. Get ready for possessive mafioso meets shit-stirring incubus – it's gonna be grand.

And if you're too impatient to wait, you can read WIP chapters as I write them on my Patreon.

If you want to stay in the know, you can sign up for my newsletter for updates and news on upcoming releases. And I can always be reached by email if you just want to say howdy. I love, love, love hearing from my readers!

graebryanauthor@gmail.com

ALSO BY GRAE BRYAN

Vampire's Mate Series

Roman (Book One) – Danny and Roman

Soren (Book Two) – Gabe and Soren

Lucien (Book Three) – Jamie and Lucien

Johann (Book Four) – Alexei and Jay

Wolfgang (Book Five) – Eric and Wolfe

Cassian (A Vampire's Mate Novella) – Blake and Cass

ABOUT THE AUTHOR

Grae Bryan has been reading romance since she was far too young to know any better. Her love for love stories spans all genres, and while her current series is of the paranormal variety, she knows she'll be exploring other worlds further down the line.

She lives in Arizona with her husband, who graciously shares space with all the imaginary men in her head. When not writing, she can generally be found reading more than is healthy, walking her monster-dog, or cuddling her demon-cat. She loves anything and everything gothic, strange, lovely, or cozy.

Find her online: graebryan.com
    Join her Facebook reader group: Grae Bryan's Reader Den
    Patreon: patreon.com/GraeBryan
    Facebook: @GraeBryanAuthor
    Instagram: @authorgraebryan
    Sign up for her newsletter: graebryan.com/contact

Printed in Great Britain
by Amazon